THE NARROW CELL

PONY BOOKS

PONY BOOKS are designed to bring you the best in fiction and fact at a price which is a mere fraction of what you would pay for the same books in their original editions.

PONY BOOKS are printed in large, clear, readable type, yet are light, compact and easy to carry with you in your pocket or handbag for reading whenever you have spare moments.

Printed on strong, opaque paper and bound in sturdy covers, PONY BOOKS will remain in good condition indefinitely.

PONY BOOKS are distinctively and attractively designed, and are immediately recognized by our pony insignia. Every selection invites the reader to many hours of enjoyment since each PONY BOOK is selected only after careful consideration by our Editorial Board.

From the thousands of books published each year we select the best and most popular available for the PONY BOOK editions. For, obviously, the margin of profit on these books is so small that many thousands of copies of each title must be sold. Every PONY BOOK, therefore, *must be good.*

THE NARROW CELL

By DALE CLARK

WILDSIDE PRESS

The Narrow Cell

Published by Wildside Press LLC
www.wildsidepress.com

for Ruth

AUTHOR'S NOTE

It must be confessed that the City of San Diego, with its camouflage and aircraft plants and Market Street Police Headquarters, does exist in actuality; but the persons who are presumed to inhabit it for the purposes of this Tale are altogether the product of the writer's invention.

As for La Jolla, the suburb hereinafter described is not the one to be found on any map; it lies closer to Baker Street than to Highway 101; it and its population are wholly fabricated for the Story's sake.

When an author sets the stage of his Mystery in New York, Chicago, or London, it is conceded without any question that he does so because a stage must be set *somewhere,* and preferably among surroundings with which the writer is, and some few of his readers may be, familiar. The size of these cities lends impersonality; and no one supposes that the police officers and suspects attributed to such locales have any existence in the flesh. Smaller cities do not wear this cloak of impersonality, and it is a natural consequence that when people find such familiar scenes portrayed fictionally, they will scan the author's pages in the expectation of finding their neighbors recognizably described therein.

Let me say at the outset that in these pages the search must prove a totally profitless exercise. No person described hereinafter has, or is intended to have, any resemblance whatsoever to any real person, living or dead; in San Diego or La Jolla, Mankato, or New Gilead, or anywhere else upon the terrestrial globe.

I have simply paid San Diego County the compliment (as I trust) of employing that locale for fictional purposes. I have borrowed the climate and some features of the scenery, and nothing else, and hope I have returned these in as good a condition as I found them.

DALE CLARK.

I

Grandfather had a simple rule . . . He said you could always tell a man's character by what he laughed at.— THE AUTOBIOGRAPHY OF CATHERINE HOPE.

CAPTAIN HARRY WHIPPLE, special duty division commander, stood nearest the desk and picked up the phone.

"Halloa," said he in a voice ripened by several high-balls. "What? . . . Yeah, he's here. John!"

Lieutenant John Kenmore came over from the group of plain clothes men who were toasting the departure of police chemist Earle Ames, lately commissioned into the United States Army Chemical Warfare Corps. The lieutenant was a tall man of spare and athletic figure. His grey eyes looked out of a face full of competence. It was a longish and rather angular face that coupled the chin of a stubborn fighter with the keen, reasoning glance of a strategist. As commanding officer in the Bureau of Internal Security of the San Diego Police Department, he ran the homicide detail and missing persons' office, and, since Pearl Harbor, the war duty office as well.

"Yes. Kenmore speaking."

"This is Henry Bowling—in La Jolla." (Pronounced, of course, *La Hoya*.) "I suppose you remember me."

Kenmore did; but it was a feat of trained memory. As war duty officer, he had come into contact with a host of civilian defense volunteers. But among the hundreds who had attended the police schools of instruction, Bowling stood out very slightly . . . A short, thick, red-faced man of pompous and self-important manner—Kenmore's recollection placed him beside Dr. Lauren Wallace, the La Jolla incident officer.

The voice in the receiver said something about an "UXB lecture." And that was it. Bowling had brought up some question about excavating a bombproof shelter in his backyard.

"You're an air raid warden out there, aren't you?" This was the sum and total of Lieutenant Kenmore's recollection of Henry Bowling.

"Senior sector warden," emphasized the voice.

Kenmore grinned. He recognized the pompous, the self-important manner. But it disappeared; the voice lowered to a pitch of sly, confiding, wheedling urgency.

"Look here, lieutenant . . . like to see you tonight. Say, if you could make it after the drill . . . eight o'clock. I want to introduce you . . . somebody you've been wanting to meet . . . long, long time . . ."

"Speech! Speech!" Across the room, Earle Ames had been hoisted to the top of another desk.

"What?" said Kenmore. "Just a minute."

He looked around.

"Pipe down, you mugs, hold it."

And then again, "What?"

Henry Bowling (if in fact it was he) did a surprising thing. He chuckled. And a moist, heavy, definitely unpleasant sound he made of it.

It was almost as if Kenmore were being kidded; but not quite that, either. It was a confidential chuckle, the lieutenant thought. He wasn't being laughed at; he was invited to join in the jest.

Heh. Heh-heh.

"To hell with Hitler-hito," declaimed the departing Ames, "is all I got to say."

"I want to introduce you," the voice in the phone confided, "to a *murderer.*"

"The murdering sons of bitches!" shouted Earle Ames.

"What's that? Hello? Damn it!" cried Kenmore—into a dead wire.

His caller had hung up in the middle of a second, lumbrously risible chuckle.

Lieutenant Kenmore clenched the telephone in his fist, scowling.

It had certainly sounded like *murderer.*

Kenmore hesitated; reached for the desk directory; opened this to the suburban pages, and ran a forefinger down La Jolla's B's.

Bowling, Henry R. 222 Laguna Terrace. Seaview 3-3609.

He dialed.

No one at Seaview 3-3609 answered.

Now, he thought, what kind of a gag was that?

And answered himself: It was no gag at all.

How did he know?

He *thought* it sounded like Henry Bowling's voice; or rather (since he had heard Bowling's voice but once, and then not on the telephone), he thought it sounded like Henry Bowling . . . judged by those nuances of speech through which a detective does judge anyone's relative education, social status, personality. Kenmore was no babe in the woods at this sort of thing. He had got tips via the phone before. Sometimes the informant preferred to be anonymous. Sometimes the tipster chose to borrow a name for the occasion. Kenmore had never found it hard to see through these deceptions, largely because most people do not know what their own voices sound like, and so don't know which features to disguise.

There was something else.

Kenmore thought the inveterate telephone jokester

would not have hung up so quickly, without having **had** his fun out. Would not have let a suspicion of levity **into** the matter, either. Would *not* have chuckled.

The chuckle clinched conviction.

He looked up at the wall clock. Its minute hand **had** just slipped past 7:16. The call, therefore, had been **made** at about 7:15.

"Speech! Speech!"

Captain Whipple had the floor, as Kenmore turned his back and walked out, and down the hall from the detective division headquarters to the B.I.S.

"There was just a call for you," said Sergeant Lyon, the uniformed officer assigned to the Bureau. "I told them to switch it—"

"Yes. I'm going to try to trace that."

"You're kind of late, aren't you?"

"It was from La Jolla . . . Most phones out there aren't on extended service. You can't dial a downtown number direct. You call operator, she puts you through, and puts the toll charge on your account. If it wasn't an extended service call I can trace it."

Lieutenant Kenmore called operator and asked for the supervisor.

"I would have to check the ticket," said she.

"All right. Ring me back here. Franklin 1101, extension 6."

"Okay if I go down the hall, then?" said Sergeant Lyon thirstily.

"Go ahead." Kenmore shook his head. "I had one drink too many already. Earle Ames has joined the Army. This makes Harry Whipple a great guy and the plain clothes department's choice for Chief of Police. I must be befuddled with booze, because that doesn't add up in my book."

Kenmore sat down facing the telephone. His thoughts

were not very important. He wished he knew more about Henry Bowling. He also wished he knew where Captain Whipple got the free bourbon to celebrate Earle Ames' departure. He wondered how long it would be before the department found another chemist to replace Ames. And he wished the supervisor would hurry.

"Franklin 1101," said the supervisor's voice presently, "was called from Seaview 3-2119."

"Where's that?"

"222 Laguna Terrace, rear."

"Name?"

"The subscriber is listed as Air Raid Warden Post B. As in Boston."

Kenmore dialed Seaview 3-2119.

No one answered.

He bent an elbow and stared at his strapwatch. Fourteen minutes had elapsed; the time was now 7:31.

He walked down the hall. He might have learned, had he listened to Harry Whipple, how the understaffed police department proposed to carry on nobly in war-swollen San Diego. He stood in the doorway, gestured to Lyon:

"Sergeant, I'm running out to La Jolla tonight. Now."

II

From the moment I saw La Jolla, beautiful Jewel by-the-sea, I knew this was where I wanted to end my days.— THE AUTOBIOGRAPHY OF CATHERINE HOPE.

Lieutenant Kenmore entered La Jolla with mingled feelings.

The physical distance from the Market Street headquarters was fifteen miles, and there was open country between, and a tidewater bay.

There was also a spiritual distance, and a sociological gulf.

La Jolla was fashionable, which San Diego was not. It bore the stamp of social distinction, which San Diego had not. Its name was a verbal coin that could be dropped with a quite satisfactory golden ring at a box in the New York Metropolitan, or passed across the glistening napery of an Astor Street dinner table.

La Jolla, as a resort, was only slightly less publicized than Palm Springs, Sun Valley, and Del Monte. There was generally one or another Hollywood personality registered at one or another of the La Jolla hotels; an ex-President of Mexico stopped there frequently, and so did the Director of the Federal Bureau of Investigation.

It was a place where people came to spend a six weeks' vacation, and remained for the rest of their lives. It was an artists' and writers' colony (in a small way); and a retired Army-and-Navy officers' colony (in a much larger way); and its population included a great many elderly,

6

often wealthy and sometimes distinguished persons who had retired to spend their declining years in the **Riviera**-like climate.

La Jolla was cosmopolite; and it was provincial, **was** more a village than a suburb. And San Diego, just a little bit jealous on the first score, was also just a little **bit** scornful on the second.

But Lieutenant Kenmore's mingled feelings had **noth**-ing to do with civic rivalry. His bias was personal **and** professional.

There had once been a murder in La Jolla, and **he had** ever since hoped devoutly there might never be **another.** It would be hard to say which aspect had been **the more** disagreeable:

—The cosmopolitan, with its resulting intense **and** even nationwide publicity?

—Or the provincial, climaxed by the descent **of a** delegation of villagers upon the mayor and city **man**-ager?

—Or the professional, the difficulty of solving a **resort** town crime which might have been committed **by any** one of scores of week-end casuals?

It had been just one hell of a hopeless mess **from the** start.

To John Kenmore, homicide detective, **La Jolla meant** a painful memory of the Catherine Hope Case.

He had got stalled by a USMC truck convoy **crossing** Pacific Boulevard. There had been a Marine **Paratroop** landing on the mesa during the afternoon, with **simulated** Commando raids at La Jolla and Linda Vista. **It was** eight o'clock when Kenmore reached the suburb; **and** La Jolla after dark was not at its scenic best.

The sidewalk eucalyptus and palm trunks **melted in an** overlying stratum of gloom. In the yards, the **colors of** bougainvillaea, poinsettia, and hibiscus **were night**-

drowned. In the homes, house lights were confined within shrouds of window drapery.

The village veiled itself from the Pacific, whose other terminus was Japan. The sea—visible at every street-end —wore a veil of its own in the form of a fog bank beyond the kelp beds. The water had a nasty, blackened, and dense look. The surf struck with a note of menace, growling against the shore.

(On the night Catherine Hope died, the beaches had glittered with bonfires. A full moon was rising brilliantly, if she had lived to see it. And her scream—presumably she had screamed—was lost in the shrieks of wave-wetted grunion hunters.)

Nowadays, beach fires were prohibited. The only nocturnal strollers along the shore were military sentries with their formidable dogs. (And it was too cold for strolling, anyway. A frost-warning night.)

But La Jolla, if not at its scenic and climatic best, at any rate functioned at civic par. The civilian defense drill following on the heels of the mock Commando attack, Henry Bowling had mentioned was drawing to its conclusion.

At the street corners, Kenmore passed armbanded volunteers. In front of the public library, heavily bandaged "casualties" were being lifted into emergency, station wagon ambulances. The Martian apparition on the postoffice steps was a helmeted and gas-masked warden; he was erecting a placard that said *Danger— Mustard.* A trailer pump unit, manned by volunteers, was just now pulling away from the fire department's substation.

John Kenmore, war duty officer, was by no means unhappy about La Jolla.

At the corner of Laguna Terrace and Toyon Street a street-lamp, its upper surface daubed with peeling dim-out paint, shed barely enough light to reveal the Bowling house rising from its maze of shrubbery beyond a head-high Laurustinus hedge.

Lieutenant Kenmore was, it appeared, expected. An air raid warden came to the curb and played his flashlight onto the vehicle's official insignia.

"It's around back. This way—the guesthouse." There was a beard under the white-painted helmet, and Kenmore made out the vaguely familiar features of the La Jolla attorney, William Wyeland. "His air raid post, you know."

Mr. Wyeland darted ahead on the double-quick.

From the corner, the Laurustinus hedge ran its impenetrably thick, bristling greenery along Toyon Street. On a small gate at the upper corner of the property appeared the red-and-white insignia of the wardens' organization. *Sector B,* a placard announced. *Henry R. Bowling, Senior Warden.*

William Wyeland flung open the creaking gate, recalled his manners, and let Lieutenant Kenmore through first onto the flagged walk.

Branches of rhododendron and white-blooming escallonia brushed Kenmore's shoulder. To the right, he caught glimpses of a tennis court glimmering in the night with a faint, liquescent shine. Ahead, the boughs of a silk oak wept down their concealing leaves.

The big house, beyond the tennis court and the silk oak, offered a cream stucco exterior rising three storeys tall to the steep pitch of an English-style roof. A few glimmers of light, as coy as harem ladies, peeped around the carefully draped windows.

It was not a very imaginative house, but it was indubitably a solid one. It had cost a lot of money to build, and only a rich man could have afforded to live in it.

Kenmore emerged from under the silk oak boughs.

There was another light, this to his left, fanning from what was obviously the guesthouse doorway. The light fan touched the pyramidal form of sandbags enclosing a window. (Henry Bowling had his shelter, though not an excavated one.)

The light fan continued, and silhouetted a kneeling figure that genuflected in deep, prayerful attitudes.

Cadenced, the rhythmic movement suggested an anciently pagan rite.

Air raid warden Wyeland directed his flashbeam ahead. And the kneeling figure became merely a man practicing Schafer Method artificial respiration upon another who lay stretched on the grass.

This might have been an air raid drill incident.

But in the darkness a woman sobbed—a sound that smote the lieutenant's ear tragically and feverishly, and gave his nerves a sharply tightening twist.

Kenmore snatched his companion's flashlight and sprang forward.

The disc of light fell on the victim's turned and averted features—the thickish features of Henry R. Bowling.

Bowling's mouth gaped open. His face, suffused now with a mottled cherry blush had on it that peculiar expression which is most expressive of all, because it is no expression at all.

It was a look of wide, stunned-eyed, and utter vacuity.

"Good God!" thought Kenmore. "Good God!"

He knew, from the moment he saw Bowling's face, the attempted resuscitation was so much wasted effort.

Henry Bowling was dead.

III

Men have more intuition than women any day, if they would stop and listen to it.—The Autobiography of Catherine Hope.

Unnatural death affected John Kenmore to about the extent a physician is emotionally affected when confronted with a repulsive disease. It was shocking, but it was also his job.

He dropped to one knee and stared at Henry Bowling's cherry-mottled face, and a change came over him. He ceased to be the John Kenmore who preferred tap beer to the bottled variety, considered Leon Errol funnier than Laurel and Hardy, and would rather spend his day off reeling in swordfish than spend it playing golf. As a normal human being, he felt all the complicated and instinctive emotions normal men do feel in the presence of death; but he put aside his personal feelings. They were not any more important than the color of the necktie he happened to be wearing.

"What happened here?" said the homicide detective.

"Gas heater." The kneeling man bent forward on the pivot made by his cupped hands. A strand of dark hair fell, dangled before his lowered face. "Fumes—got him —I guess."

"You've sent for a doctor?"

"Think so." The other leaned back and rested with his hips on his heels, showing Kenmore a thin intent face from which the lock of dark hair had fallen away and down one flat cheek. "Can't talk—doing this."

The eyes burned with their own preoccupation, and it was possible this man did not really see Lieutenant Kenmore.

"*One,*" he said under his breath, and his body rocked forward, his cupped hands pressed against Henry Bowling's ribs, and the strand of hair dropped from his forehead. "*Two. Three. Four.*"

Kenmore straightened.

"Mrs. Axiter would know about that," suggested the warden at his side.

Kenmore's grey glance made out the woman's form. She leaned against the pyramid of sandbags. She was watching, and weeping as she watched.

Kenmore, as he came a step closer, saw that tears had washed paths down her faded, and he thought curiously heavily powdered face. Her hands hung lamely and limply at her sides.

She had to gather herself, and gather her breath, to answer him.

"I think," Mrs. Axiter faltered, "the gardener went and phoned."

Kenmore could not be sure, from the indecisive sound of this, that a doctor had been called at all.

(Not that he thought it would make any difference to Henry Bowling. However, that was the doctor's province, and not a homicide detective's.)

The lieutenant took two more steps to the guesthouse door. It was a redwood cottage, and its interior had the ripened and dark look common to very old redwood. The end wall had been freshly paneled, and the new wood made an odd, eye-catching contrast to the other three, seasoned walls and the floor.

The room was very hot; the heat came flooding up

from a portable gas heater beyond the flat-top desk where the telephone stood.

Kenmore lifted the telephone from its base, and dialed Seaview 3-3000, the La Jolla control room number.

"Elliot?" said he. "You'd better rush your nearest casualty station physician to 222 Laguna Terrace—" and had to repeat the instruction to make the district warden understand he was not simply reporting a drill incident.

William Wyeland had come in, a step behind the lieutenant.

Very pale, he muttered: "I was in the A.E.F. last time, you know."

Kenmore understood perfectly what the apparently uncalled-for remark meant.

"It gets you, anyway," said he.

"I suppose it's—we were just talking . . . It'd already happened then. Of course, Theodora never dreamed," said the other confusedly. "He was a good sector warden. She often said, no one could have done more. This is a heavy blow for all of us."

"Theodora?" Kenmore remembered, or half-remembered, the name.

"My wife."

"*You* found him, did you?"

"No," said Wyeland. "I was at home, that's my post. My daughter—she's in the messengers—was the one."

"Your daughter . . . When was this?"

"Just now."

"Five minutes ago? Ten?"

Wyeland said, "Let's see . . . I opened the envelope at 7:47—that was the time marked on it. Then I had to make up my report in writing. Mr. Bowling insisted on that; he said it saved time on the phone. I suppose it was a couple of minutes later when I tried to phone him here."

"He didn't answer?"

"No, but I thought nothing of that. I supposed the wires were down as a result of some earlier incident in the sector, you know. That was all prearranged, that if he didn't answer the phone we were to send a messenger. So I sent Dorothy. But she had to go upstairs and get her armband—it took a minute or so more."

Wyeland colored faintly above his brown beard.

"That," said he, "was what we were talking about. My wife didn't see why Dorothy needed to bother about the armband. Since the child was wearing a white dress, anyway. But, as I said, it might be a dark dress next time, and that white armband's a good thing to wear in a dim-out, running about the streets. And of course Mr. Bowling would notice if she neglected to wear it. He was very keen about details—old-maidish, as Mrs. Wyeland put it.

"But"—hastily—"we were lucky to have him in charge. I know, the wardens found him difficult at times. And the ladies didn't appreciate having him come poking into their attics after fire hazards. Still, if we have a real raid instead of a practice one fine day they may be grateful to him after all."

Kenmore nodded; he imagined it had been 7:55 or later when Dorothy Wyeland arrived and found Henry Bowling dead.

"Here," said he, returning the flashlight. "You'd better be out front when the doctor gets here."

And having dismissed Wyeland, Kenmore turned and stared at Henry Bowling's desk.

On the desk lay two sheets of pink paper. The lieutenant glanced at these; at first casually.

Both were filled out in large, pencil-printed characters. At 7:03, there'd been an UXB reported from 30 Pheasant Lane; and at 7:17, an explosion and spreading fire at the Richfield filling station at Toyon and Balboa Streets.

Kenmore's mustering frown owed to the fact that the pink sheets were mimeographed, and not the standard printed forms supplied by the War Duty Office.

There was nothing else on the desk except half a dozen pencils methodically arranged in a wire holder; an ashtray and a briar pipe; a pair of horn-rimmed spectacles, an eraser, a flashlight, and an alarm clock.

Kenmore observed that the pencils were sharpened after the fashion of professional draughtsmen, being pared to a wedge point rather than a round one. The pipe had been tamped full, lighted, and then let go out with the tobacco scarcely blackened.

The lieutenant's frown became an expression which pressed up pads of muscle under his grey eyes, and knotted other muscle pads at the corners of his wide mouth.

He stepped back, glanced around the room, and then walked behind the desk.

In the top, right-hand drawer lay two copies of the *Handbook for Air Raid Wardens,* a pamphlet on extinguishing incendiary bombs, and a booklet, *What You Can Do.*

The second drawer held only some loose sheets of typing bond paper. These were letterheaded: *The Valley Press, Mankato, Minnesota. H. R. Bowling, Publisher.*

The third and lowermost drawer was larger. Its contents included a civilian's white-painted steel helmet, a training gas mask in its canvas carrier, a fly-spray gun, and an 8-oz. bottle that bore the label *Formaldehyde 3 %.*

The central shallow drawer had nothing in it except a miscellany of paper clips, penknife, pipe cleaners, and (curiously) a clip of '06 cartridges.

On the left side of the desk was space for a typewriter, and a lower drawer in which were stacked some copies of the dim-out proclamation under a city telephone directory.

That was all for the desk. Placed against the wall behind it, stood a steel filing cabinet.

This, when Kenmore turned to it, disclosed an index of the homes in the sector, divided by posts; it cataloged the residents in detail: the children under six, and adults over sixty-five, and the infirm and otherwise handicapped, and the household pets . . . together with the location of each house's water taps and garden hose, and electric switches, and gas cut-offs.

Then there was another section, given over to correspondence, mostly mimeographed, and much of it directives from the war duty office.

Lieutenant Kenmore looked into the other rooms—there were only three; a tiny kitchen, a tinier bath, and a bedchamber.

Henry Bowling had kept these rooms closed off; they were chillish and damp, and looked unused in a long time. Perhaps he had never put them to any use at all. The wicker furniture of the bedchamber, the flat-spring bed without a mattress, the picture of Yosemite that had come unglued from its frame—none of it suggested the accommodations the owner of the big house would offer a guest.

All the windows, like the one in front, were sandbagged; the kitchen door, locked and made secure with a bolt besides. Kenmore looked attentively to this bolt, which wore an undisturbed film of dust.

He stood in the other, front room, staring at the desk; considering.

He had found absolutely nothing to explain Henry Bowling's sardonically amused phone message.

But he had found enough to feel very sure Henry Bowling had not died by accident.

IV

"So he fled with all that he had; and he rose up, and passed over the river, and set his face toward the mount Gilead."—GENESIS *31:21*.

Grandfather did likewise, and that is how New Gilead got its name.—THE AUTOBIOGRAPHY OF CATHERINE HOPE.

"It's no use, that's that," said James Myatt, M.D.

Lieutenant Kenmore made the notation in his pocket memo book: *Pronounced dead by physician 8:43 p.m.* In this interval two uniformed officers had hastened from the La Jolla sub-station with an inhalator. District warden Sam Elliot and the local civilian defense corps chief, Dr. Lauren Wallace, had come from the control room.

And Darwina Roydan appeared—she being the drill umpire who had handed Wyeland his incident envelope.

Kenmore brightened. For if the ill winds brewed by the Catherine Hope Case had blown good to anyone, his acquaintance with Darwina Roydan was that good . . . But at the moment Miss Roydan merely stood by in the shadows. Kenmore intended to renew the acquaintance, and was otherwise occupied now.

"Cause of death?" said he.

"Why, carbon monoxide—it was that heater in there, of course," thought Myatt.

"Those unvented heaters play the very devil," Elliot muttered.

The man who had tried to administer artificial

respiration sighed, "Well, you'd better go inside, Jessie," to Mrs. Axiter. "There's nothing we can do here."

Kenmore said: "Just a minute."

He got from the other a dark, narrowly questioning look.

"We have to file a report on accidental deaths," the lieutenant observed. "Names of witnesses, who found the body, and so on."

"I thought you knew. It was the girl, Wyeland's little girl."

"And she notified you?"

"She came to the house," the other said. He produced a wallet, and from it a card that read: *Kane & Ffleming, Insurance,* with *Foster V. Ffleming* printed in its lower corner. "She told Mrs. Axiter. I came out with her and we got Mr. Bowling into the fresh air. I'd seen carbon monoxide poisoning before, and I guessed it was that, all right."

"This was at approximately eight o'clock, I understand? He was entirely unconscious when you found him?"

"Yes, he'd fallen out of his chair. On the floor behind the desk. He might have struck his head in falling, I thought." Ffleming added, "I don't think Mrs. Axiter can tell you any more than this."

Kenmore did not put any questions to Mrs. Axiter. He said, indeed, he thought it would be a kindness on Darwina Roydan's part to see Jessie Axiter into the house.

Darwina did so, assisted by Ffleming and Dr. Myatt.

And as Wyeland had gone to telephone the mortuary, it left the lieutenant with the district warden and the incident officer.

"Oh, Elliot," said he, turning to the guesthouse door. "Dr. Wallace."

The two men followed him inside.

Kenmore asked, "You phoned your test signal blue at what time?"

"Why," said Elliot, "at 6:30."

"And reached Mr. Bowling here?"

"Why, no. In the house. It's a different line entirely."

"And the test signal red—?"

"Just before seven o'clock."

"And he was here then? I'd like," said Kenmore, "to fix the time as closely as I can."

"Well," Elliot thought, "you can come closer to it than that. Because he phoned in a couple of reports tonight."

"Yes," Kenmore agreed, thumbing the pink sheets on the desk, "these. At 7:03 and 7:17."

"A *little* later than that. Those are the incident times. It'd take a few minutes for the post wardens to put through their reports to him, and for him to call the control room."

Kenmore said, "So death occurred, say, between 7:20 or thereabouts, and approximately eight o'clock."

He jotted this into his pocket notebook.

Dr. Lauren Wallace interrupted. "But, inspector—" he paused, "—I mean, lieutenant."

This slip of the tongue recalled the unpleasant memory.

John Kenmore had been only a detective-inspector when Catherine Hope was slain. Dr. Wallace had been Director of the Marine Research Institute at that time. (He was Director Emeritus now.)

La Jolla took the institution rather for granted, but M.R.I. enjoyed a very substantial reputation in scientific circles, and to the establishment of this reputation Lauren Wallace had contributed notably. The Director Emeritus was not a great scientist nor scholar; and did not pretend to be. Dr. Wallace's talent inclined to administration, and his genius to money-raising. By means of this genius he had made possible the 1923-'29 Expeditions, whereon was founded the Institute's unique position in its field. Those were the years of the seven fat kine. And in the starveling years that followed, the good doctor's administrative talent had at least kept the institution afloat in shoal waters.

The shocking demise of Catherine Hope—whose nude body had been discovered in one of M.R.I.'s aquarium tanks in April, 1937—served to darken the final months of his directorship.

It was not so much the three-day wonder (and that had been bad enough, with the headlines, with the curious wearing footpaths across the grounds, with the morbid threatening to dismember the aquarium in their search for souvenirs). It was the dismal three-week police investigation which did the damage. The revelations had led to the enforced resignations of three professors—not that these marine biologists were probably any better or worse than other mortals; they had been merely more naive in their transgressions.

The scandal cost M.R.I. a number of annual contributors; and it cost Dr. Lauren Wallace his hope of building the edifice which would have been Wallace Hall and the fitting monument to his life labors.

Inspector, said Lauren Wallace, and brought home the jarring fact:

The murder of Catherine Hope remained unsolved to this day.

That affair had run the predictable course of violent crime in a small locality; it had fattened indecently upon the unfortunate professors, and then withered profitlessly away.

Kenmore could hardly blame himself; Captain Harry Whipple had commanded the homicide detail then; but

Kenmore had worked on the case, and the recollection of frustration made his grey eyes momentarily bleak.

"Yes?" said he. "What is it?"

Dr. Lauren Wallace shook his white-maned head. "I was going to say, lieutenant, there should be three of those."

"Three pink sheets?"

"Yes. It's a new form we were trying tonight. Mrs. Rhine didn't mimeograph enough copies to waste any. The sector wardens each got exactly three, because we planned three incidents in each sector."

Kenmore considered that.

"Well, did Bowling actually get three? Is there any certainty he did?"

Dr. Lauren Wallace said, Yes, the copies had been handed around at yesterday's sector warden meeting; a meeting he had called especially to acquaint the men with the new form.

"And as a matter of fact, Bowling came up to me before the meeting. It was about his messengers, the Chapman twins. They are table tennis addicts, and are playing in a tournament in San Diego tonight. Bowling wanted to know whether he should make other arrangements, and I told him the boys wouldn't be needed. We talked about the pink sheets, I gave him them to look over, and counted them as I did so."

Dr. Wallace spoke positively. He was a positive figure of a man; a big ruddy individual with a tall forehead under his shock of white hair; with the forceful manner of the experienced executive and administrator.

Kenmore respected the incident officer's ability.

"Well," said he casually, "then Bowling misplaced the other."

"That would hardly be like Henry Bowling," Lauren Wallace objected, puzzled. "He was so systematic in everything. Still, none of us are perfect, are we? I suppose he must have lost it."

But Dr. Wallace was not through thinking of the third pink sheet. Rather sharply, his glance rested on Kenmore. "You must have hurried here," said he.

The lieutenant told exactly as much of the truth as he considered Dr. Wallace, or any of them, were entitled to hear.

"It happened I was in La Jolla. I had an appointment with a chap nearby."

"I see." Wallace dabbed at his tall forehead with a folded square of handkerchief. "How very hot it is . . . Nobody seems to have remembered to turn off that heater."

"Yes," said Kenmore, attending to it. "If you'll excuse me, I'd better notify the coroner's office."

Then, having dismissed the two gentlemen, he lifted the phone to dial operator and give her the headquarters number . . . and summoned the police photographer-and-fingerprint-man from the farewell party on Market Street.

Kenmore, when he had finished talking, stood frowning at the two pink sheets. His frown was cautious in its concentration, for police work makes a literal man. Dr. Wallace had pounced on an interesting detail. If he had noticed the pipe and the eyeglasses and the alarm clock as well, he was as near to a solution as Kenmore himself. But that was not anywhere near enough to satisfy the district attorney. District attorneys want clues—forthright clues whose value as evidence will impress even an unsympathetic jury.

In this sense, Kenmore did not have a case at all and he knew it. He could not prove a crime had been committed; and if he could not prove that, obviously he could not arrest anyone on suspicion of having committed it. He could ask questions, to be sure; but he could not demand answers. The fact that a man has died apparently by accident does not give a police officer the right to probe into the private affairs of his family —and families of relative wealth generally know their Constitutional rights. If Kenmore asked himself *why* he believed Henry Bowling had been murdered, the answer would be, firstly: because of the telephone call. From the legal point of view, there were three things wrong about the telephone call. It might be excluded from the testimony altogether. It might be objected that Kenmore could not positively identify the voice as Bowling's. It might be argued, supposing Bowling had made the call, he had nevertheless died by accidental means. Just as, if he had set forth afoot to deliver his information at the substation, he could conceivably have been run down and killed by a motorist having no connection with the case. No law of nature exempts informers from the hazards of traffic, defective heaters, and electric short-circuits. In fact, being preoccupied with the business in hand, Bowling would have been less than ordinarily apt to notice gas fumes in the room.

Secondly, there were the items of a missing pink sheet, a pipe, eyeglasses, and alarm clock. Kenmore considered these were items he assuredly could not *act* upon, but he could *think* from them . . . He lighted his own pipe; walked around and sat in Henry Bowling's chair; and locked his hands behind his head.

"You can't just rush in and grab the bull by the horns," he excused this inaction. You couldn't, because you needed a preliminary knowledge of the bull's anatomy. Or you would find yourself helplessly hanging onto the brute's tail.

He had to establish a line of inquiry. Or else it would all be hit-and-miss; and worse, because he wouldn't know when he *had* registered a hit.

Kenmore leaned farther back in the chair. Henry Bowling at 6:30 o'clock had received a test signal blue at Seaview 3-3609; he might have called police headquarters then; but he had not done so. He had not done so until 7:15 o'clock, when he was engaged in the Commando defense drill, expecting two more incident reports from his sector, and expecting these reports by telephone. And, you would have thought, would have left his phone open for the purpose of receiving them. Instead of which, at 7:15 o'clock, Henry Bowling had undertaken to expose a murderer.

The bull's anatomy was becoming dimly visible in a cloud of pipe smoke.

"Try that again," thought Kenmore. Henry Bowling had got the blue signal at home . . . come out here to his post and received the red signal . . . within a minute or so of 7:01 had taken and dispatched a reported UXB incident at 30 Pheasant Lane . . . had lighted the gas heater . . . telephoned John Kenmore at 7:15 o'clock . . . then received and transmitted the 7:17 o'clock Richfield station incident . . . and then he had replaced his pencil in its wire rack, lighted and laid aside his briar pipe, removed his eyeglasses, and almost immediately died.

Kenmore would have to fill in the gaps in this account.

He was irritated by a thought on the periphery of consciousness . . .

You had to take those actions apart, put them together into a new combination.

The thought crashed violently from the periphery to the exact center of his suddenly focused realization:

"He wouldn't have known the number!"

The lieutenant leaned down, dragged open the lower left-hand drawer, and slapped the directory onto the desk before him.

He opened its pages to *San Diego, City of*—and the thing lay square before him.

A square envelope, grimed with dust and somewhat yellowed with age, it bore on its surface (wrinkled as if it had been partially balled into a wad and then smoothed out) an uncanceled three-cent stamp.

The address, composed in a flowing feminine hand, was to Mrs. E. H. Burrett, New Gilead, Michigan.

"Good God!" said Kenmore, and turned over the envelope.

Across its torn back flap ran a printed legend: Miss Catherine Hope, 1116 Balboa Street, La Jolla, California.

There was, however, nothing inside.

He got up, jammed the thing in his pocket, and went outside hurriedly.

The guesthouse occupied the rear, north-east corner of the large yard; its entry stoop faced upon the tennis court. This court, running north-and-south, had a high wire fence inside the Toyon Street hedge; the garage provided a backstop at the other, south end.

Thus the court offered a short-cut to the big house. Kenmore stepped out onto it and was halfway across the concrete when he heard the voice.

V

*. . . washed my mouth with soap and to this day that
word makes me think of Pine Bros. tar soap.*—THE AUTO-
BIOGRAPHY OF CATHERINE HOPE.

John Kenmore came to a stop; listening.

"Skunk-kitty," the voice in the darkness said. "Dirty,
nasty little skunk-kitty. That's what you are, you drunken
bitch."

The words made up a meaning of violence and anger
and reproach. Only the voice (a man's) was not that kind
of a voice. I-told-you-so, its tone said, and the only passion
in the saying was a small lip-smacking note of triumph.
That's what you are, it said with a taste of relish on the
tongue.

Kenmore was shocked. The lieutenant was used to the
casually indecent vituperation of the lock-up and bull-
pen; but this struck the ear differently, it was genuinely
and studiedly impure.

Unfortunately, he couldn't·see the speaker. The sound
came from the rear, around the house corner, so that
even by broad daylight he couldn't have seen anything
from where he now stood.

Kenmore, who had been heading toward the front
door, veered his direction swiftly.

"Come on," the voice said, quietly and almost sooth-
ingly. "Don't stumble, don't break your damned neck.
Upsi-daisy, watch the step, you sow."

Kenmore could subsequently testify to these words. What his testimony could not reproduce was the quality of the voice: its blend of pleasure and contempt, mockery and self-satisfaction. And of something else he could not define at all, but was surely evil.

He had overheard a blasphemy, the lieutenant thought. But he could not imagine the district attorney making anything out of that ancient and Biblical impiety. The incident was not to be that easily pinned down . . . "At 9:03 p.m., while proceeding across the tennis court in the direction of the house, the officer heard a sacrilege committed upon the back step—" no.

All the same, Kenmore knew something more than the skunk-kitty was being mocked.

Another figure, likewise arrested by the sound of the voice, loomed unexpectedly before the swiftly advancing lieutenant.

He heard a startled gasp.

And a flashlight blazed full upon him.

"John Kenmore!" Darwina Roydan's voice exclaimed.

After that, of course, when Lieutenant Kenmore got around the house corner to the rear, the service porch back step was clear of everything except a trio of milk bottles.

Miss Roydan, not for the first time in her career, had outspokenly upset the beans. And Kenmore, not for the first time in his, proved himself a patient man.

After all, it was hardly her fault. Darwina, emerging by way of the front door, had been on her way to the guesthouse. She had simply not recognized him as he bore down toward her out of the night.

"Darwina," said he, "will you come along, please. There's something I want to ask you."

Darwina Roydan, Sc.D., Ph.D., was Fellow of the American Zoophytical Society and the author of the renowned two-volume monograph on *leucetta losangelensis*. Among marine biologists, Kenmore understood, her name was almost exactly synonymous with the *leucettidae* for the same reason that the name Einstein is popularly and practically synonymous with relativity.

"This carbon monoxide?" he asked. "How much is enough? A fatal concentration?"

"You mean in here?" Darwina's hat (it resembled a Spanish galleon more than anything else) tacked sidewise and back again as she glanced around the guesthouse. "But concentration isn't the point. It's a question of saturation. So it doesn't require any particular concentration. The process is absorption, the inhaled gas combining with the victim's red blood cells, which it does about 250 times as readily as oxygen will."

"Yes," said Kenmore, "but how much—?"

"I'm trying to tell you," interrupted Darwina, somewhat pedagogically. This was an impression furthered by her physical proportions. Darwina was almost Amazonian; she chanced to be one of the sturdiest distance swimmers on the Pacific Coast. Her eyes flashed with a vitality she was accustomed to harness for conversational purposes.

"I am trying to tell you," said she, "it isn't the concentration in the atmosphere, it's the amount in the bloodstream. Death results from an eighty per cent saturation, but you could get that much eventually from the merest trace of the gas in the air—one part in 5000—if you breathed it long enough."

"But how long?" said the lieutenant. "What's certain here is that Bowling was alive as late as 7:20, and dead— at any rate unconscious—when I tried to reach him by phone at 7:31."

Kenmore's grey eyes wore a gleam of intense thought. The whole face had a wiry look of energetic cerebration.

"Now! It would take a pretty powerful concentration to account for your eighty per cent saturation—in ten minutes, or less, wouldn't it?"

"Yes," said Darwina, "one part in 100. Only it doesn't necessarily follow he was killed in ten minutes, or even half an hour."

"Why not?"

"Because carbon monoxide is insidious. It can sneak up on one. Suppose," suggested Darwina, "he lighted the heater before seven o'clock. He might have absorbed up to perhaps a thirty per cent saturation and not have noticed any definite symptoms—and then just suddenly collapsed."

This was not what Kenmore had hoped to hear. His expression changed; his face did not exactly fall, but it became profoundly contemplative.

He confronted a difficult decision.

How far should he trust Darwina Roydan?

Kenmore didn't question her personal integrity. It was just the opposite . . . He knew where the young woman stood in La Jolla's estimation; she was candidly radical. Only her radicalism had nothing to do with anything so remote as Communism, for instance. She believed ardently in reform, and concretely, in reforming the village.

And she believed in direct action. Thus she had been known to patrol the beaches, snatching up discarded ice cream paper cups and fragments of sandwiches. "Here," she would say, thrusting the offensive article under a picnicker's nose, "do you realize you've left a rat a day's rations?"

It was in this forthright manner that she undertook to renovate and enlighten La Jolla. Undoubtedly, Darwina was something of a busybody; but at least she was busy in the public interest . . . Only as so often happens, the public needed to be shown where its best interest lay.

Kenmore knew she was an optimist, as every sincere crusader must be. To believe in Causes, she had first to believe in human nature; she could never permit herself a moment's disillusion about the essential *goodness* in people. Or what would have been the use of trying to change mere conditions?

Darwina Roydan, who was a scientist in respect to *leucetta losangelensis,* was an idealist in respect to the human race.

And that, thought Kenmore, was just the trouble. Her honesty was too transparent. *She* was too candidly transparent.

You could pledge her tongue to silence, and her eyes would nevertheless speak eloquently.

But the lieutenant had reached a point where he needed help; and Darwina was assuredly his best bet.

"That's no good, then," said he, and took the plunge. "I'm trying to get around it—the heater part. I'm not satisfied about it a bit."

Darwina's eyes opened widely in the shadow of the galleon's prow. "But then you must mean—!"

"Yes," said Kenmore, "if it wasn't accidental, it was on purpose."

Murder . . . That chasm yawned too wide.

Darwina shook her head.

"If it wasn't the heater, you would have to get the carbon monoxide in by some other means. And then it probably wouldn't have worked at all. It might be possible to kill a sleeping man or a drunken one that way. And while the poison is insidious, still in a majority of cases your victim would be warned by headache and dizziness and nausea. He'd simply step out for some fresh air. It would be a stupid and improbable way of trying to kill anyone, really."

Lieutenant Kenmore smiled at the corners of his mouth, an unconvinced smile. He wasn't going to rule out the possibility of homicide merely because the apparent method seemed stupid and improbable to Darwina Roydan.

"Would this mean anything to you?" said he.

She peered at the face of the envelope.

"No."

"This, then."

He turned it over.

"Good heavens!" said Darwina thinly. She moistened her lips. "You mean he was killed after he phoned you about her? Because he had *this?*"

"Was he, though?" Lieutenant Kenmore looked perplexed. "Maybe. If that's it, he must have read the letter inside. But the letter itself is gone. And that's only one difficulty. Bowling seems to have run onto this thing in the last few minutes of his life. Or why didn't he act on it sooner?

"From that point," he shook his head, "it gets worse than confusing. The thing contradicts itself. For if Bowling only stumbled onto this in the last few minutes of his life, apparently his death was a last-minute necessity, too. But to kill a man and make the murder look like accidental death caused by a defective heater needs preparation and planning. Such a crime is not thought-out and executed in ten or eleven minutes. If it was the kind of murder the set-up indicates, of course it was plotted hours in advance. But why plot to kill a man because of this envelope he hadn't yet seen?"

He stepped to the filing case, opened its upper section, ran his thumb along the index cards to the one headed *Henry R. Bowling, 222 Laguna Terrace.*

"Darwina," said he, "I suppose it has occurred to you this envelope may be a plant?"

"A—?"

"A plant, a decoy, a red herring."

She looked momentarily enlightened. And the next moment, distrustful. "Why? This was supposed to be accidental death. Not murder. And people don't leave false clues scattered around a scene of accidental death."

"Unless it was desired to have two strings to the bow. I had a case once in which a man pushed his wife off a cliff. He hoped it would pass for suicide. When he saw we wouldn't swallow that, he got busy and helped us find some footprints along the top of the cliff. He had gone to a second-hand store and bought a pair of oversized boots, figuring if the suicide theory wouldn't wash, the crime might be pinned on some unknown tramp or hitchhiker.

"Well, then, Darwina. It might have been hoped Henry Bowling's death would pass as accidental, but if not, the envelope would point away from the murderer."

And the detective got down to brass tacks:

"That brings the family into it. They may be innocent. I hope so. If they are, they'll probably be glad to cooperate with the police. But I can't rely on it. Because if they are guilty, after all, I don't dare put them on guard, point out the little discrepancies in the thing, in fact show them the little lies they must tell . . . It's a delicate job. And you can help with it. You know them, you can tell me what I'm going into here.

"First—" his grey glance dropped to the card "—Mrs. Axiter. Who and what is she?"

"Bowling's sister. She managed the house for him." Darwina pursed her lips. "I think if you told her Henry was murdered—well, perhaps murdered—I suppose her first reaction would be to faint. Then she would burst into tears. Finally, she would be insulted."

"Insulted?"

"Because murders don't happen in nice families," said Darwina, "and Jessie is wonderfully adept at closing her eyes to unpleasant truths."

"Yes," said the lieutenant. "What truths?"

"I don't suppose it has anything to do with **Henry Bowling**," said Darwina hurriedly. "I mean Lally. **Lalitha** is Jessie's youngest. Younger. There are two daughters. Lally married a man named Al Dearborn, and the marriage turned out badly. They've separated. Lally's staying with her mother. The gossip is—I don't like to repeat gossip, but you should know—she's consoling herself with alcoholic beverages *and* pick-ups at the local bars.

"I suppose," said Darwina thoughtfully, "she's in psychiatric difficulties, as almost all dipsomaniacs are, and perhaps the same difficulty was what upset her marriage. Though I'm told Al Dearborn is no bargain, either. At any rate, if you broke your suspicions to Lally, the chances are she'd react by needing another drink. I don't suppose it would go deeper than that with her."

"Corinne Axiter," said Kenmore, from the card. "She would be the other daughter."

"The elder one. The dark one. She's a glacial, bitter brat. I wouldn't predict how she'll respond."

And for the first time, Darwina's tone sounded perturbed.

"Corinne has intelligence! It takes brains to be that sarcastic. She could do something, she could be useful. I don't understand people who have intelligence and simply won't use it."

There were three more names on the card. Mary Yellick, said Darwina, was the cook. Ella Marion, the maid. And Fred Crush, the gardener. "But I don't suppose the servants count, do they? Or Lally, either. It's what Jessie and Corinne will think, and I don't imagine you'll find them very cooperative."

"No," said Lieutenant Kenmore. "Well. I had better let on I think it was accidental death, for a while at least."

VI

. . . a houseful of women. My grandmother said, no roof was ever built big enough for that.—THE AUTOBIOGRAPHY OF CATHERINE HOPE.

It being Thursday, and the maid's night out, Kenmore's ring at the front door was answered by Corinne Axiter. (The dark sister. Darwina's glacial, bitter brat.)

"Yes. Please come in." Corinne's face was expressionless, as smooth as her straight-combed dark hair. Corinne missed prettiness by a little margin—a margin of reserve and sharp intelligence. She had what Kenmore considered bookish features, thin and cool and introspective.

From the front hallway, he followed the girl down three curved steps into what tried to be a baronial room. It only needed a suit of armor or so in its distant corners, the lieutenant felt. An enormous dragon-limbed table at the foot of the steps emphasized the expanse of glistening, parquetry floor; so did the succession of massive, blue velour-clad settees along the walls.

Window drapes of this same blue fell from ceiling-high valance boxes to spill yards of velvet upon the parquetry. A fireplace, unlit, was repellently large, austere, and cold. This last was flanked by somber oils, overwhelmed by their own great, gilt frames.

Jessie Axiter, a tiny figure on a blue settee, was now bearing up bravely with an obvious effort.

Kenmore said he regretted the necessity of questions. "For the coroner's records, you know.

"Name of deceased, *Henry R. Bowling*," murmured he, over an opened memo book. "What is the *R* for?" to Mrs. Axiter.

Jessie Axiter, seen now by light, was a fair-haired and ineffectual-seeming woman, amorphously flowing. Kenmore recognized at once that she hadn't any force or thrust of personality; he imagined, though, she could cling to beat the very devil.

"Ross," she told him. "It's the family name on my mother's side. She was Scottish. So were the Bowlings, only they were really English originally."

"Mother," said Corinne. "The officer only wants the name, he doesn't care what it means."

She misjudged Kenmore. He certainly had no objection to letting Jessie Axiter render an account in her own diffuse way.

"His age?"

"Sixty-two," said Mrs. Axiter.

Kenmore continued in a disarmingly mechanical manner. Date and time of death, he had that. Reported by, place of death, character of premises, ditto. Last residence of deceased, 222 Laguna Terrace. Without the slightest change of tone, Kenmore asked: "How long had he lived here?"

"We came in '39," said Jessie Axiter. "That summer."

That was to say, two years after the Catherine Hope Case. It was not quite what Kenmore had expected to hear. Henry Bowling might not even have heard of Catherine Hope.

Mrs. Axiter took advantage of the detective's momentary preoccupation. "Though Henry always said he'd been a resident much longer than that—in spirit. He visited here the first time, I think in '33. No, it must have been '32. I remember he cast an absentee ballot, I had to get the papers and send them on, and after all the bother it didn't make the least difference. Because Mr. Hoover wasn't elected, anyway. Well, Henry simply fell in love with La Jolla, then. Of course, it's changed since. It's not at all the same place."

"Last previous address?" said Kenmore.

"Mankato. We're old Minnesota stock. Grandfather Bowling—my father, but I always called him that after my own children came—settled there at the time of the New Ulm Massacre."

Lieutenant Kenmore had become almost resigned to it . . . Of every two persons you met on a San Diego street, one had lived here not more than a decade; of every three, one had come in the last year or so. Most people, like Henry Bowling, had their roots elsewhere.

It posed a peculiarly boom-town police problem, since so much a detective needed to uncover was somewhere else, maybe a thousand miles away.

The lieutenant asked, "Your brother's birthplace was Minnesota, then?"

"Yes, in Mankato."

"Occupation?"

"Why, retired. He was a newspaper man. A newspaper publisher."

"Oh, mother." Corinne was smoking a cigarette, or rather letting it smoke itself away in her slender, tapering fingers; with continual, small, birdlike pecks toward an ashtray. "He wasn't *really*. What he did was sell the printed insides to little country papers. I don't think you can call that being a newspaperman."

Kenmore recognized ironic hostility in this comment, and reproach in Jessie Axiter's answering glance. "Dear, I don't think the police care exactly what he published. It was a newspaper supplement, at any rate. I'd call it being a newspaper publisher, and I'm sure he considered himself one."

"Civil condition?" He interpreted. "Married? Widower?"

"Oh, no. Not *Henry*."

"His father's name?"

"David. David Bowling."

"And his birthplace?"

"It was Linlithgow. That's in Scotland."

Kenmore scribbled. "And you say his mother's maiden name was Ross."

Mrs. Axiter smiled; said to Corinne, "You *see*, dear." And to Kenmore: "Yes, Jessie Ross. She was a Linlithgow girl. They were childhood sweethearts. Grandfather Bowling came away to America to make his fortune, and then years later he went back and they were married, after they'd both waited for the other all that time. It was terribly romantic, wasn't it? But he always said, she was worth crossing the ocean twice to win. She was a great beauty—you won't see it in me, I take after *him*— but Lally's the very image."

Mrs. Axiter's shoulder suddenly quivered, and she gave a little gasping sob.

"I'm sorry," she said faintly, and touched a handkerchief to the corners of her wet eyes. "It's just that a death in the family takes one *back* so." She paused. "Do you think Saturday's too soon for the funeral?"

"Well," said Kenmore, "you've got to allow time for the coroner's autopsy."

He would sooner this question had not come up so abruptly.

"Oh." The eyes widened above the handkerchief. Jessie Axiter looked to her daughter. "We hadn't thought of *that*."

"No," said Corinne, and stared at Kenmore. "It didn't occur to us. I should think Dr. Myatt's signing the death certificate ought to satisfy the red tape. The other would be just a formality—and a pretty disagreeable formality."

She bent forward.

"You saw off the top of their heads, don't you, officer? And split them up the middle. I don't think Uncle Henry would have cared for it a bit."

Mrs. Axiter cried out painfully, "Oh, *no!*"

"Well, mother, that's what an autopsy *is*," observed the bitter brat.

She was certainly smart enough to know what she was up to; Lieutenant Kenmore didn't yet know; but he felt completely certain she hadn't objected to the sawing-and-splitting out of squeamishness. For what Corinne's composed and unmoved face could not mask was a bland indifference to the effect of this lurid description upon her shocked and distressed mother.

"No," Mrs. Axiter trembled indignantly, "we could never consent to anything of the kind. Never."

It was not the first time Lieutenant Kenmore had encountered opposition to an autopsy.

He began reasonably and sympathetically. "But, after all, it's only surgery. It's performed by a physician for a necessary and legitimate reason, like any other surgical operation. And it's quite often to the family's advantage . . . Henry Bowling carried life insurance, I suppose?"

"I can't see whatever his insurance has to do with this," Jessie Axiter protested.

Kenmore replied, it might. "If there's a double indemnity clause covering accidental death. The underwriters would have to be convinced it *was* accidental, that actually enough carbon monoxide had been inhaled to cause death."

"Yes," said Corinne, "only his wasn't that kind of insurance."

Kenmore glanced curiously at the girl.

She said, "Uncle Henry purchased insurance as an

investment, not to buy protection he didn't need. I don't understand all the complexities of it, but I know it wasn't the kind of insurance you're thinking of."

Jessie Axiter brightened. "Well, then, there's no need for an autopsy," she declared in relief. "So we won't talk about it any more."

"It's not a question of insurance, Mrs. Axiter. I mentioned that as a possibility, as an example. I hoped you'd see it was reasonable—"

"No," said Jessie Axiter, interrupting sharply. She got up from the settee, with little flags of color in her too-powdered cheeks. "I don't see it, I don't think it's in the least necessary or reasonable. It's absolutely horrible and barbaric! And," her voice had grown shrill, "there's no use trying to change my mind, because I shan't even consider it."

This was meant to be final.

But what else did it mean? Kenmore could not be sure whether Mrs. Axiter objected to the autopsy, or to what it might disclose. Or whether she had not been goaded into this stand by the sardonic Corinne.

At any rate, it demanded a final answer. He was not going to get anywhere with this investigation without determining the cause of death. The issue had to be faced—and forced.

Kenmore stood, too.

"You needn't change your mind, of course," said he. "Mr. Bowling's body is in the custody of the State of California. It cannot be released until the authorities have investigated and certified their findings."

Jessie Axiter gave him a rigid stare.

"You mean you think you can just go ahead and *take* him?" she asked incredulously.

"Technically, yes. But in practice, we don't 'take' the body anywhere. It will remain at the local mortuary."

"And that's all we have to say about it?"

"Legally," Kenmore dryly assured her, "you've no property right to the body of the deceased. But actually there won't be any objection to a member of the family attending—or you may ask your family doctor to be present. I suggest you do so."

There followed a pause; Mrs. Axiter used it to moisten her grey lips; the flags of color were hauled down, and left her face rice-white.

"Well!" she burst forth. "We'll *fight* that! I never heard of such a law. If it is one. The idea a man's own family can't, his own sister can't—just because he died accidentally!"

Behind her came a slightly blurred giggle. "Mother, that's baloney. You know perfectly well Uncle Henry was murdered, and we're all tickled pink."

Jessie Axiter flung around: *"Lally!"*

Her mother hadn't exaggerated; Lally Dearborn was certainly a beauty. The portiere drapes of a side doorway provided the suitably somber background for a helmet of dazzling, wheat-gold hair, and for a figure sheathed in clinging white. The gown left bare Lally's arms and her shoulders, suntanned to the complexion of richly creamed coffee.

She'd made an indisputably effective entrance.

Unfortunately, the effect dissolved as Lally advanced into the room.

"She's not herself," Mrs. Axiter told Kenmore hurriedly; and she was not, at any rate, very sure of herself. He remembered seeing drunken drivers trying to walk chalklines, before breath and blood tests for intoxication came into police use. Lally walked like that, placing her feet upon the parquetry with painfully preserved steadiness. It wasn't that she staggered; she only looked as if she would, the next step.

Corinne Axiter, her head tipped to one side apprais-

ingly, studied her sister. "I don't know, mother," said she
critically. "I should say she's very much herself. Almost
more so than usual."

And Mrs. Axiter observed: "She's been taking those
headache drops again. They always make her dizzy. I
think there's sulfa or something dreadful in them."

The curious thing to Kenmore was that Lally's condition excited these comments; but what she'd said made
no visible impression upon her mother and sister.

It was left for him to pick up that . . . "Here," he
directed. "Sit down. What do you mean, *he was murdered?*"

Lally, as he bent over her, was not quite so beautiful
as she had seemed in the doorway. And yet her features
were flawless. The tiny termites of dissipation hadn't
actually loosened a lineament; it was only that you could
sense what she'd look like next year, and the year after.

"What a pity," thought the lieutenant, who knew
better than most how inexorable the change would be.
"Why doesn't she take the cure?" Or, if Darwina was
right, put herself into the hands of a psychiatrist. But
he knew she wouldn't. Kenmore had observed before
now, there is no one more recalcitrant than a young
woman who is determined to go to hell.

But the thought was by-the-way.

"Well?" he demanded. "Why do you say he was murdered?"

In vino veritas. But what degree of truth? Lally replied
with childlike logic:

"That old heater's been there for years. It never killed
Mrs. Rhine. So you see."

Kenmore drew back a discomfited step. It was only
that?

Corinne was stabbing her cigarette to its death. "But,"
the dark sister observed superiorly, "when Mrs. Rhine
lived there she had the chimney."

"Chimney?" said Kenmore.

"There used to be a fireplace. Uncle Henry tore it out. He thought if a bomb dropped anywhere near, the bricks would fall through the roof."

Kenmore thought, that explained the new paneling.

Corinne continued briskly. "The north lots didn't come with this house. He bought them two years ago, to have room for a tennis court partly, and partly because the old redwood cottage was an eyesore. It was built, oh, years before this section of town was restricted. And Mrs. Rhine never watered, never pulled a weed, and she hung out her washing practically under our noses, things like that. Of course, Uncle Henry intended to remodel the cottage inside and out and make it really a guest-house. Only priorities came along and he couldn't get the materials, and let it go until after the War. That's how it became his air raid post, because he didn't want to pile sandbags around *this* house.

"Anyway," said Corinne conclusively, "it's perfectly true the heater never poisoned Amy Rhine, but she hadn't the place sealed up as it is now."

Lally listened, or didn't listen, petulantly. "Anyway, you're glad it happened. You can't deny you are."

"But I do deny it," said the dark sister. *"You* may be tickled pink, but that's because you're so deliciously primitive, darling. When actually it won't make the least difference. You'll go on just as before, boozing and sleep-ing-around, until one fine day Al Dearborn slits your pretty throat."

Jessie Axiter broke in, fluttering: "Corinne! Girls! What will the lieutenant think of us?"

"Mother," said Corinne, "her habits aren't any secret from the police. They call her by her first name at the sub-station—if they are charitable. Otherwise, God-knows-what."

"Are you a cop?" Lally murmured to Kenmore. "You

don't look like one. I think you look like a football coach. College, not high school."

"That," said Corinne, "is what she tells all the boys who are too old to look like football heroes."

Kenmore ignored the bitter brat. He stared down at the younger girl. "Yes, I am . . . Why should you be glad? Any of you?"

Under his searching scrutiny, Lally gave a little blurred giggle.

"I bet you think I haven't any brassiere on." In fact, the white gown was almost shamelessly low-cut. "Well, I have so. A very special one, from New York, and it cost—you guess."

The settee caught Jessie Axiter's collapsing, spent weight. "Oh, my God," she whispered, and burst into tears. "Corinne, take your sister upstairs."

"No," Kenmore insisted. "I want her to answer that."

Lally's entrance had obviously been fortified by a very stiff drink, the effects of which were rising in her clouding blue eyes.

"Twen'y-fi' dollars," she mumbled.

"I mean why you should be glad."

"Because Uncle Henry saw through us," Corinne told him, "is why. When you perform your autopsy, take a good look at his tongue. He had a blunt one."

She stood.

"Come along, darling, before you're sick on the nice parquetry, and you know Ella hates that."

"No," said Kenmore, "she isn't that drunk . . . Look here. Don't touch this. But have you ever seen it before?"

Lally's blue eyes focused with some difficulty on the envelope.

"No," she denied.

"Miss Corinne?"

The dark sister shook her head. "I've no idea—what is it, anyway?"

"I don't know. That's what I am trying to find out," said Kenmore. "What it was doing in the guesthouse."

"It probably fell out of the carpenter's pocket," Corinne thought. "We don't know anyone named Burrett, and I never heard of New Gilead, Michigan."

"Mrs. Axiter?"

Tears trickled down Jessie Axiter's too-powdered cheeks. She looked up at Kenmore, and for the first time he saw the faint and ancient scar on her throat under the thick powder.

"That isn't Henry's handwriting," said she. "Mr. Kenmore. Lally *does* have headaches. I'm sure that is why . . . She is simply not responsible when she has these spells."

And so wonderfully made is the human mind, Kenmore thought it even possible she believed what she said.

"Yes," said the lieutenant. "But have you any reason to think what she told us *might* be true? If your brother had an enemy—?"

"Oh, no!"

"I don't necessarily mean a blood feud, Mrs. Axiter. But if he was involved, let's say, in a lawsuit? If he had been annoyed by a crank in some way recently?"

And he ran down the list of commonest motives for murder.

"No," Jessie Axiter repeated, "no, no."

"Did you notice," persisted Lieutenant Kenmore, "anything unusual in his manner? He was worried . . . or wrapped up in something he mightn't have talked about?"

"Not at all," said Corinne. "We had dinner at the Loquat House tonight. Uncle Henry left early, before the dessert, because of the Commando raid drill. That was the last we saw of him, and he was certainly in the best of spirits then."

Lieutenant Kenmore went outside and, pausing on the verandah, tamped tobacco into his pipe. There was a great deal wrong in the house of death, but what was significantly wrong? He couldn't tell . . . The scene was too like one of those pictures in which the artist deliberately includes several score errors, and challenges you to count them accurately.

He was not to smoke the pipe of contemplation as yet.

A light showed now above the garage's triple doors. The lieutenant found a flight of outside stairs. He climbed, and knocked.

Stifled tones told him, "Yup, come in." Kenmore entered a small, slope-ceilinged room that had an ill-kept, masculine, bachelor appearance. A box couch fitting against the lower wall, between bookshelves, wore a rumpled blanket cover. Copies of *Time, Sunset,* and *Popular Machanics* lay strewn over a table in the middle of the room. The pine floor lacked any covering.

"Hello, where are you?"

Kenmore heard footsteps, and then a small, bald, moustached man came around a partition at the room's end. He appeared in an undershirt and trousers, with his suspenders falling to his knees.

"Fred Crush?" the lieutenant asked, and showed his badge.

Crush nodded; then held the nozzle of a medicinal-looking tube to his nostril; flattened the companion nostril under his thumb, and sniffed noisily.

"Yup," said he in a congested tone. "What you want?" And as an afterthought: " 'Scuse me. Lots of pneumonitis around. A working man can't take chances with his health, it's all he's got."

Kenmore replied: Fred Crush had been a witness tonight, had he not?

"Uh-huh. Pull yourself up a chair." The gardener

seated himself on the box couch. He squeezed out a thumbnail's length of the nasal jelly, tossed that into his mouth, and swallowed, grimacing. "I guess I can't tell you much. They had him outside on the grass by the time I got down there."

"They called you?"

"Nuh, I heard her carrying-on, crying. Miz Axiter."

"And then?"

"Well, sir," said Crush, "that's just about all there was to it."

Kenmore looked at him. "Nobody told you to *do* anything about it?"

"Oh. Yup. She said to call a doctor, so I went in the house."

"Ran across the tennis court?"

Crush nodded.

Kenmore said, "All the way to the house, when there was a phone right there?"

"Well, I went in *there* first. There was a phone, all right, but I didn't see any book. I had to look up the number before I called. That's why I went to the house, mister."

"And which doctor did you call?"

The gardener gave a headshake. "I didn't, I told Corinne about it."

"And then," said Kenmore, "you weren't interested enough to go back to the guesthouse and see what was happening?"

Crush's eyes refused to meet his inquisitor's. "I dunno what good I could 'a done."

"Where did you go, then?" Kenmore asked.

When he didn't get a reply to that, the lieutenant arose from his chair.

"Put on your shirt," said he, "and a coat."

The box spring cried out, the gardener jerked visibly

as from a blow. His lips worked under their shelter of greying moustache. He whined: "If you got to know. I had to go look for Lally. I went down to the Shore Club, only she wasn't there."

"Lally! What is this? Why didn't you say so?"

Fred Crush's face got brick red. On his cheekbones traceries of hairline capillaries gorged into blue prominence.

He exploded: "Well, God A'mighty! Corinne told me not to mention it! Lally's on a drunk-bat, I suppose. They're trying to hide that, they expect me to lie and get myself in Dutch with the police . . . What does Corinne care about me? They're all alike, that family!"

Lieutenant Kenmore could not imagine Corinne in the role of Lally's defender. There was certainly more to it than that . . .

The gardener had jumped up excitedly.

"If you had to put up with them yourself!" Fred Crush exclaimed. "The way they impose on a man! Take just one thing—*eating*. Of course they've got my ration books, so's to do all the shopping together. But you take meat . . . The government never intended a big roast should go on Henry Bowling's table for him to carve off more than the family can eat, and then send the bone out to the kitchen for the hired help. I don't care if you are a cop, you have to admit that's not right."

But he didn't give Kenmore a moment to admit it, he plunged on:

"Oh, they'll tell you what a fine fellow Henry Bowling is—was. How much he did for civilian defense. Well, maybe, but there's more to it than that. You take those sandbags down there—" the gardener gave a short bark of laughter. "On account of the housing shortage, he was afraid the government'd step in and *make* him rent that little cottage to some War worker. But a family in it would mean kids. Not that there's anything they could hurt. Only you know how it is. Kids holler and yell. They'd be a nuisance. He saw it coming, and he figured if he made the place into an air raid post, he wouldn't be bothered."

Fred Crush wiped a bent and nervous forefinger across his moustache, both ways. And went on, headlong:

"There's your Henry Bowling. *He* knew which side to spread the butter on—his side. And when butter's rationed, it makes a man stop and think . . . At that, he was the best of the lot. When I see those girls that never lifted a finger in their lives—one of them drinking herself to death—and Corinne just as bad, driving everybody else to drink—! What the hell have they got to kick about? I'd like to know. They've got every advantage and luxury money can buy. Everything in the world. And they're bawling because the moon wasn't thrown in. I tell you what it is—

"Selfishness! It's spoiled selfishness. I'm not any crazy Red," he shook his head at Kenmore, "but the whole family makes me good and swearing mad. Miz Axiter, too. Damned if she doesn't think those girls ought to have the moon!"

"Yes," said Kenmore, "if it's true, I can see how you feel."

But this lengthy outburst hadn't distracted his attention from the original issue.

"You brought Lally home, then?"

"No," said Crush, "she wasn't at the Club."

"One more thing. This."

The gardener peered at the envelope, and shook his head.

Lieutenant Kenmore carried that object back to the guesthouse where Donald Heyes, police photographer and fingerprint technician, was now busy.

"You had better take a picture of this, and see if there are any prints on it."

Donald Heyes took the picture.

He said there were only unidentifiable smudges on the envelope. "Plenty of other prints here, if you got any suspects to match 'em up with."

Kenmore replied everyone involved might conceivably be suspected. "Only we can't start fingerprinting them yet."

He had to be content with bundling together the pink sheets along with the gas mask and helment; these last articles he could fairly claim, since they were property issued through the war duty office authority.

"Too bad he wasn't wearing that," said Heyes.

"You mean the mask? It wouldn't have made any difference, this type isn't designed to exclude carbon monoxide."

Nevertheless, Lieutenant Kenmore examined the mask attentively; the white, very thin rubber inlet valve was lifelessly weak. "He couldn't have worn it, anyway." And the lieutenant transferred his attention to the heater. This had two valves; one upon the heater base, and the other at the wall tap, whence ran a reinforced tubing to the heater.

"Check these prints here," said Kenmore, discovering the grilled top of the heater bore visible impressions.

He had next to pay a call at the mortuary and, according to regulation procedure, remove and list Henry Bowling's clothing and personal effects to seal and deliver to the police department's property clerk.

In this occupation, Kenmore generally found both food and opportunity for reflection. It followed the first interrogation of witnesses, and with the conflicting testimonies fresh in mind.

Though Kenmore knew he was not going to get any

useful perspective of Henry Bowling by walking around and seeing him through a dozen pairs of eyes. (The arm-band and whistle he laid aside. Wallet, wristwatch, keys, spectacle case, tobacco pouch, stickpin and signet ring went into another heap.) For what any man sees in an-other is the reflection of the observer's self-interest, at-tributes and attitudes. Kenmore thought, "A missionary doesn't look the same to a bishop and a cannibal."

(He tied the shoes together by their laces.)

And how the missionary would look to a homicide detail detective would be neither the sum of those ob-servations, nor a balance struck between them. Henry Bowling as employer, as sector warden, and as family head didn't engage John Kenmore's professional atten-tion. No matter what the man had really been like; only, how must he have seemed to the murderer he meant to denounce?

(The clothing, neatly folded, made another pile.)

And with the clothing went the individual; what re-mained was The Victim. Who had to be seen as such; and not in any perspective Kenmore could get by adding Wyeland's estimate with the several contributions of Lauren Wallace, Mrs. Axiter, Corinne, Lally, and Fred Crush.

Leave the exact weighing of pros and cons to the Recording Angel; leave Kenmore's own personal and human philosophy and feeling out of the matter; what he had to do now was see eye-to-eye with the killer . . . a nebulous figure concealed in an unexplored shadow Henry Bowling had cast sometime and somewhere.

Eye-to-eye with the killer?

Lieutenant Kenmore had not reached that point. It was, he thought, "Like playing chess blindfolded," against an adversary who operated at no such disadvan-tage and besides had every move plotted in advance.

VII

"The grave is a very small hillock, but we can see farther from it . . . than from the highest mountain in the world."

Grandfather always quoted this when he preached a funeral sermon.—The Autobiography of Catherine Hope.

The Marine Research Institute grounds occupied a picturesque headland; they were not otherwise picturesque; consisting principally of redwood cottages surrounding the architecturally barren central buildings.

"Wait here," Lieutenant Kenmore told Donald Heyes, and went hurrying along a footpath to the third cottage beyond the pier entrance.

Darwina Roydan, opening the door, widened her eyes at her caller's request.

"The monograph? Whatever for?"

"I'd like to consult it," said Lieutenant Kenmore.

"Volume I or II?"

"Both."

Darwina crossed a comfortably furnished living room to her bookshelf and tugged forth the life history of *leucetta losangelensis*.

"If you would only *ask* me," said she. "There are 824 pages of text."

And very luxurious pages they were, being printed on enamelled stock and bound in three-quarters calfskin.

"You're just looking at the pictures!" said she some moments later.

"No . . . These tables of chemical analysis. Did you do all that by yourself?"

"Of course!" said Darwina with almost Amazonian indignation. "Do you suppose I hired a ghost to do my research for me?"

Kenmore had not supposed anything of the kind; as a matter of fact, he had not known what he would find in the famous monograph. The only marine research that had ever interested him was the behavior of a swordfish or yellowtail on the end of several hundred yards of deep-sea line. The solid scientific reputation of the monograph had made him fight shy of ever peeping inside its calfskin covers. He felt if it had been comprehensible to a layman, it wouldn't have been scientific.

"It seems you are a practical chemist," said he abruptly. "You should make an excellent substitute for our police test tube expert who is going into the Army and can't possibly be present to testify at the trial. If there ever is a trial."

"I don't know that I want to testify at a trial . . ."

"Of course you don't. But you will, my model citizen."

Darwina colored. "Well-l, if it is *really* necessary."

"It is absolutely necessary . . . You have a key to the Institute laboratory, haven't you?"

The key let them into a dark and cavernous tunnel of hallway extending down the middle of the laboratory building. Darwina frowned as her companion drew the envelope from his pocket.

Kenmore said: "Here's the exhibit. It's been fingerprinted and photographed in its original condition. Also, I've shown it to the family. I didn't get a nibble. If the thing is authentic, it's up to me to find that out by other means than confirmatory testimony. It will have to speak

for itself, since no one of them will identify or explain
it. That's where you, as a chemist, come in."

"Whatever do you want me to do with it?" said Darwina uneasily.

"We'll begin by making an analysis of the ink."

Darwina reached a hand to the doorknob. "Oh, no, we
won't. I won't. I know my limitations—"

"It will be only an elementary analysis," said the detective. "I suppose it is ordinary, blue-black gallotannic ink.
That is, it is probably a sulphuric or hydrochloric solution of tannic and gallic iron salts in combination with an
additional aniline dye, sugar, gum arabic, and so on.
As you know, the blue in ink doesn't actually turn black.
It is the aniline dye which is blue, and the iron salts
which in time are oxidized and cause the writing to
blacken."

"Yes," said Darwina. "I knew that, but I never knew
chemistry was one of your hobbies."

"It isn't. I once had a case involving an altered will,
and so I had to bone up on the identification of inks.

"Well," Kenmore said, "this is black ink. And if it is
black owing to oxidation, that can be proved by making
a test for iron salts."

"Hydrochloric solution of ferrocyanide and rhodanid
of sodium in nitric acid," nodded Darwina, "but I suppose there is no use telling *you* that."

"It is no use *telling* me. I know the theory of the thing.
It's the practical technical touch I lack."

Darwina led the way along the hall to a large room
equipped with work benches, concrete vats, and racks of
retorts and test tubes. She slid her arms into a rubberized
apron, helped herself to a supply of chemicals from a
cabinet, and set to work.

"Well?" said the lieutenant presently.

Darwina looked up from the eyepiece of a Spencer

microscope. "There is an iron reaction," she reported.

Some of the tension relaxed on Kenmore's angular features.

"It is gallotannic ink, then," said he, "and we can plunge it into Ermel's solution."

"What's that?"

He opened his pocket memo book.

"You make up five grams of silver nitrate, one gram of citric acid, half a gram of tartaric acid, and three drops of nitric acid in a hundred grams of distilled water . . . You have a photographic darkroom in the building? This has to be used under a ruby light."

"Yes, but what is it *for?*"

"You will see—if Miss Hope put a letter into it. She wasn't a *wasteful* person, she always wrote on both sides of a piece of paper," said Kenmore reminiscently.

"The darkroom is down in the basement."

There followed an interval of activity under the darkroom's ruby light (in the course of which the envelope got slit open).

Some minutes later:

"There is writing on it!" cried Darwina.

"It is not writing. It's a latent image, a picture, that is transferred from one piece of paper to another if they are brought in contact, and if one piece has been written upon with gallotannic ink. Don't ask me why," Kenmore forestalled hurriedly. "I am not chemist or physicist enough to understand the phenomenon, but it is so. Criminologists have been getting evidence out of discarded envelopes for years, but it is not very likely a forger who prepared a plant like this would think to prepare a forged enclosure as well."

"Unless it was to fool Henry Bowling," said Darwina.

"Yes. In that case, it will be helpful to know how he was fooled.

"Only," unhappily, "of course it is not possible to recover more than a fragment—the portion of the letter that was in direct contact with the envelope surface."

Darwina bent closer to the developing tray. "I can't read it at all, it is backwards—no. It is like a blotter impression. You hold it up to a mirror."

"We'll have Heyes photograph it first," said Kenmore. "Because in the fixing bath the image is very apt to fade."

Fascinated, Darwina peered into the tray. ". . . a-n-d s-a-y-s period H-e i-s a b-o-s-t-o-," and paused. "No. B-*a*-s-t-*a*-r-d. Well! I must say I am surprised at her language!"

Catherine Hope, in fact (if in fact it was she) had written:

. . . and says. He is a bastard but of c . . . . e I don't let on all I . . . . . ow . . . n't you either. You had better burn this and fo . . . . . . ver told you. I have not got any work . . . . ll week on . . . nt of it. I tore up my . . . irst letter but then tho . . . . . know in case anyth . . . . . . pens to me, *destroy it* for his wife's sake.

Has . . . . ing sister,
KATIE

"But!" cried Darwina. "Whatever was the *rest* of it?"

VIII

Sometimes I think the real me is not in this book at all.—THE AUTOBIOGRAPHY OF CATHERINE HOPE.

Lieutenant Kenmore, when he returned to the Market Street headquarters this Thursday night (but it was very nearly Friday morning when he did so), walked briskly into the B.I.S. files room. He got from the files of *Open* (which meant unsolved) *Cases* a tremendously thick folder.

This contained the official reports of the uniformed officers, detectives, coroner's surgeons, and district attorney's investigators; and the official photographs; and the newspaper clippings and magazine articles and their unofficial photographs; and the letters from various and sundry citizens; and a great mass of manuscript from the victim's own hand—

In short, the tremendous folder enclosed the Catherine Hope Case.

MONDAY, 16th APRIL, 1937, ALMOST ON THE DOT OF 8:00 A.M., August Vabois, janitor, unlocked and opened the Marine Research Institute aquarium at La Jolla, California. 'Aquarium' ought perhaps be enclosed in apologetic quotes; for the structure was no more than a single-storey outbuilding of weathered and paintworn, batten-and-board construction. It was in fact a shed, twenty feet by forty-two, furnished with a roof that was part tarred paper and part ordinary window sash skylighting.

Vabois reached it by means of a footpath along the sea-wall; the path began at the M.R.I. laboratory building, it pierced through the adjacent shrubbery to the water front, and then proceeded northwards for seventy yards to the aquarium and another forty yards to the M.R.I. pier. Mr. Vabois was not the first to traverse it this morning. He had been preceded by Darwina Roydan, who used it to go swimming; and by Strickland Smith and Edward Torrance, who were bait-fishing from the pier.

Every inch of this path, every square foot of the terrain about the aquarium, was presently to be scrutinized with the most minute circumspection; Mr. Vabois presumably had no foreknowledge of the fact; he paid no attention whatever to his familiar surroundings.

Vabois, if he had looked about, would have observed a footpath of clay-and-sand, having a surface barely susceptible to the impression of his soles; this was bordered on the one side by plantings of waist-high pittosporum bushes, and on the other side by a dense green mat of ankle-deep ice plant sloping down to the sea-wall. The wall, of concrete, enclosed and reinforced a natural, twelve-foot bluff against the highest of plus tides.

Vabois, from his doorway, could not have seen that the beach below lay washed clean by the previous night's tide. But he might have observed the pier wading, on its ponderous telegraph pole stilts, some two hundred feet into the sea.

And he might, if he had glanced around, taken note of the Institute laboratory and office buildings some two hundred feet in the other direction; and the scattered redwood cottages about the grounds, housing the Institute's staff.

Vabois unlocked the door and thrust it open—it was

a sliding door, hung upon a somewhat rusty track. The janitor peered inside. The interior was ill-lighted, at least by contrast with the morning sunshine; the illumination proceeded through the roof skylights, and then was filtered through the glass walled fish tanks.

These tanks ran around the two sides and the rear of the building. They were all of a unit, comprising the interior walls of the aquarium. August Vabois paid no attention to them, either; he looked at the concrete floor; it was his job to sweep out debris of cigarette butts, gum and candy wrappers, and peanut shells dropped by Sunday afternoon visitors.

Vabois had brought a broom for the purpose, and he set himself to wielding it.

Presently, idly, he looked up from his occupation. And beheld what was to be, in succeeding months, the cover illustration of almost every true-crime magazine in the United States.

Mr. Vabois saw an entirely nude woman jammed head-first into the sting-ray tank.

It is true that the cover illustrators embroidered lavishly upon this theme. Miss Hope's hair did not rise from her scalp in a rippling blond submarine growth; her hair was confined in a tight bun at the nape of her neck. And it was not blond hair; it was grey, really. The illustrators were obliged to deduct some years from the victim's age, and to alter by inches her physical proportions; and their flesh tones were all wrong. Catherine Hope, as Vabois saw her, was of a ghastly washed-out green hue.

What August Vabois said was not of record; but he ran out of the building, shouting.

Strickland Smith and Edward Torrance heard him shout.

As did Professor E. W. Martin, meteorologist, just then

quitting his cottage front step. Professor Martin established the time; it was now 8:03 a.m.

Darwina Roydan was nearer than anyone else; returning from her swim, she had reached the top of the concrete steps at the pier gate when Vabois dashed out onto the path.

He ran toward her—along the path. "Somebody has *drowned* herself in with the fish," he said.

Witnesses Smith and Torrance did not overhear these words; but they saw Vabois running, they saw his excited gesticulations, and Strickland Smith handed over his fishing rod to his companion.

Torrance paused to reel in both lines, and then he followed Smith.

Professor Martin testified he would have thought nothing of the shouting, "They had caught a fish, I supposed," but when he saw Vabois, Darwina Roydan, and Smith all running toward the aquarium, he likewise headed in that direction.

Darwina Roydan and Vabois got there first, of course. Darwina looked into the tank; she immediately said, "Gus, you had better hurry and call the police."

Vabois dashed out and down the path, toward the laboratory building.

Strickland Smith, as he came along the path from the other direction, snatched up a stick. "I thought the yelling was about a snake," he subsequently explained. Smith, summoned by his wife's outcries, had killed a rattlesnake in a flowerbed the previous afternoon. On discovering his error, he dropped the stick—a length of driftwood—on the walk outside, where, a minute or so later, Professor E. W. Martin stumbled and fell over it.

"I am going to get Dr. Wallace," Strickland Smith overheard the meteorologist say. "I am going to *tell* Dr. Wallace," was Darwina's version of the remark. At any rate, the professor made off and took the stick with him; it was found later a few yards from the Director's door, and there were bloodstains on it.

Smith and Torrance burst through the pittosporum planting and found a ladder lying beside the aquarium wall. They raised this and first Smith, and then Torrance, climbed and peered through the shattered skylight. Torrance called to Darwina Roydan that he had touched the body, and it was cold.

Darwina had been trying, by peering through the fish tank side, to recognize the victim. She hastened outside, saying, "You mustn't touch anything until the police get here."

This was excellent advice; but unfortunately, the footpath had already been repeatedly trod by Darwina herself, August Vabois, Professor Martin, Strickland Smith, and Edward Torrance. The last two named had handled the ladder, and they now guiltily returned it to its place beside the wall; and on one could ever say certainly which of the several ladder impressions in the soil had been left there by the murderer, and which by Smith and Torrance.

Officers Earl Harley and William Buckholtz came promptly from the sub-station. That, however, was all that could be said for them. They likewise added their footfalls to the miscellany upon the path; they pushed through the pittosporum; and Harley eyed the ladder dubiously. They were both large men—Harley, the smaller of the pair, weighed 210 pounds. Using his revolver-butt for the purpose, the patrolman repaired a loose-nailed rung; then he climbed to the aquarium roof.

He wanted, as he said, to make sure the woman was dead.

Dr. Lauren Wallace arrived. Professor E. W. Martin

returned, this time with his wife. Presently the whole staff of the Institute was assembled at the scene.

Dr. Wallace observed, "This is murder. We must all keep our heads," and he then called the roll of the females employed by, or living at, the Institute.

Catherine Hope was not identified until the homicide detail detectives arrived. The detail operated under the command of Captain Harry Whipple (in 1937, the Bureau of Internal Security had not as yet been created). His principal assistants were Inspector John Kenmore, Sergeant Benjamin Trafton, and First-Grade Detective Lem Bixby.

They were not a congenial unit. Captain Whipple had not his subordinates' confidence. No man is born a cop, and Harry Whipple had become one because he was too shrewd to choose the career of ward-heeler instead. He was a political cop; he had acted as a kind of contact man or go-between linking a former chief of police with the gambling fraternity; and he was himself frequently spoken of as the next chief.

The captain had sought, and he had got, transferred to the homicide detail because his earlier command, the vice squad, was not quite the foothold from which an ambitious officer could spring to the throne. That squad was not in too good odor, in fact. Whipple had neither the special talent nor the special training which makes an efficient homicide investigator; but he felt one good murder, with its attendant publicity, was exactly what he needed.

"By God, boys," said the captain, when he had peered into the sting-ray's tank, "we've got a juicy one."

Kenmore, Trafton, and Bixby understood that credit for a successful investigation would reside entirely with the captain; but if discredit resulted, somebody else would have to bear the blame. Whipple would sacrifice any or all of the three to further his personal advancement, and they knew it.

The coroner's deputy arrived, and the reporters. Whipple conferred with the deputy, and then made a statement to the press. "Miss Hope," said he, "was beaten and strangled. The weapon was a blunt instrument. The strangling was done with the killer's bare hands. It happened between eight and eleven o'clock last night. It was the work of a fiend, of course."

One of the reporters asked, "A sex fiend?"

Captain Whipple hesitated; he could not positively say that the victim had been sexually assaulted; but he wanted to give the boys a good story.

"It has all the earmarks of that," said he.

The captain later had to retract the sexual assault; for the autopsy proved quite the contrary. He had to renege on his bare-handed killer; the only identifiable prints found on the ladder were those of Strickland Smith, Torrance, and Earl Harley. Even the blunt instrument was questionable—the victim's contused injuries might have been caused by a fall, by being bumped violently against some object whilst she was being strangled.

Captain Whipple detailed Inspector Kenmore and the La Jolla officers to assemble and preserve the physical clues on the scene. (He himself proceeded to Miss Hope's home at 116 Balboa Street.)

The physical clues on the scene consisted of some trampled earth, a broken skylight, and the ladder. The ladder was a home-made affair, of ten foot 2x4's to which were cleated some 1x4 risers; it was reinforced by strips of 1x4 reinforcement tacked diagonally onto the rear. August Vabois used it when the fish tanks were cleaned;

it had been lying there next the wall since that was last done.

At another stage of the investigation, Kenmore put this ladder to a breakage test. It succumbed under a burden of 412 pounds; but no one could say what weight the weakest rung would have borne before Harley secured it . . .

Inspector Kenmore, when he had thoroughly hunted over the immediate area about the aquarium, pursued his investigation along the footpath past the laboratory building to the Institute's parking lot. He looked with particular attention into the shrubbery; because a criminal, owing to nervousness, frequently relieves himself by means of a bodily function.

Kenmore found nothing of the sort. He turned his attention in the other direction, toward the pier and the shore. And on the rocks fifty yards north of the pier, discovered a lard pail, a waterlogged flashlight, and a woman's bathing suit.

These articles were identified as Catherine Hope's; but the discovery was almost ignored in the newspaper account of the crime.

The newspapers had something much more sensational. Captain Harry Whipple, in a second statement to the press, had proclaimed Catherine Hope a Scarlet Woman; and he had furnished a *portrait parle* of her probable assailant.

"The Hope woman," said he, "was a goddam Red and a sex cultist," and read the reporters some excerpts from her diary to prove it.

In fact, Miss Hope had been a dismayingly virginal spinster; her only fault being that she was a penwoman, and frequently inflicted on her acquaintances selected readings from her (unpublished) *Autobiography*.

What Captain Whipple had discovered in the victim's writing desk, and prematurely released to the press as evidencing her secret eroticism, was a Selected Reading —and instantly identified as such by the several score La Jollans to whom the author had read it aloud. This purple prose scoop constituted a description of the life in an offshoot theological community where Catherine Hope had spent her childhood; the man involved—and Whipple had pieced together his description with a view to apprehending the bigamous rascal—had been her maternal grandfather.

The 'diary,' in short, was Chapter III of the *Autobiography*.

How had the captain made his incredible error?

He had made it, in the first place, because of Miss Hope's failure to master the typewriter. She wrote in longhand, and frequently, wrote at the beach, using odd scraps of paper (and both sides of it) for the purpose.

In the second place, because she was an amateur who had never learned a professional technique or discipline. She wrote when she was inspired; that is to say, when she felt like it, and wrote what she felt like writing. And her inspiration wasn't chronological. Chapter XXXVII, *I Meet Hitler* (she had seen him, with the aid of her opera glasses, at the Berlin Olympics), was written on shipboard in 1936; but Chapter XIII, *I Sail on the* Titanic—*Almost*, existed only as a heading in a table of contents. Miss Hope's literary method was that of jotting down her recollections as they came to her, dew-fresh and generally in the present tense; and of interpolating material drawn from her correspondence, and newspaper clippings, old theatre programs, and the like; and trusting to the typist, Amy Rhine, to make it all come out coherently.

But in the third place, and mainly, the fault was Whipple's own.

He hadn't verified his finding, he regarded the rules of evidence as legalistic obstacles that existed only to be outwitted, he hadn't hesitated to launch a possible ir reparable blow at the subject of his *portrait parle*.

Consequently he had to retract the 'diary,' along with the sexual assault, the bare-handed killer, and the blunt weapon.

What remained?

The facts concerning Catherine Hope were these: She was a female, aged fifty years, who had resided in La Jolla since 1923; her income, which she had inherited, amounted to $3000 a year. On this amount of money, a single woman of modest taste could live more than reasonably well. Miss Hope found it possible to travel; she had twice been in Europe, once to Mexico, Vancouver, and Panama; and in 1927 she had taken a world cruise. The *Autobiography* was principally a record of these excursions. Inspector Kenmore, when he came to read it, found very little light shed upon the author's sojourn in La Jolla.

But by all other accounts, Catherine Hope's fourteen years in the village had been remarkably unremarkable. She wasn't beautiful (she had never been that), or exceptionally energetic, or equipped with an uncomfortable degree of intelligence. The last day of her life, Sunday, 15th April, 1937, was quite typical of her leisurely, unexciting, but pleasantly occupied life. Miss Hope, on this Sunday morning, rose at her usual hour, 7:30 o'clock; she prepared with her own hands a breakfast of coffee, buttered toast, and a boiled egg, and this (for it was a fine morning) she ate in the patio. Her patio was overlooked by her neighbors, a Mr. and Mrs. William Wyeland. Catherine Hope, when she had breakfasted, talked to Mrs. Wyeland about the inroads caused by snails in her garden. During the forenoon, she attended church;

after church, she lunched at the La Jolla Buffet; then she strolled home by way of the waterfront walk.

Miss Hope did not own an automobile; the Wyelands, who did, suggested she accompany them on a Sunday afternoon drive. "We felt sorry for her," said Theodora Wyeland, and the majority of Miss Hope's female acquaintances felt more or less that way about her . . . when they did not envy her instead. Her life seemed extremely empty to them—or extremely carefree, depending on your point of view and your children's behavior at the moment.

They drove to Escondido, and back; Catherine Hope purchased some grapejuice at a highway stand; this she insisted upon presenting to Theodora Wyeland.

At 5:30 o'clock, when Amy Rhine stopped by, Miss Hope was engaged in writing some letters. Mrs. Rhine, who was employed as stenographer in William Wyeland's law office, had been glad to add an honest dollar to her income by typing nights on the *Autobiography*. This was the purpose of her call; she meant to pick up Chapter I (*I Am Born*); but Catherine Hope, because of the drive, had not worked on that.

"Well, then," said Amy Rhine, "suppose we go to the movie tonight. It's Clark Gable."

For Mrs. Rhine, though compelled to earn her living, was a gentlewoman and in every way Miss Hope's social equal.

Catherine Hope declined. "I am going after grunion," she explained. "But if you're walking downtown tonight, would you mind mailing these letters?"

Amy Rhine took the letters. But she did not mail them that night, being asked to make a fourth at bridge; they stood overnight on her mantel, and she took them with her to Wyeland's office in the morning. Mrs. Rhine intended to drop them at the postoffice when she went there for the lawyer's mail, but hearing of the murder, took them to the police sub-station.

On examination, two of the envelopes contained checks payable to San Diego department stores, a third was addressed to a literary agent whose advertisement Miss Hope had seen in the *Writer's Digest*, a fourth accepted an invitation to tea on the 19th, and the fifth conveyed to her congressman Miss Hope's disapproval of a pending item of legislation . . . Wyeland had talked about this bill in the course of the afternoon drive.

Catherine Hope, when Mrs. Rhine had left her, presumably dined alone; she was next seen, by several witnesses, en route to her grunion hunt. She was, in fact, about to introduce the grunion to the newspaper readers of America. The grunion is a small, smelt-like fish which, at certain high tides, at the full and the dark of the moon, comes ashore on the tip of one wave, lays its eggs on the beach, and returns to the briny deep on the next wave. Miss Hope carried a lard pail in which to place her captured grunion, a flashlight with which to spy them out before the moon rose, and she wore a bathing suit in the expectation of being drenched at the sport.

The shore, when she reached it, was a-twinkle with fires, and populated with some hundreds of persons on the same errand as she. The tide reached its full at 9:17 o'clock; the wet sands flashed with myriad, quicksilver tiny fish; firelight, and the stabs of flashlights, painted the forms of the grunion hunters.

Catherine Hope plunged anonymously into this scene, and was never again seen alive.

These were the incontestable facts presented at the inquest. And what Captain Whipple's intensive, month-long investigation subsequently discovered was either not fact, or was not relevant.

A Mrs. Edwards had heard "loud shrieks" from one of

the Institute cottages on the night of the murder; it was true, apparently some hours after Miss Hope's body was flung into the fish tank. Inquiry revealed that there had been a party culminating in a game of strip poker in which three professors had participated.

Captain Whipple, just then being roundly criticized for inactivity, gave this item to the newspapers. The poker game provided a headline tidbit; it cost Drs. R. M. Stanley, Allen Wade-Brooks, and J. F. F. Bolgard their connection with M.R.I.; and it shed no light whatever upon the crime.

Three La Jolla housewives reported men had tried to peep into their bedroom windows that Sunday night; no trace of the miscreants was ever found.

Nearly a score of known sex offenders were rounded up for questioning; without result.

The bloodstained stick was presently found and accepted as the blunt instrument; until Professor Martin recalled that in falling he had scraped skin from his right palm.

Captain Whipple proved himself a persistent man, if sometimes an impulsive one. He relentlessly ran down every tip, and every shred of scandalous suspicion that offered itself. Only it all came to nothing. Catherine Hope in her grave remained what she had been in life: a virtuous spinster without a lover or an enemy. No motive, unless it were insanity or mistaken identity, could be ascribed to her slayer. The sole gainer by her death was a sister, Mrs. Ellen Hope Burrett, widow, of New Gilead, Michigan, who had not lived six months to enjoy the gain.

The official record dwindled away to its bitter, inconclusive end.

The time, when Lieutenant Kenmore had turned the

folder's last page, was 3:00 a.m. The lieutenant had paused, from time to time, to scribble a name onto his memo book flyleaf: Darwina Roydan, Dr. Lauren Wallace, Amy Rhine, William Wyeland . . . Henry Bowling's name was not on the list.

IX

I began to think you needed political pull to get even so simple a thing as a passport.—THE AUTOBIOGRAPHY OF CATHERINE HOPE.

"Captain Whipple wants to see you," said Sergeant Lyon.

"Yes: What the devil about?"

"Come over, was all he told me."

Lieutenant Kenmore stepped from the war duty office into the sun-lighted patio—for the San Diego police headquarters *has* a patio. The Market Street station does not look like a police station at all. It is for the most part a single-storey structure (with a lower tower or so) and to the passing Coronado ferryist it presents a picturesquely Spanish-styled exterior of stucco and dark red roof tile.

At the moment, ten o'clock of Friday's forenoon, a great Consolidated flying boat roared not very many feet above the roof tiles in its descent toward the block-distant bay. Kenmore didn't even glance up at it. Flying boats were overhead so often, you became as used to them as to street trolleys.

And Kenmore was preoccupied, not pleasantly, with the coming interview. The Catherine Hope Case had cost Captain Whipple his command of the homicide detail; but he'd been politician enough to manage being kicked upstairs rather than down.

Lieutenant Kenmore advanced warily into his superior's office; and Captain Whipple, just now cradling his desk phone, remarked by way of greeting:

"That was the district attorney's office. My God, John, you've kicked up one hell of a hornet nest in La Jolla."

The captain had an impressive physical façade. He was cast in the noble-Roman mold, but cast in inferior metal. His face, with its large features under crisply curling, iron-grey hair, photographed forcefully. Posed, he was magnificent; but he couldn't hold the pose forever.

In action, in conversation, the forceful face too often dissolved into a series of fleeting, faintly treacherous expressions.

Kenmore thought he read treachery in the captain's face now.

What's he up to? thought the lieutenant.

He waited, watchfully; on guard.

"Well," said Harry Whipple, "I've been on the wire with the coroner, too. There's a lot of pressure being brought to bear, one way and another. Tom Larned has been after the district attorney, and I understand Mrs. Axiter went to the coroner herself . . . trying to get a death certificate and the body released to her without a post-mortem."

Jessie Axiter had threatened to fight; Kenmore had not thought she could do so successfully. He did not think so now. "I told her last night, she hasn't a legal leg to stand on."

"She's not trying to make a legal issue out of it. Mrs. Axiter," said the captain, "is a smart woman. Or she's been smartly advised. She knows a person can get a hell of a lot in this world by seeing the right people."

Kenmore didn't like the sound of it. Because he knew, of course, that was true.

"Here is her out," Whipple continued. "She's learned that technically the police don't and can't order autopsies.

If you want to follow the law to the letter, post-mortems are performed at the coroner's discretion. He doesn't perform one in every case of accidental death that comes along. He does, if in his judgment it's necessary; otherwise not. And she doesn't see why an exception should be taken against her feelings in this case."

Kenmore knew very well there were cases in which coroners and medical examiners had been persuaded to spare the feelings of the bereaved. Sometimes they certified as accidental death what they must have felt morally certain was suicide. It would depend on the circumstances, on the amount of persuasion involved, and on the medical officer.

"Yes," said he, "but isn't she sticking out her neck? Her fighting it is a whale of a big reason for going ahead."

"Not necessarily. She says the idea of butchering-up her brother is repulsive to her. And that ain't so damned unusual. A good many people, perfectly innocent people, are prejudiced against an autopsy on a loved one."

Kenmore shrugged: "A good many murderers are prejudiced against it, too . . . The coroner isn't going to refuse my request for a post-mortem, is he?"

Captain Whipple chose not to answer this question directly.

He opened a pocket cigar case.

"Well, John," said he, "you've got eyes and ears. You read the papers, you see the billboards around town, you listen to the radio. I shouldn't have to remind you there's an election coming up."

"What's that got to do with me?"

"Nothing in the world. Except somebody's got to take the rap for this thing. It isn't just the Axiter woman, it's all her friends, and she runs in the best circles. You know La Jolla, you know those people out there have an influence out of all proportion to the votes they cast."

The cigar's tip vanished at a penknife stroke.

"Frankly, the coroner doesn't want to tell this woman to go to hell, and the d.a. doesn't want to, and neither does Councilman Larned on *his* own responsibility. What they want to do is pass the buck to us. They're sorry, but their hands are tied because the police insist—that's their line."

"Okay," said Kenmore. "If they want to put it that way."

The captain lighted his cigar.

"Yes," said he, breathing away a wreath of smoke. "However, is that fair to Chief Royce? I put it to you. He's not in such a sweet spot! Bringing him in here— an outsider—didn't sit well with a certain local element. Some of the boys want a more wide-open town than he's willing to run, and they're after his scalp.

"John, you must have seen some of the doorstep throwaways. You must have heard the Home Front hour on KGOY. All those blasts at us—all that talk about the streets being unsafe for women war workers—is aimed at Royce. They're gunning for him, and of course this thing'd be more ammunition."

Kenmore realized this statement of the political situation lacked candor. Had he been perfectly candid, Captain Whipple would have added that the open-town element was exactly where his own strength lay.

The lieutenant could surmise who the 'boys' were; he knew that Whipple had been their liaison man in the past; and would be their logical candidate for Royce's job, if they could oust the chief.

Transparently, Harry Whipple wasn't interested in defending Royce as a matter of departmental loyalty. But there the transparency ceased. The rest of it was hidden in that smoke-screen of political complication which was the captain's special domain.

"I don't know what you're getting at," observed Lieutenant Kenmore truthfully.

"Well," said the captain, "what do you expect from this autopsy? You already know it was carbon monoxide."

"All right, if it was carbon monoxide, I want that definitely down in the book. I don't want to fool around with this thing for weeks, have to get a court order to exhume the body, and then find he died of a heart condition, after all."

"And that's all?"

Kenmore said, "There's a possibility of a head injury, too. But it's beside the point. I don't expect an autopsy will solve the case, and it may not prove anything at all. Still it's an absolutely essential preliminary to an investigation."

Captain Whipple rendered first aid to his cigar, moistening and meticulously pasting down a shred of brown leaf.

"Well, but what happens? You cut Bowling open, and there's nothing inside him you didn't already know. It's going to look like officious meddling. It is going to stir up a La Jolla hornet nest, and then it will look like a piece of damned bureaucratic red tape when it doesn't prove anything new. That's why the coroner and the d.a. are afraid of it, they can see it'll arouse antagonism, and no elected public official wants that on the eve of an election."

Lieutenant Kenmore's glance hardened. It was with just this sort of argument he had no patience whatever. The one thing he could not tolerate in police work was politics . . . He said so, sharply.

Captain Whipple surprisingly agreed. "Right," said he. "We want to keep the police department out of politics. I don't see why we should put ourselves in the middle. Take La Jolla; there's Tom Larned's machine out there, and then there's also that reform element—like Darwina Roydan. I understand *she's* mixed up in this—"

Whipple paused; as if thought-struck. He suddenly grinned.

"By God! John, what do you think? *She* might appear as a complainant . . . I don't mean, swear out a warrant. But, you know, demand an investigation. She's a do-gooder, a crusader, just the type who would put her nose in . . . And then *we* wouldn't be criticized, we wouldn't have a delegation of La Jollans demanding a shake-up in the police department."

Lieutenant Kenmore stared.

The captain continued briskly: "The whole thing is— we don't want another Catherine Hope Case on our hands now . . . I don't like to ask Royce to go along, the way the thing stands. Because we should offer him a little more than you've apparently got, when you ask him to take the rap."

Kenmore recognized the trap—and disdained it.

"I'm not asking Miss Roydan to take the rap, either," said he. "I command my Bureau. I don't run to you or to the chief, asking can or should I do this, that, and the other."

Harry Whipple seemed to hesitate.

"It's political dynamite," he replied, "and I told the coroner I'd sound Royce out. But if you feel that strongly about it, if you want to take the plunge on your own responsibility—"

"Yes," said Kenmore.

And knew, as he said it, this was what Whipple had wanted all along. It was heads-I-win, tails-you-lose from the captain's viewpoint. If the autopsy proved nothing, *he* not only couldn't be blamed for unfeeling officiousness, but the resentment in La Jolla could be skillfully fanned to affect the approaching election. And if the autopsy proved murder, the whole thing might result in a hopeless tangle—another Catherine Hope Case, as Whipple said—and what could suit him better?

Lieutenant Kenmore didn't like politics in police work, on principle. He didn't like Harry Whipple, personally. And Whipple didn't like him. The day the captain became chief the Bureau of Internal Security would have a new commander.

Whipple was smug. "Okay, John, okay. Any time I can be any help—"

Kenmore was bleak. "Any time I want your help, I'll ask for it."

The captain sat diplomatically silent. Kenmore walked out, wondering what else, if anything, Harry Whipple had up his sleeve. He had a notion his job lay at the point of the autopsy surgeon's dissecting scalpel.

X

. . . whipped me for lying. But I was not a liar. Like most children I simply had a terrific imagination.—THE AUTOBIOGRAPHY OF CATHERINE HOPE.

Lieutenant Kenmore did not attend the autopsy. As war duty officer, he had to attend a conference on war plant protection Friday forenoon, and then a luncheon in honor of the visiting F.B.I. sabotage expert. Working under pressure, it was not possible for Kenmore to give all his time to any one case. The police department representative present was Ralph Arnold, acting-lieutenant, of the La Jolla sub-station.

Through Arnold, eventually, Kenmore figured out what happened. Dr. Myatt attended for Jessie Axiter. At a certain stage in the proceedings, he stepped out to the telephone and told his office girl he would be detained awhile. He also told her why. The mortician's wife, who was going out to a motor corps meeting, overhead the reason. So it happened that several dozen motor corps members knew all about it before the autopsy was completed, and well before Lieutenant Kenmore returned to the Market Street station to receive Deputy Coroner Ed McGheen's telephoned report:

"Blood of a bright cherry-red color . . . lungs saved for independent toxicological analysis . . . quantities of cyanogas in blood and lungs—"

Not carbon monoxide, Kenmore thought, not the heater at all. He had never believed that, but . . . !

The deputy coroner's voice ran on. "The funny part is, monoxide and cyanogas result in identical external physiological symptoms," and he began a recital of the symptoms, beginning with the cherry blush and suffused conjunctivae . . . to which Kenmore hardly listened.

"Cyanogas!" said the lieutenant. "The stuff exterminators use?"

"Cyanogen is the way you'll find it in the dictionary. It has different trade names," said McGheen, agreeing. "The commercial formulas vary a little, but they're all based on calcium cyanide as the active ingredient. In combination with moisture, it forms a hydrocyanic gas."

"I know what it is. But, my God! It reeks to hell and gone!"

The deputy coroner agreed to that, too. "What threw Myatt, and all of you off, of course, nobody seems to have noticed the characteristic odor. Take that away, and in his shoes I'd have made the same diagnosis. You don't stand over a body with a flashlight and do a pathological chemist's job."

Kenmore considered the odor of cyanogas wasn't one you could notice or not notice; it wasn't merely characteristic, it was overwhelming. And his mind balked from the fact. There had been enough cyanogas loosed in the guesthouse to kill a man at some time after 7:20 o'clock last night? And then when he himself arrived there on the heels of eight, there had lingered not a trace of the malodorous chemical agent?

It was incredible. It defied all reason. The door would have had to have been flung wide open, it would have needed a battery of fans besides to clear the atmosphere. The door hadn't been open at all, for the room had been closed and torridly overheated.

"I suppose he died practically instantaneously," said

the lieutenant. "Hydrocyanic gas. That'd be lethal as hell."

"Murderous," agreed McGheen.

Murder was the word; the autopsy had established that much . . . Only the fact had not brought Kenmore any nearer to a solution. He stood a great deal farther from one, in fact. The mystery was enormously and fantastically magnified.

A ten second interval later, the deputy coroner's voice came over the wire:

"You asked for it," observed McGheen.

Kenmore knew that was true. He had asked for, and he had got, what looked dismayingly like another, hopelessly tangled Catherine Hope Case.

"Yes," said he. "What about the head injury?"

"Just a bruise—purely superficial."

"Enough to knock a man out?"

"You mean, was he slugged first? No, I think that injury was inflicted afterward. When he fell, or maybe when the body was moved outside."

"Okay, and thanks," said Lieutenant Kenmore. "You'd better send us two copies, and send a report to the district attorney's office, of course."

He put down the phone and told Sergeant Lyon to summon Donald Heyes from the laboratory. "We are going to fingerprint all these people and have their statements," said he.

He did not expect too much of his assistants. Donald Heyes was a useful specialist and technician; but only useful in those capacities. The sergeant was a shorthand expert and a brave and energetic man—and unfortunately, as unsubtle as he was brave and energetic.

Neither of them, Kenmore thought as the B.I.S. sedan took the boulevard past the concrete defended Convair plants, had the peculiarly adroit touch that would be needed in this affair.

Cyanogen, he thought. *The external physiological symptoms are identical.* And the killer had very nearly gotten away with it.

Would have gotten away with it, if there had not been a telephone call, a missing pink sheet, and an envelope.

The sedan sped through an area of camouflage, machine gun nests, and funnel-snouted anti-aircraft artillery. Some defense units fleeted past; the sedan swerved around a Navy boot camp company, in whites, proceeding at route step; more anti-aircraft in the hills behind La Jolla was discharging black bursts into the sky.

Lieutenant Kenmore sat in silence the whole journey. *Cyanogen,* he thought, and the ideas which followed darted off at a dozen different tangents. He had not by any means begun to explore these fully when the sedan entered La Jolla, and Sergeant Lyon presently turned up Toyon Street.

Then:

"Whoa!" cried Kenmore. "Stop!"

Darwina Roydan, at the corner of Toyon and Laguna Terrace, was gesticulating with a large, linen crash handbag.

Darwina's hat today was an enormous platter of Mexican straw; she wore a flamboyant print dress; and had huaraches on her feet. Lieutenant Kenmore, as he got out of the car, admired her taste in clothing, which was frankly ostentatious; most women of her Amazonian proportions simply would not have dared . . . Darwina, however, chose her barbaric hats because she liked them, and not because she imagined they would deduct an apparent inch or so from her splendid height.

He crossed the street toward her. "Hello, what is it?"

"It's about that autopsy finding—"

Miss Roydan was obviously in a state of unusual tension.

"Here," said she, delving into the handbag and producing a blue-and-yellow tin.

Kenmore accepted the article. *Kills Pests,* the skull-and-cross-bone adorned label asserted. *Official Antidote of the California State Board of Pharmacy: Intravenous injections of methylene blue; 3 per cent solution of hydrogen peroxide in large quantities followed by immediate evacuation of the stomach. Artificial respiration and pulmotor. Inhalations of amyl nitrate.*

"Where'd you find this?"

"It's from the hardware store. From the Victory Garden counter," said Darwina. "I bought it. I didn't need a prescription, or have to sign a register, or anything. Anyone can buy it. Or steal it off the counter, for that matter."

Lieutenant Kenmore had been aware of that difficulty. He had seen cyanogen displayed in the downtown department stores, just as openly, along with other insecticides and rodent poisons.

"Well," Darwina said, "smell it."

The squatly square container had a twin-capped spout, for air-tight closure. Kenmore unscrewed this. He shook into his palm a few dark grey grains of the preparation. The odor which assailed his nostrils was pungent, biting, alarming—and sickening.

"Yes," said he. "I know. It has got to be explained why no one noticed it—"

"But Dorothy Wyeland did!" interrupted Darwina.

"What?" said Kenmore incredulously.

The Mexican platter bobbed.

"I've just come from a Motor Corps meeting," said Darwina, "in fact, I left early before the meeting began.

"Because Theodora Wyeland was there, and it seems

Dorothy ran home crying after she found the body, terribly upset, and *told her mother how awful Henry Bowling smelled*. Theodora thought it was all imagination because the child claimed *she could still smell it, the odor had got on her clothing*. Theodora has a perfectly good nose of her own and as she couldn't detect anything of the sort, she supposed it was all just the child's imagination. But," said Darwina grimly, "it occurred to me there might be another explanation. And I think this is it."

She tugged from her handbag a child's play shoe. (A rather grimy, and not very attractive article.)

"Dorothy Wyeland's," said she. "I got Theodora to drive me home, and we looked in the child's clothes closet, and found this. Just sniff at it once."

There was an odor of perspiration, and of the rubber sole, and at least the ghost of what had originally been another pungent, biting, and nauseating scent.

But it was not, Kenmore thought, quite the odor of cyanogen.

The detective recalled Edmond Locard's famous dictum: "It depends upon the taste of the individual whether the smell of a rotten pheasant makes him think of corpses and cadavers or places him in a condition of culinary happiness."

Little Dorothy Wyeland had identified this odor as the very effluvium of death; Darwina Roydan thought it cyanogen; for Kenmore it had quite a different, lurking association.

"Suppose we walk around to the Wyelands'," said he, and glanced across Toyon Street. "I suppose the kid cut across back lots last night. She was delayed, getting on her armband."

In fact, the lots opposite the guesthouse were vacant, and crossed by a footpath.

"You see what it means," Darwina was saying. "The

shoe couldn't have that odor still, from merely having been in the same room in which cyanogen was released. And it is only the one shoe—her left, not the right one at all.

"There's only one answer to that. Some of the poison, a grain or so, got *into* the shoe. Where did it come from? Again there's only one conceivable answer. It came from Henry Bowling's garments. It was brushed off his clothing, and brushed in the child's direction."

Darwina drew a deep breath.

"I'm afraid," said she, "Foster Ffleming has got a great deal to explain."

"Ffleming has?"

"Foster Ffleming," repeated Darwina. "Because if the child noticed the odor, why didn't he smell it? And if he did, how could he imagine for a moment Henry Bowling had been killed by carbon monoxide, which is perfectly odorless?"

Kenmore came to a stop.

"Ffleming was not the only one there, you know."

Darwina moistened her lips.

"You mean Jessie Axiter . . . But she simply stood by—not too close—and she was in tears. And in that condition, a woman's nose is much more useful for blowing than for smelling."

Kenmore said: "And Fred Crush went into the guesthouse within a minute or so of the discovery of the body."

"I know, I've just come from talking to Crush, said Darwina, "though I didn't ask him about it. I didn't have to. Because he had a terrific cold in his head."

Kenmore recalled, "He was using a nasal jelly last night."

Darwina's eyes were solemn under the Mexican platter's brim. "So you see. There were four persons gathered around the body in those first few moments. One was a half-hysterical woman, another a man with a head cold, the third a child who smelled something but she didn't know what—but what ailed Ffleming? Surely *he* had the best chance to notice. It's no use pretending Jessie Axiter or little Dorothy Wyeland could have been any help, it's clear Ffleming got the corpse outside practically by his own unaided efforts. And then, he knelt directly over Bowling. Where he couldn't possibly have missed discovering any smell of cyanogen on the man's clothes. Not only that."

Standing in the middle of the vacant lot, Darwina involuntarily lowered her voice.

"The child doesn't count . . . And of the other three, Ffleming was the only one in La Jolla when Catherine Hope got killed!"

"Was he involved with her?"

"I can't say . . . But he was *here.*"

"Yes, so of course were three or four thousand other people."

Darwina said slowly, "All right, then, I'm prejudiced against him. I think he is absolutely cold-blooded and mercenary. He inherited some money three or four years ago, and it changed him. He divorced Ginny and dropped all his friends who had helped him along when he was just a struggling insurance agent, and that's when he started running after people like the Gyfells and Maxtons and Henry Bowling.

"I'll admit, I don't know his motive . . . All I've said is based on the cyanogen odor entirely."

Kenmore agreed, he didn't think motive was overwhelmingly important at this stage. "Sometimes it doesn't exist outside the murderer's distorted mentality. A few years ago, I arrested a young Italian boxer who'd fed a man poisonous *boleti* because he imagined the fellow was putting the 'whammy' on him in the ring. Motive is a thing you've got to see through the killer's eyes."

Darwina's stare followed him. "Where are you going?"

"I'm about to show off my education . . . Homicide dicks and criminal lawyers pick up funny stuff. Gallo-tannic ink is one example. For another, by the time the pugilist came to trial I and his attorney had come to know every mushroom in San Diego County by its Latin name. I never thought it would be any use to me again. But, Darwina," he gestured downward, "look here."

"What on earth—?"

"It's one of the *phallacae*. What happened last night was, the kid stepped on this stinkhorn mushroom . . . But she was running," said Kenmore, "so she didn't no-tice until she stopped, which was when she reached the guesthouse."

Darwina peered strickenly at the fleshy stalk of fungus, trampled into its pool of liquescent decay. Her nose wrinkled from the fetid stench (pungent, biting, and nauseous) of the stinkhorn mushroom.

She became a schoolgirl pink.

"Go on," Darwina uttered dismally, "and laugh. Tell me to stick to my *leucetta losangelensis*."

"No. I'm grateful for your help."

"A fat lot of help."

And she added remorsefully:

"I wonder how I can look Foster Ffleming in the face again."

"Ffleming? You've done him a hell of a big favor. For Dorothy Wyeland's story was bound to get around, it would crop up eventually, and it would have grown in the telling. Those things always do. Like the bloodstained stick in the Catherine Hope Case," Kenmore observed. "And it might have obscured the main point."

"What?" said Darwina, frowning.

"The fact," replied Lieutenant Kenmore, "that cyano-gen has that terrific odor, and yet nobody smelled it at all."

XI

It is true polygamy was practiced in New Gilead in those days. The women did not mind so much as you might think.—THE AUTOBIOGRAPHY OF CATHERINE HOPE.

Leaving Darwina to return to her motor corps meeting, Lieutenant Kenmore walked back to Laguna Terrace. "A guy just went in here," said Sergeant Lyon, and inside the baronial living room the headquarters trio found Foster Ffleming seated with Mrs. Axiter.

Ffleming rose from his chair, and to the occasion. He greeted Kenmore by his correct name and rank. He volunteered his assistance: "Anything I can do—anything at all. I'm afraid," wryly, "we all got off on the wrong foot last night? But who could have *dreamed*—?" And with a gesture that included Jessie Axiter, "Of course, we're absolutely shocked, stunned, by the autopsy's result."

Throughout this speech, Kenmore stood inspecting the man Darwina didn't like. It was hard to tell . . . The insurance man was slender, gracefully clad in conservative blue serge, had a clean, scrubbed, pleasant appearance. But from Kenmore's point of view, the suspicion of scientific salesmanship was on him. As a detective, he had long ago learned that salesmen are harder to read than stevedores, schoolma'ms more enigmatic than housewives. Their occupations compel salesmen and schoolteachers to conceal their real personalities in their public, professional shells. Foster Ffleming's slick exterior might

camouflage cold-blooded selfishness—or it might shield
secret timidity, shyness, or even poetic sensitivity.

"Thanks. But I want to see Mrs. Axiter alone," said
the lieutenant.

His attention fixed on Jessie. He saw a rather grim
woman, who looked nervous enough, but certainly did
not look either shocked or stunned. Kenmore got the
curious impression her thoughts were abstracted and far-
away. Her pale eyes wandered uneasily, never focusing on
the detective in the way that persons with guilty con-
sciences generally fix surreptitiously and apprehensively
upon an officer.

Ffleming had stooped to a coffee table, was sweeping up
an impedimenta of professional forms.

"Before you go," said Kenmore, "there *is* one thing
. . . Henry Bowling's insurance."

Ffleming had the answer on the tip of his tongue.

"Why, of course, I didn't write his policies. They were
purchased years ago. But he had talked to me about making certain conversions, and from what he said, I suppose
the total might be $200,000 or more."

Sergeant Lyon, making his fluent pothooks across a
steno-book page, whistled . . .

Ffleming smiled:

"He had most of his money invested in insurance.
He told me, because he foresaw this War. Though I doubt
that. I think he was alarmed by the New Deal spending,
he watched the deficits piling up, and he anticipated a
period of extremely high taxation. Well. It's always been
a principle of the Federal income tax program that the
proceeds received under an insurance policy are tax-
exempt until the aggregate return exceeds the paid-in
premiums. And there are special provisions relating to
annuities and endowments. I don't suppose you care
about the details of all that, but Henry was primarily

insuring himself against what he considered the prospect of confiscatory taxation."

"No double indemnity for accidental death?"

"None. Because you get what you pay for. And double indemnity is a feature which costs an added premium. From his point of view, it would have been money thrown away . . . Good God!" said Foster Ffleming. "Do you hear that?"

They had all heard it.

Sergeant Lyon's pencil halted in the middle of a pothook. Mrs. Axiter, staring ceilingward, revealed the irregular scar on her throat.

It had been overhead—the sound of some object striking heavily.

What followed Ffleming's exclamation was absolute silence in the house. There were sounds outside. A watery hiss of lawn sprinklers entered the open window. A long way off, the machine guns on the Marine Target Range chattered. And in the hills, an anti-aircraft battery fired practice bursts which shook the opened window sash.

But these were sounds so familiar nowadays that La Jollans had ceased to more than half-hear them. The War rattled by like a passing street trolley . . .

The very house seemed to wait and hold its breath, listening.

A thin whimper of sound from Jessie Axiter broke the spell.

"Lally—!"

"I'll go see," said Ffleming, up from his chair.

Mrs. Axiter gave Lieutenant Kenmore a tremulous look of sick apprehension in which was mingled evasion and shame.

"Lally—her dizzy spells," the girl's mother managed. "Once she fell from the top of the stairs. I'd better go, if you'll excuse me."

The lieutenant followed.

"No," said Mrs. Axiter desperately, at the foot of the stairs. "Please. Really, you mustn't bother."

Kenmore supposed Lally was drunk again.

But then Ffleming's shout rang out.

Sergeant Lyon and Donald Heyes flung into motion now, past the dragon-limbed table and up the curving steps to the front hall. Kenmore, who had sprung past Jessie Axiter, was climbing a flight of stairs that seemed interminably long.

Ffleming gestured at a second floor doorway; Kenmore brushed him aside.

He stared into a mauve boudoir; every article in the room was swaddled in silk—the chairs clad in skirts and flounces, the bed a tester affair with a canopy that dripped ruffles and bowknots and with a rumpled coverlet that was all ribbon and embroidery. And everywhere were hassocks, pillows, footstools, doilies . . . It was not in good taste; it was not in bad taste; any more than a child's garish crayon drawing could be in either.

It was simply Lally's room, and she lay face down upon its floor.

Lally wore a mandarin's robe of Chine orange, a great splash of sultry color out of which one tanned leg thrust crookedly, with an arm lamely curled around to shield her ghastly pale cheek.

Lieutenant Kenmore felt the assault of a tide of angry pressure flood against his temples.

The room was close with an odor of perfume, and a sharper odor of whiskey.

Lally's fall was not the result of a dizzy spell.

Beyond her, in an open dressing room doorway, a smashed whiskey bottle leaked its contents into a towel wrapping.

"Is she—is she—?" Ffleming started forward.

"Stand back," Kenmore ordered. "Did you open the door?"

"What?"

"Did you put your hand on the knob and turn it and open the door?"

"Yes, I opened it, but—"

"Stand back, and don't touch anything else in here," said the lieutenant.

On one knee beside Lally, he discovered a tiny and fluctuating thread of pulse in the girl's wrist.

The blow had not lacerated the scalp. But the wheat-gold hair did not quite hide an ominous bruise. She had been struck from behind. Kenmore feared a skull fracture, considering the force needed to shatter a quart whiskey bottle.

"She's not dead," said he. "You'd better call a doctor in a hurry."

"Right away," gulped Foster Ffleming, and vanished.

The lieutenant could not help letting his grey glance rest pityingly on the girl.

Another voice intruded harshly:

"This is Al's work . . . He hated her."

Kenmore looked up, startled. The alien voice issued from a formidably altered Jessie Axiter.

On the mother's throat, that ancient scar stood forth purple. And her mouth, drawn askew, had the look of another, torn, and badly healed scar.

"Has *he* been here?" Kenmore asked.

Mrs. Axiter had not meant anything so logical. Her reply wasn't in response to his question. It burst from an inner compulsion of wrath and loathing.

"That beast. Oh, that beastly swine."

There was enough vengeful passion in her at this moment to have annihilated a regiment of Al Dearborns . . . She was, Lieutenant Kenmore saw, capable of murder.

"Sergeant," he called to the officer behind Jessie Axiter, "search the house! I'll help—Don, you make a check for prints in here."

He stepped past—almost stepped over Lally to the dressing room. The door, wide open, suggested the assailant might have sprung from this inner room and then, dropping his weapon, fled by that exit.

Kenmore advanced into the dressing room; this had two more doors; one into a bathroom, and the other into a second bedchamber.

He opened the bathroom first.

Behind him, Jessie Axiter cried out shrilly.

Kenmore swung back. "What—"

Mrs. Axiter gestured wildly:

"*He's there!* Behind the door! I saw it move!"

Donald Heyes, revolver drawn, was ahead of the lieutenant.

"No," said he. "It just moved by the draft of air when you opened that other door . . . Hey. Look."

Heyes had found a wastepaper basket in that corner of the room. He lifted from it a newspaper page:

"Why was she cutting a clipping from the sports page?"

Lieutenant Kenmore marked the location of the missing item; it was from the third column of today's *Union*.

"We'll remember to check that," he said, and went on into the second room.

The second room was Corinne's, and it was Spartan.

It contained a prim single bed. The other, few items of furniture were green-painted pine. Almost the only adornment consisted of three tennis trophies arranged on a shelf; two of the trophies were old and tarnished souvenirs of Mankato, Minnesota. Corinne and somebody named D. Wayne had won the third at the La Jolla Shore Club.

Lieutenant Kenmore emerged into a central hallway. This led to a back stairway. He descended the steps:

The lower hallway branched to the kitchen in one direction, and toward the front of the house in another (where Foster Ffleming was now speaking urgently into a telephone). Then there was a door back under the stairs, and a side door providing an exit from the house.

Kenmore chose this last door. He stepped into the sunlight and saw Fred Crush at the moment sweeping some leaves from the tennis court.

The gardener, leaning against his push-broom handle, professed having seen no one leave the house.

"I wasn't watching, of course," said he in nasally congested tones. And gestured toward the southerly sky, across which a Navy utility plane was towing a silver target sleeve. "I been figuring, how much would a guy lead that?—I always was a hell of a good duck shot. Yes, sir, many the mallard I knocked down with my ol' double-barrel."

"Then you don't know whether anyone left the house in the last minute or so, or not?"

"I don't guess anybody did," replied Crush. "Why-so?"

But he obviously didn't care why-so. For practically without a pause he continued: "Yup. Ducks with a double-barrel. Rats with a .22. Had rats under there—" he gestured toward the guesthouse. "Bowling wouldn't let me plink at 'em, though. Set out pizen, instead."

Lieutenant Kenmore, in the act of turning on his heel from the monologist, turned back again.

"Pizen," observed the garrulous gardener, "never set right with me. Got to kill something, I say shoot it. Live and let live, or anyways make it a quick, clean kill."

"What kind of poison?"

"Red squill," said Crush. "It op'rates on the principle, a rat can't vomit up what ails him . . . Henry Bowling didn't have a drop of sporting blood. He's the kind, he'd shoot sitting ducks, anything to get his limit in a hurry.

And to hell with the cripples. Wouldn't waste his valuable time to put a wounded creetur out of its mortal agony."

"Squill," Kenmore repeated. "Was there ever any cyanogen around the place?"

"I don't know . . . I could look."

"Never mind looking," said the lieutenant, and turned back into the house.

Ella, who had been polishing silver in the pantry, had not heard anyone come down the back stairs; she was positive no one had passed through the kitchen.

Lieutenant Kenmore opened the door under the stairs. This gave upon the basement stairs.

Corinne was in the basement.

He found the dark sister in a surprisingly smudged and disheveled condition. Corinne wore slacks and a sweater, with a white turban wound around her hair. Knee deep in a debris of opened boxes, she held up a rubber boot:

"Would you give this to the salvage or the Welfare—?" she began. And then: "Oh. You. I'm going through Uncle Henry's things. Most of this hasn't been opened since we left Minnesota."

Kenmore glanced around. "No one else down here?"

"Who do you suppose?" said Corinne, flinging aside the boot. "Servants are so independent nowadays, you won't catch Ella or Mary lifting a finger they don't have to. And mother's no good, she's such a sentimentalist, she'd simply sit down and cry over these souvenirs. Perhaps it's just as well, someone has to shed a tear for our callers."

And the dark sister grinned cynically.

"Frankly, I'm in hiding! Because if there's one thing I won't do, it's receive condolences from the friends of the family. And it's been the door chimes or the telephone all day—"

"I asked," said Kenmore, "are you alone?"

"Of course I am. You're not looking for Lally, by any chance? Because if you are, this is definitely the wrong atmosphere for her. You don't see any nice shining bar, any softly shaded lights, with cozy booths with a juke box in the background—"

"I've just left your sister," began the lieutenant flatly.

Corinne, as she listened, put on her expressionless mask.

"I expect I'll have to go up, then . . . By the way, I want to take back what I said about Al Dearborn last night."

"Yes. You said he would slit her throat."

"And I was wrong," said Corinne. "I imagined he was the type who'd use a long, flashing knife—a cloak and dagger villain. Instead, it seems he is just a common barroom brawler. My God, hitting her with a bottle!"

A strange, too self-possessed girl, Kenmore thought. He had an extensive professional acquaintance with toughs of both sexes; the toughness was generally mere emotional and mental vacuity . . . Corinne wasn't a moron, she was tempered metal, but what had forged her so?

He had a look around the basement, into the furnace room and storage bins before he returned to the first floor hallway. Foster Ffleming stood waiting here.

"I think," said Ffleming, "there's something I ought to tell you."

"Tell me what?"

"It's the reason I'm here, why I was here last night, in fact. That was a professional call. I wouldn't mention it —point of ethics—since it's a client's affair. But in view of what's happened, I think you *should* know."

Ffleming paused.

Kenmore waited.

"Well. Al Dearborn and Lally took out a husband-and-wife policy when they married," said the other. "Al is still keeping up the premium payments, and Jessie hasn't liked it a bit. In fact, she means to stop it. She feels he hasn't an insurable interest in Lally's life since they've separated. Though they're not legally divorced, of course."

Kenmore frowned: "A joint policy payable to the survivor? How much?"

"Five thousand dollars—" Ffleming turned a thin face hurriedly.

It was Sergeant Lyon; reporting.

"There ain't a hide or hair in the house," said he. "That ain't all. Some stuff is gone—a brooch, some rings. The old lady says."

"You had better get a description of those things, then," said the lieutenant. "Where were they kept?"

"Jewel box. Dressing room."

"Of course, have Don go over that for prints."

He considered the possibility that Lally Dearborn had been assaulted for the sake of her brooch and rings. Undoubtedly, a trapped thief would have struck Lally with the bottle. The difficulty was the towel wrapping; Kenmore presumed the towel had been taken from the bathroom.

But then the assailant had time to make that preparation; and had freedom of movement through the dressing room. He (if it was *he*) hadn't been trapped, for he could have retreated through Corinne's room.

So it had not been the act of a desperate, cornered thief.

Kenmore thought, Lally had not made any outcry. She had been struck from behind. She had not, probably, seen her assailant at all. Much more logically, the attacker had lain in wait for Lally.

"But how the devil could anyone get away so fast?" Ffleming asked.

Lieutenant Kenmore was not convinced anyone had
Corinne, he thought, was a possibility. Or even, Ella. O
Fred Crush.

"You stick around," he told Ffleming, and opened th
side door a second time.

Fred Crush had disappeared.

And in the middle of the freshly swept tennis court, a
stub of cigarette sent up a blue spiral of smoke.

Kenmore walked out and stared down at that. The
cigarette lay almost on the center service stripe; farther
on, in the doubles alley, a spill of ashes showed where it
had first struck, bounced, and rolled.

Lieutenant Kenmore walked to the guesthouse door.
He gave its knob a quick, hard twist and gave the panel
a quick, hard bunt with his shoulder.

The electric light was a sicklied yellow shine in contrast
to the sunshine. It glimmered on a line of steel aimed at
the lieutenant's chest. This was a knife blade. Behind it
was an apostrophe of a face, an extraordinarily long face,
held with chin in and lowered. A pair of pear-shaped,
almost-maroon irises peered up from under wavy reddish
eyebrows.

"Drop that!" said Kenmore.

The man had been standing directly beside the door;
with this knife in hand, poised. He didn't drop it; he
gathered himself in a deepening crouch of head and
shoulders.

Kenmore pivoted off the doorsill. His arm lashed out
—this was not a blow. The lieutenant's fingers trapped
the wrist behind the pointed knife, tightened, and instantly twisted outward—an application of police Judo.

The knife fell. Its owner nearly fell, too. Flung sidewise, he saved himself at the end of several stumbling
steps.

"Now, who the hell are you?" said Lieutenant Kenmore. "Let's see your draft card."

XII

It wasn't polygamy which destroyed New Gilead. It was the discovery of copper on the Videll farm. Grandfather called it the Devil's Manna. The simple, faithful wife was over forever.—THE AUTOBIOGRAPHY OF CATHERINE HOPE.

The registration certificate had been issued as of the 16th October, 1940, from the 3rd La Jolla precinct, to Alvah LeRoy Dearborn.

Kenmore stared at Al Dearborn. He realized many women would have considered the long face handsome, would have been fascinated by Al Dearborn's peculiar, almost maroon-hued eyes. The detective wondered why he thought of that. Then he realized he was wondering whatever had led Lally to marry the man.

Dearborn was brightly clad in a Hollywood pattern of rolled-collar-and-rolled-lapel sports coat, a pastel green polo shirt, and slacks which were positively pink. He had a very sporty, gay dog appearance; or would have, if he had not looked so dejectedly hang-dog at the moment.

"Your classification card," impatiently.

Dearborn fumbled in a bright yellow, glossy billfold that seemed well supplied with banknotes. "Here," said he surlily.

It occurred to Kenmore that hang-dog was not quite the word; hang-wolf seemed the phrase for Al Dearborn. He peered at the classification card: "4-F?"

"I got a bum ticker, if it's any of your goddam business."

There was certainly a wolfish snap to this. Kenmore looked his man over thoughtfully. The pear-shaped and almost maroon-colored pupils were equivocal.

"Everything about you is my business," said the lieutenant. "Who were you laying for with that knife?"

Al Dearborn sneered. "Are you nuts?" and put his teeth into the wolf-snap. Lieutenant Kenmore's grey glance sharpened. He was familiar with the underworld stratagem known as *copping a plea*. It consists of pleading guilty to a lesser charge to escape being tried for a greater. The notion entered his head that Al was trying a variation of the trick. Kenmore surmised Al's character was such he couldn't hope to convince anyone of his milk-white innocence. He couldn't pretend to be a model citizen, but conceivably he could pose as just a dumb, low-grade tough guy. He might plead guilty to the charge of being a cheap heel and hoodlum and so escape the suspicion of having committed any crime requiring intelligent planning.

Bluster and bravado, Kenmore thought, were a good deal safer than a display of cool-headed cunning—for a man in Al's situation.

Possibly the other saw that he'd over-played it. More soberly, he gestured: "I was fixing a screw in the switch there."

Kenmore glanced at the light switch; it consisted of a brass plate enclosing two pairs of push buttons; one pair must originally have controlled an out-of-doors bulb since removed during the dim-out era.

The plate was loose when he touched it.

"See?" said Al Dearborn. "When I turned on the light, that almost fell off in my hand. I was using the knife for a screwdriver."

"Why didn't you drop it, then?"

"I was too surprised when *you* busted in."

"Who'd you expect?"

"Bowling," said Al Dearborn.

He saw the detective's face change . . .

"You don't think I was laying for the old boy with a shiv, do you?"

"No," Kenmore said. "Inasmuch as he's been dead twenty hours, I didn't think that."

Al Dearborn peeled his eyelids very high. He stared rigidly at Kenmore. His upper lip jerked at one corner of his mouth. The twitch ran on up through the muscles of the cheek, a nervous quiver that washed out at eyeball and cheekbone.

"Dead. Henry Bowling? Oh, my God."

And suddenly his long face broke all apart. The eyelids fluttered down, the jaws unlocked behind the too-tense mouth, and below the jaws the Adam's-apple rose agitatedly. There pumped up from his throat a shrill shudder of sound.

Al Dearborn was laughing.

"You fool," said Kenmore, "what's funny about it?"

But it wasn't mirth, it wasn't that kind of a laugh.

Al Dearborn stopped short.

"*You* are. Trying to hand me *that*."

Kenmore shrugged. "Don't you read the papers? Where've you been? Anyone in La Jolla could have told you."

"I've been in Los Angeles," Al Dearborn said. "I didn't see it in the L.A. papers."

"Los Angeles . . . When did you go?"

"Last night . . . Say, what the hell is this?"

"Henry Bowling was murdered," said Kenmore. "And this is your alibi. If you can make it stick."

Al Dearborn was entirely straight-faced now.

"I'm sorry," said he. "I didn't realize. I couldn't believe you at first. My God, that's awful. How did it happen—?"

Lieutenant Kenmore smiled. "No, Al," said he. "You

tell me. And then I'll tell you. No, wait." He walked around the desk, lifted the phone, and dialed. Ella Marion answered. "Send Sergeant Lyon to the guesthouse," said Kenmore, "and tell him to bring his book."

He looked up at Dearborn.

"We'll have this in black-and-white. In case you should change your mind about a detail or so."

The other's expression became crafty.

"Can I have a lawyer?"

"Yes," said the detective.

Al Dearborn looked surprised.

"You're entitled to an attorney," said Kenmore. "I'm not going to sit around here and wait for you to make up your mind which one. But I'll have Lyon book you at the sub-station until your lawyer can be present at the questioning."

"Oh, —— ——! I've got nothing to hide, anyway," said the other. "Let's get it over."

Kenmore waited for the sergeant to seat himself at the desk.

"All right, Alvah LeRoy Dearborn, you understand Henry Bowling was murdered. You are not under arrest, but you may be, and anything you say may be used against you. And you make this statement of your own free will. Is that all understood?"

"More or less."

"What do you mean, more or less?"

Dearborn said, "I'm going to make this statement, or be thrown in the can until I do. That's how free it is."

Sergeant Lyon glared: "Listen, monkey—"

"No," said Kenmore. "Put it down. It's an accurate statement. What's your address, Dearborn?"

"Beachview Arms. A-3."

"In La Jolla?"

"Yeah."

"Occupation?"

"I haven't been well lately," said Al Dearborn.

"No occupation?"

"No. Come on. Get down to business."

"I'm trying to get down to your business," said the lieutenant. "Apparently, you've no visible means of support."

"You go to hell! Ask me about my alibi. I won't answer any of this other crud."

"All right, what is your alibi?"

"I told you. I was in L.A. I went up last night."

"At what time last night?"

"I took the seven o'clock bus," said Al Dearborn. "That got me into the terminal at about ten-thirty. I took a cab to the Mayflower. I think it is. Anyhow, a hotel right in back of the Biltmore. You can check with them and find when I registered in. It was before eleven."

"Yes. What was the purpose of this trip?"

Irritation flashed into the maroon-pupiled eyes. "You said twenty hours. God damn it, what I did after eleven o'clock last night is none of your business."

"Possibly," said Kenmore. "You haven't yet proved you were on that bus. You've only said so. There's a phone book in the bottom drawer, sergeant. No, the other side."

He ran a forefinger down the page, and dialed.

"Hello, Greyhound. I want to ask about the seven o'clock bus to Los Angeles last night . . . Did you sell Al Dearborn a ticket?"

And then:

"It was a 7:10 bus, Al. And you didn't buy a ticket."

"That's right," Al Dearborn said. "I paid the driver a cash fare. It's a good thing I did. He ought to remember that."

"But why didn't you have a ticket?"

"Because I got on at the Shore Club," said the other. "Why the hell should I go uptown and ride back, when the bus stops a block from my apartment?"

Lieutenant Kenmore replied, "Then it wasn't 7:10. It was 7:15 or 7:20." But that didn't provide enough leeway, either. Henry Bowling had called police headquarters at 7:15, and had telephoned an incident report to the control room five minutes after that. It may have been as late as 7:25, the lieutenant thought. And the bus wouldn't have consumed fifteen minutes between the village bus station and the Shore Club; Al Dearborn could not have counted on any such delay; not if he had planned to use the bus trip as an alibi. And even so, it left him a bare five minutes to commit a murder *and* travel a dozen blocks from 222 Laguna Terrace to the Shore Club.

Unreasonable, Kenmore thought. Because, if that was his plan, Dearborn would have got his murder done at least ten minutes earlier.

"Well, then," said he, "you returned on the bus today?"

"Yeah."

"In ignorance of the fact this murder had been committed?"

"Sure," said Al Dearborn jauntily. "How could I know? I hadn't seen any San Diego paper. I didn't even stop to talk to anybody. The bus pulled in half an hour ago, I parked my bag in my apartment, and came on up here."

"Unaware of Henry Bowling's death, and therefore expecting to see him?"

"That's right."

"Yes," said Kenmore, "but did he expect to see you? Was this prearranged? You didn't call at the house, did you?"

"No, and I'll tell you why I didn't," replied Al Dearborn. "And I hope your stooge writes this in letters a foot high. It was on account of that God damned old hag, my mother-in-law."

"You were avoiding Mrs. Axiter?"

"On account of Bowling, I was. She'd scalp the old boy alive if she caught him talking to me. I mean, if he was alive."

"Why? What had your meeting to do with her?"

Al Dearborn laughed.

"You won't get it out of me that way," said he. "What I wanted to see Bowling about was personal, none of your business, and I'm not telling."

Lieutenant Kenmore stepped back, gestured to Sergeant Lyon:

"That's enough for now, Joe. I'll have Don fingerprint him later. Meanwhile, you can book him at the substation."

"Book me? What the hell for? I told you my alibi!"

"What makes you so sure it is one? That boarding last night's bus puts you in the clear? But it's not that alone," said Kenmore. "The charge is suspicion of assault with a deadly weapon. A whiskey bottle. You've just got through denying any alibi for what happened to Lally in the last half-hour."

Al Dearborn said softly, as if to himself, "Lally? Assault—?" and for a moment forgot to be noisy and tough . . . The strength he counted on wasn't on the surface, after all. And he went in, deep, after it. Little fires of secret thought seemed to play in the maroon eyes.

He came up out of it with a headshake, a snarl: "What're you handing me? Was she—too?"

Lieutenant Kenmore would have given a good deal to know whether Al had been startled to hear Lally had been attacked with a whiskey bottle, or startled to hear it was only assault and not murder . . .

"No. Not quite killed. Or not yet dead, anyway. But if

she dies, Al, you'll be a rich man. The insurance you've carried on her life is the least of it.

"It's the sequence of all this," Kenmore said. "Bowling first; he leaves perhaps a quarter of a million dollars or more; I don't know how much. And I don't know how much of that to her directly. But whatever her share is, you'd inherit at least a husband's legal third. All of it, maybe. Suppose you didn't and couldn't have killed Bowling? It doesn't follow, when you heard of that, you couldn't have made an attempt on your wife's life.

"Perhaps you came here to kill her; possibly that miscued; then you took refuge in the guesthouse. I don't say positively, but it's a suspicion I can't overlook. Unless you can give another explanation—and it had better be good —for being caught here."

The suspect listened saturninely. "———— you, you cruddy cop!" said Al Dearborn. "Go to hell. I'm not saying a word. Not till I see my lawyer."

"You can see him. Who is he?"

"Wyeland—no, I'll get a good one. I'll get Stacey."

If Lally dies, Kenmore thought, you can afford Stacey. But why had you thought of Wyeland first?

The door flew open and Donald Heyes entered the guesthouse excitedly, bringing with him a white handbag.

"Lieutenant—look here."

Kenmore stretched forth a hand and the fingerprint man surrendered the purse.

"Lally's?"

"Yes. Look *in* it."

Kenmore did so. The handbag contained nearly a dozen Christmas cards. They were a shabby lot, yellowed with age and begrimed with dirt. All were addressed to *Dear* or *Dearest Amy*.

"Can you beat that?" Heyes asked curiously "Why

should she be carrying around a bunch of old Christmas cards that weren't even hers, for hell's sake?"

"But—" began Al Dearborn, and stopped abruptly.

Kenmore snapped: "What?"

"Nothing. I'm not talking, not'll I see Nathan Stacey."

Lieutenant Kenmore, when Sergeant Lyon had led away his prisoner, took out a pocketknife of his own and attacked the light switch plate. "Look, Heyes."

Donald Heyes said he would be jiggered. "I've heard of people putting pennies in a busted fuse. But why in a switch?"

"It isn't a penny," said Kenmore, removing his find from the conduit box. "It's a five dollar gold piece."

The fingerprint man had not seen one of those in a coon's age.

"Of course you haven't. Gold hasn't circulated since the bank holiday in '33."

XIII

The men wore full beards because as grandfather preached, man is made in the Lord's image and who can imagine a clean-shaven Creator?

Anyway, a beard seems to me a very manly thing.—THE AUTOBIOGRAPHY OF CATHERINE HOPE.

"I can't understand it *at all*," said Amy Rhine helplessly.

Lieutenant Kenmore, who recalled Mrs. Rhine from the Catherine Hope Case, thought the intervening years had not changed the lady in the least. Amy Rhine was a lady, in the old-fashioned sense of the word; she was a gentlewoman who had come upon hard times, and not one of your modernly crisp business girls.

At her desk in the outer office of William Wyeland's law office, Mrs. Rhine received callers in the manner of a hostess who would presently pour tea.

"They are yours, are they not?" said Kenmore.

"Well, *yes*. But, good gracious, what was Lally Dearborn *doing* with them?"

Mrs. Rhine fastidiously picked up a particularly grimy and disreputable looking card, by her extreme fingertips. Her appearance was altogether fastidious. She wore an exceedingly impractical white shirtwaist, pleated in front and elaborately ruffled at throat and cuffs. From the cuffs emerged a pair of very pale, slight, but wiry-seeming hands; above the throat, the face was prim, aquiline and shrewd. Astride the delicately whetted blade of nose, lenses rode in a pince-nez frame.

She focused the pince-nez upon the card in question. "It's *incredible*," said Amy Rhine, "This is from *Marjorie* Diehn. And she died, oh, *years* ago. *Ten* years ago, at least."

"Are they all that old?"

"I'm not sure. I'd have to *think* . . . No. This is a card Mrs. Wyeland sent me from Bermuda, that would have been the winter of 1938."

Kenmore sought to adjust himself more comfortably into a chair which did not permit of comfort. "It seems likely you left these behind when you moved from the guesthouse."

"But I didn't leave anything there. And I never *saved* Christmas cards. So that is not the answer. It is a perfect *mystery* to me."

But perhaps it was not altogether a mystery. For Amy Rhine suddenly frowned. "I wonder if *that* was what he meant," she murmured.

"Who?"

"Henry Bowling. He telephoned the other day, Wednesday, no, it was *Tuesday*, yes, Tuesday. Something about a *card* or *letter* he had sent me. I wonder if he could have meant *these*."

"What did he say?"

"I don't *know*. I couldn't make out. It sounded to me as if he had been *drinking*," Mrs. Rhine thought. "I hung up because there was something Mr. Wyeland wanted just then, and I couldn't waste time with a *drunken fool* on the telephone."

"I didn't know he drank."

"Whatever ailed him, then. *Henry Bowling was such a queer pair of shoes,* anyway," Amy Rhine asserted. "And when you live *next door* as I did—well, I can only say Mr. Bowling was very *far* from a gentleman. Of course, that no longer matters does it? Nobody cares what you are, it's only the almighty dollar that counts, regardless of how you got it."

"That's a general indictment," said Kenmore. "It would apply to a great many others beside Bowling."

"Wouldn't it?" said Mrs. Rhine grimly.

"But speaking of the almighty dollar—" and the lieutenant showed her the five dollar gold piece.

Amy Rhine could not say *positively* it was her gold piece. She could only recall the following circumstances: Firstly, that Mr. Wyeland had *always* given her *five* such coins at Christmas (when gold coins circulated); secondly, that one year (1929) she *had* lost a five dollar gold piece by giving it (as she supposed) to the milkman as a *penny;* thirdly, as a consequence she had changed milk-men.

She had not, asked Kenmore, made a practice of con-cealing money about the house; for example, in electric conduit boxes?

She had not.

Amy Rhine thought, if the gold piece had been found about the guesthouse, it was hers. But if Henry Bowling had found it, she was *not surprised* he had said nothing. "He was not very honest in *financial* matters, you know."

"I haven't had time to look into his business affairs, unfortunately."

"Well, of course, I haven't, either. I found out *ac-cidentally.* It was at the USO, I'm a chaperone at the dances," said Amy Rhine, "and I met this boy; quite a nice boy; from Minnesota. A sailor . . . I don't recall the name, and of course you never ask them what ship. But he was really a fine boy—with *manners*—and how unusual that is in these times." She sighed for the times. "Well, we were just *talking.* And he told me that was where he was from—Mankato, Minnesota. And I *said* there were Mankato people in town. The Bowlings. Well, he knew them very well. Indeed, lived in the *same block*. Of course," said Mrs. Rhine, "I hadn't *any* wish to draw him out. It was only that a boy like that, so far from home, wants to *talk*. To have a good visit, so to speak. For instance, I said he must have known Mr. Axiter . . . And do you know, Lally comes by her traits honestly? Because the stories Jessie Axiter tells are *not* true. The fact is, Mr. Axiter ran off with *another woman,* and there was a *dreadful scandal*. But perhaps I shouldn't say this."

Try to stop you, thought Kenmore.

"Because," Mrs. Rhine resumed, "we were talking about *business honesty,* weren't we? Well, according to this boy, Henry Bowling wanted to run for Congress, but the Republicans wouldn't have him because he'd been mixed up in a bit of highway paving graft. I think he accepted a bribe, or something of the sort, in return for *publicity* in the newspapers. And Bowling had the *face* to put himself up for Congress, blowing his own horn in his own newspapers. Then it all came out, and that's why he came to California."

Lieutenant Kenmore smiled.

"Your sailor," said he, "must be an extremely handy lad at the scuttlebutt."

The pince-nez shed a suspicious glance at the detective. Mrs. Rhine was not exactly certain that remark was one which a gentlewoman could properly hear.

"Navy slang," said Kenmore, "for rumor."

She said: "I shouldn't call it *rumor*. It all fits too well. For if you ask me, Henry Bowling didn't give a *hoot* about civilian defense. He was simply trying to make a good impression and get into *politics* again. I mean, we elect Congressmen in California, too, don't we?"

"Yes," said Kenmore, "but do we murder our fledgling

candidates? Bowling may have been as politically ambitious as Caesar, but what Brutus had he offended? If
you will pardon a literary allusion, Mrs. Rhine."

Mrs. Rhine looked approving, and flattered.

"I don't suppose he had a Brutus," said she. "Or even
a *lean and hungry* Cassius. No, but I do think he was
trying to patch up things between Lally and Al. Because if they ever went into divorce court and started
telling on each other, it'd be awful. For him. A politician's family, you know, ought to be like *Caesar's wife.*
At least, not exposed *in flagrante delicto.* I daresay Henry
Bowling could have *made* Lally do what he wanted—
after all, he held the purse-strings—and it was just a
question of getting Al to take her back. And Al would do
anything for enough money. But then, Jessie hates Al,
so there was that obstacle. Though I don't believe *she*
has a penny of her own, either."

Then Mrs. Axiter had killed Henry Bowling?

It seemed to be Amy Rhine's point. Lieutenant Kenmore returned to his own point.

Gathering up the cards, he asked, "Then you can't
explain these?"

"Certainly not. I supposed they had all been burned
years ago."

"Yes. Well, if I might see Mr. Wyeland—?"

William Wyeland was not a man who showed to his
best advantage under a tin hat, as Kenmore had encountered him last night.

But Mr. Wyeland, now, with his brown beard and
meditative brown eye, his massive gold watch chain crossing his waistcoat's piped front, was the picture of your
old-fashioned family attorney.

"I suppose," said he, "you have come to ask about
the wills?"

Lieutenant Kenmore raised an eyebrow. "There were several?"

"Three, to be exact," the attorney replied. "Henry Bowling's, Lally's, and Alvah Dearborn's. Though the last two are reciprocal forms. That is, the husband bequeaths to the wife all his property of whatever description and wherever located; and the wife, similarly.

"It is a very simple matter," he added, "to draw a will where there's no property involved."

"Dearborn has none?"

"No," said the lawyer. "No real estate, for I inquired into that possibility; no personal property beyond the clothes on his back and an automobile which in effect belonged to a finance company."

"And Lally?"

The attorney shrugged. "She had nothing except her prospects. And at that time, Henry Bowling looked good for another dozen or twenty years. I didn't give Lally's marriage—the wills were drawn at that time—I didn't give it a dozen months."

Kenmore said he was interested in Lally's prospects. "In other words, Bowling's will."

"A beautifully intricate document," observed the lawyer. "I may say so, since I did not frame it. It was drawn before he came to me, but he added a codicil when he purchased the Laguna Terrace house. And as I handled that, I am acquainted with its provisions. Roughly speaking, he bequeathed a few thousands outright to a cousin back in Minnesota. He provided Jessie with a life tenure in the Laguna Terrace house and an annual income. The rest, he left to Corinne and Lalitha, in the form of a trust; they were to inherit the principal upon marriage, or on attaining the age of twenty-five."

Kenmore considered. "And he needed a beautifully intricate document to say that?"

William Wyeland leaned back, stroking his beard. "I have only defined the general substance of it. You understand, lieutenant, it is necessary to distinguish the definition of an article from the article itself.

"For example. The dictionary states that a battleship is a heavily armored ship of war of the largest size; that is true; I can tell you in a dozen words what a battleship is. But in practical fact, of course, such a ship is also a beautifully intricate mechanism.

"What I have told you," said the attorney, "is a satisfactory statement as between laymen; but it would not fulfil the legal requirement . . . Consider. There are taxes on the Laguna Terrace property. Who shall pay them? Jessie? But if she fails to do so, then the title fails, and the daughters do not inherit what it was intended they should inherit. Then are they to pay the taxes? If they do not, again the title fails, and the mother is deprived of her life tenure.

"And that is only one detail. Mr. Bowling retained control of a publishing business in Minnesota, not as an individual, but through a family corporation which was apparently a device he'd adopted with an eye to the Federal income and inheritance tax laws.

"Well!" said William Wyeland. "You see, it is not very easy to build a battleship, or to prepare the last will and testament of a man whose estate is large, as Henry Bowling's was, and whose intentions are involved, as his were. The document was an instructive one; I enjoyed examining it."

Lieutenant Kenmore listened respectfully.

"It comes down to this, then," said he, "Lally inherits $100,000 or more? And if she dies, Al Dearborn gets it all?"

Wyeland nodded agreement.

"It's odd," said Kenmore after a moment's reflection. "Granting his sister an income and awarding his nieces their share outright. I would have expected it the other way around. Mrs. Axiter is not incompetent in financial affairs, is she? She manages the household, I'm told."

William Wyeland's beard did not quite conceal a tightening of his lips.

"You will excuse me from discussing Henry Bowling's motives. It is not a matter of privileged communication," hurriedly. "I simply do not know them."

And Wyeland gave the beard an uncomfortable tug. "The fact is, although I acted as his attorney, a coolness arose between the families. Because, Theodora resented what she considered his abominable treatment of Mrs. Rhine."

"How was that?"

"Why, my wife believed Bowling used Amy very badly. It was when he purchased those lots where the tennis court now stands. The cottage, the guesthouse as it is now called, had been her home for so many years, and he evicted her practically on a day's notice."

Mr. Wyeland sighed.

"Theodora felt he used *me* very badly," said he, "considering that I helped conduct the negotiations. He did not commit himself to anything in writing, or verbally, and yet he gave a certain impression . . . 'I hope you won't jack up Amy's rent,' Theodora said to him, and he replied he would not.

"Nor did he. He simply sent her packing instead, as my wife puts it. When she had lived there so many years, and had all that sentimental attachment to the place. Women, you know, set great store on sentiment."

William Wyeland said this with feeling, and it oc-curred to Kenmore that the lawyer (or perhaps it was his wife) had a weakness for unattached, mid-elderly females. The Wyelands, he recalled, had been on somewhat better than good-neighborly relations with Catherine Hope.

"However," said the attorney, brightening, "it turned out all for the best. Mrs. Rhine is really a great deal better off on Penguin Street, as she does not have that long walk uphill. But there *was* a coolness, and Theodora never set foot inside the Laguna Terrace house from that day. She had not liked Bowling, anyway, because of Miss Hope, you see."

Lieutenant Kenmore put the question: What had Henry Bowling to do with Catherine Hope?

"He knew nothing about it, of course," replied Wyeland. "There was still some talk about her death when he came here, though. Henry Bowling fancied himself an amateur detective. He had had some experience along that line, or so he let on. Well, we were asked to dinner there one night—this was a long time ago—and in the course of the conversation the murder was mentioned and he proceeded to solve it."

"And what," said Kenmore interestedly, "was his solution?"

"Oh, a ridiculous one. He had poor Catherine leading a double life, one with Lesbian implications. He didn't know that he was blackening the memory of a very dear friend of Theodora's . . . Or perhaps he did know. I've a fancy he disliked Theodora from the start. He was always cordial enough to me at our men's bridge club, and yet I could not cultivate the friendship of a man I didn't feel free to invite into my home. Not that he cared about coming there. My point is," said William Wyeland, belaboring the point, "he was crude and insensitive enough to offend my wife's feelings and at the same time not understand why I should resent his doing so."

XIV

After all, a man must value women pretty highly to marry two of them at once. It is the old bachelors who really have no respect for womanhood.—THE AUTOBIOGRAPHY OF CATHERINE HOPE.

At the sub-station, Kenmore found Sergeant Lyon and Donald Heyes; their mood was congratulatory.

"It ticks like a clock," said Heyes, "and I think Mr. Al Dearborn's hour has struck. I took his prints, and his prints were in that girl's room. Not on her jewel box or the bottle. He wiped those off. But he didn't wipe off a chair in the dressing room, or the dressing table, either. Not only that. He left his prints in the guesthouse. I don't mean today. Last night."

Acting-Lieutenant Ralph Arnold, officer in charge of the sub-station, was of a similarly optimistic opinion. "No kidding," said he, "we've had an eye on Al for quite awhile. It takes money to live as he does, throw the parties he throws, and Al gambles quite a bit, too. Where does the money come from? I won't be surprised if this pinch clears up a number of burglaries."

Kenmore thought the wish was father to the thought.

"You didn't find the brooch and rings on him, did you?"

"No; he was smart enough to ditch the stuff."

"He may have stolen Lally's jewels but I don't imagine he's a professional burglar," said Kenmore. "It's an amateur's trick to steal from one's relatives. Because amilies as a rule won't press that kind of charge."

Arnold shrugged. He had sent two officers to the house to search for the missing brooch and rings.

"He threw those things away somewhere between Lally's room and the guesthouse," the acting-lieutenant thought.

Kenmore approved. "Yes, you take charge of that end." Donald Heyes was to get a warrant and search Dearborn's apartment. Sergeant Lyon would visit the Shore Club.

By the way, he added, what was the latest word on Lally's condition?"

"She's in the hospital," said Heyes. "Myatt is making some X-rays."

"He was to call and leave word here, when I could see her."

"He hasn't yet. There's one call for you," said Arnold. "For you to stop by at the control room."

The lieutenant had been going there anyway.

The La Jolla control room was in the American Legion Hall. Kenmore found Darwina Roydan in front of the building. She had exchanged her straw hat for a steel one; she was conducting a Motor Corps gas mask drill.

"By the counts," she called. *"One* . . . No, Ella May, don't drop your helmet on the ground—you don't want to lay it in a pool of mustard. Hold it between your knees."

She glanced around. "Just one minute, lieutenant . . . *Two!"* The line of ladies had been holding their masks a painfully exact eight inches before their noses, now the noses disappeared from view. There was a general, rubbery whispering as harness got tugged over coiffures. *"Three,"* pronounced Darwina, and the sound became a rubbery trumpeting; each outlet valve was capped by a hand; each wearer blew forth energetically and thereby forced the trapped air from the cheeks of her mask. *"Four,"* said Darwina, and all the eyepieces, which had fogged with their wearers' breaths, cleared with newly indrawn atmosphere. "And don't forget to close your carriers," said Darwina. "Forward *march!"*

The Motor Corps, not too perfectly, stepped off across the Legion Hall lawn. Darwina turned to Kenmore.

"Frieda Chapman is here," said she. "Something she said set me to thinking. She's the twins' mother, you know."

"Bowling's messengers?"

"Yes. Well, Frieda is a perfect fool. She's under the impression it's only by the grace of God the twins weren't murdered, too . . . And while she was telling all that, it suddenly struck me. They wouldn't have been in danger anyway."

An appreciative gleam came into the detective's grey glance.

"You mean," said he, "the murderer knew very well those boys would not be there. It was an essential element in the scheme."

"But it was in the La Jolla paper— *Company!"* cried Darwina. *"Halt!"*

And just in the nick of time; the Corps was nearly into the flowerbeds.

"No," said Darwina. "I mean *Henry Bowling wasn't killed in the guesthouse.* That's why no one noticed any cyanogen odor in the room. Because someone came to the door, or called on the phone, and told him Lally had been hurt in an auto accident, for instance. He was lured somewhere else during the evening, and then his body got brought back and dumped on the floor . . . *About face!* Remove masks!"

Across the yard, the Motor Corps ladies crouched

low; each inserted a finger inside the cheekpiece of her mask; each sniffed suspiciously; and being convinced there was no contamination in the immediate area, re-moved her mask.

"By George!" said the lieutenant softly.

"It is logical, isn't it?"

"You've shown me how it was done," the lieutenant thought.

He went on into the Legion Hall. Its principal chamber was furnished with a long table, with chairs for the staff ranged around it; there was a battery of telephones; and a large map of the village in which were still thrust pins denoting the location of last night's incidents . . . blue for high explosive, red for incen-diary, and green for war gas.

Lieutenant Kenmore turned left from the entrance, into what had formerly been a cloakroom and was now Dr. Lauren Wallace's office. And where Dr. Wallace now looked thoroughly distraught behind his desk.

"I have just heard," said the Director Emeritus, "it was not carbon monoxide, after all."

"Just heard?"

"Yes, the Motor Corps, chattering like so many mag-pies. I wonder why it is that a murder brings out the worst in a community? I've been sitting here listening to perfectly libelous remarks about poor Mrs. Axiter. Yes, and the girls, too. You would think it surprising they hadn't done away with Mr. Bowling long ago."

Kenmore thought that the Catherine Hope Case had left its mark upon Lauren Wallace. His remark (*This is murder. We must all keep our heads*) had not made a very favorable impression at the inquest, and there had been the tiniest breath of suspicion when the blood-stained stick was found almost at his door. How had he missed seeing it there, in those days when everyone was looking for the "blunt instrument"? No one supposed Dr. Wallace had done Miss Hope to death, but a good many people thought he refrained from telling all he knew. The Director had certainly received some hints about the strip poker party days before Captain Whipple ran down that incident.

Kenmore thought of this, and so perhaps did Lauren Wallace.

"I mean," said he, "it is one thing to divulge pertinent information to the proper authorities, and another thing to indulge in indiscriminate, vicious slander."

"That would be true," said Lieutenant Kenmore, "if we knew what was pertinent." He sat down, got out his pipe, and loaded its bowl from his tobacco pouch. "No," he went on, "I can't agree. The worst witnesses are the conscientious, intelligent ones like yourself. It is not very hard for an experienced investigator to discount the testimony of a malicious, hysterical, or untruthful person. That is merely a task of separating wheat from the chaff, and the more the individual talks the easier the task becomes. Which is why professional criminals 'dummy up,' as they say, and won't talk at all. The police know how to handle criminals, but what is a detective to do when a conscientious, intelligent, high-minded man reserves a kernel of the truth because it seems to him of no importance?"

Kenmore thought, Captain Whipple had never handled Lauren Wallace correctly. Whipple's method was that of applying pressure until the subject cracked. What kind of pressure, depended on what the captain thought he could get away with.

Whipple had not dared resort to third-degree methods with the M.R.I. staff; so he had used the social pressure of public opinion instead. He hadn't sacrificed Messrs. Stanley, Wade-Brooks, and Bolgard merely to create an illusion of official activity. He had done it as well **to** smash the cohesive unity of Dr. Wallace's organization. *We must all keep our heads,* the Director had said; but demoralized troops do not respond to such an order; in flight, it is every man for himself.

Lauren Wallace possibly lacked Kenmore's acute strategic sense; he did not understand Whipple's method, perhaps, but he knew the result.

The incident officer shook his white-maned head.

"That's all very well for the police," said he, "but I am thinking of my own job. From my point of view, this backbiting gossip is simply ruinous. If we are going to have La Jolla set by its ears, as happened before, we shan't have any civilian defense left. I told you, slanderous remarks were passed concerning Mrs. Axiter. But Jessie Axiter has her friends among the Motor Corps, too. Just now Dr. Roydan averted an explosion by ordering the ladies to *fall in,* but unfortunately even she can't permanently confine the wagging tongues inside gas masks."

Yes, thought Kenmore, Lauren Wallace was again in command; and again, the fact of murder threatened to smash his organization.

"I know," said the detective. "That is why I have got to crack this case without any delay at all. We don't want it to run on for a month, either of us."

Lieutenant Kenmore struck a match; he brought his pipe bowl aglow. Dr. Wallace was going to be a delicate witness, thanks to Captain Whipple.

"Well, then," said the detective. "How am I going to do it? I've got to have the facts to work from, haven't I? All of them, without any mental reservation of what seems to be impertinent . . . For instance, on Wednesday, the day before the murder, Henry Bowling attended a sector wardens' meeting here. At what time?"

"The meeting was called for four o'clock. Mr. Bowling arrived a little early."

"Before the others?"

"Yes. He approached me about that matter I mentioned, his messengers."

"And that was discussed between you two alone?"

"Yes . . . Among other things."

"What other things?"

"Why," said Dr. Wallace, "there was some talk about the new report form; some talk about the Thursday night drill."

"Did he know the incidents he would get?"

"Of course not! We'd all known for days the Paratroops were coming—I suppose they publicized it so no excited citizen would start shooting under the impression it was a Jap raid. But I had not finished preparing the incident envelopes and I merely told Bowling I would arrange matters so that the Chapman twins could be excused. I think that was almost all."

"Almost?"

The incident officer faintly colored. "He told me a story about an air raid warden and a WAC . . . I don't believe it is necessary to repeat it."

Lieutenant Kenmore's pipe bowl flared red. "Were you shocked?"

"Certainly I was not shocked. I did not think it was necessary or appropriate to the discussion."

"A sense of humor," Kenmore thought, "on the crude side . . . Dr. Wallace. What was your opinion of Henry Bowling, man-to-man?"

"Why, I found him extremely interested in the work, he had talent as an organizer, he was attentive to details—"

"I don't mean that."

Lauren Wallace looked doubtfully at his interrogator.

"**Now you** are asking me to gossip," said he uncomfortably.

Kenmore said: "I know he was interested and attentive and all that; but what is the other?"

"I can't see it has any bearing whatever," said the incident officer. "However, it is true he had a fault in his nature . . . He would not have anything to do with the block leaders in civilian defense. He would not have a woman warden in his sector, and he was even doubtful about using the Wyeland girl as a messenger. He was inclined to undervalue the ladies. It never seemed to me," said Lauren Wallace, "a very generous or appealing aspect of his personality. But with men, he was extremely good; the wardens all liked him, if their wives did not."

Lieutenant Kenmore recalled that at any rate Will Wyeland's wife had not liked Henry Bowling.

"There's another thing," the lieutenant said. "I want to look over last night's reports."

Dr. Wallace tugged open a drawer of his desk.

"Particularly," said Kenmore, "the incident at Toyon and Balboa Streets."

The incident officer glanced down a check list. "Number nine," said he. And a moment later, "Here."

Kenmore glanced at the pink sheet. His teeth locked on the pipe bit; the pads of muscle tightened at the corners of his mouth.

"But!" said he.

"Yes; what?"

"*This was received at 7:15. The incident did not occur until two minutes later.*"

"I hadn't noticed," said the incident officer. "Slips of that kind will happen. Who was the reporting warden?"

"E. Norman."

"That's Ed Norman. Possibly his watch was a minute

or so fast. Little errors of that kind are bound to occur," Dr. Wallace observed equably.

"It would have had to have been at least five minutes fast. Henry Bowling reported this to you, but he first had to receive a report from Norman, and the envelope would have had to be opened at 7:12 instead of 7:17."

"Yes," said Wallace, "but we have had wardens reporting casualties half an hour before the incident is supposed to happen. During a drill, Sam Elliot and I are receiving reports at the rate of one every two minutes. And last night, unfortunately, I was delayed reaching the control room, and Elliot had to handle the incoming calls alone. So it is not any wonder he failed to notice the discrepancy."

"But that report passed through Henry Bowling's hands; how could *he* fail to notice? He was not, like Elliot, under any pressure of work."

The incident officer shook his head.

"It's beyond me," said he. "It is like the missing pink sheet. Mr. Bowling's mind seems not to have been on the drill at all . . . We can ask Dr. Roydan. She was the umpire in that sector, you know."

He stepped to the doorway and called Darwina.

Darwina Roydan listened incredulously.

"Norman's watch *was* fast a minute or so," said she. "I had him compare it with mine when I handed him his envelope."

Lauren Wallace thought, in that case, Darwina might have had the wrong time.

She looked more incredulous than before.

"How could I? If I had been five minutes fast, then I would have delivered that very first incident ahead of time, and it would have been opened at 6:56 instead of 7:01. And it would probably have been reported before the drill even began."

Lauren Wallace searched through the pink sheets.

"There is not any incoming time marked," said he perplexedly. "I suppose Elliot was so rushed trying to answer both phones at once."

Darwina's forehead wrinkled under the helmet's steel brim.

"Well," said she, "we can get at it in another way. I stayed at Balboa and Toyon about ten minutes, until the fire unit arrived. Then I went on up to Wyeland's post. If the first two incidents were off by five minutes, then so was Wyeland's, for I told him the correct time, too. He would have opened his envelope at 7:40 instead of 7:45, and Dorothy Wyeland would have started that much sooner, and she would have found the body five minutes earlier than she did."

Lieutenant Kenmore sat in a brown study of his own.

He thought, even if Darwina had committed the flagrant error in time, the thing was still impossible. Henry Bowling could not, at 7:15 o'clock, have been telephoning an air raid drill incident to his district warden and simultaneously have been putting through a toll call to police headquarters in San Diego.

"Look here," said Lieutenant Kenmore. "Both of you. I've got an idea . . . I am almost certain I know how Henry Bowling was killed."

Dr. Wallace stared soundlessly. Darwina started to say something, and was silenced by the lieutenant's gesture.

"No, no. It happened right there in the guesthouse . . . What were Henry Bowling's last acts? He lighted his pipe and then laid it aside unsmoked. He removed his eyeglasses—doesn't it suggest something to you?

"Some action," said Kenmore, "in connection with a civilian defense drill which would prevent his smoking the pipe and wearing a pair of thick-lensed, heavy-rimmed eyeglasses?"

Understanding flared in both pair of eyes.

Kenmore nodded. "Yes. You can't wear any but very thin-rimmed glasses inside an M-1 mask. He put on a gas mask . . . He had just been handed an incident slip which informed him that an imaginary mustard bomb had been dropped at 222 Laguna Terrace. And that explains what became of the missing pink sheet.

"Henry Bowling, on being handed an incident envelope, started to fill out a report form. He wrote down the time and the incident address before he got far enough into the message to discover the nature of the supposed incident. Consequently, the murderer had to make off with the partially completed report.

"For," said Kenmore, "if the pink sheet had been left lying on the desk, what had happened would have been clear at a glance. Neither the time nor the address would have corresponded with the master list in this office; the false incident must have set inquiries in motion; and no one would have assumed for a moment Henry Bowling had died by reason of a defective heater."

Lauren Wallace rose up from his chair, dabbing at his tall forehead with a folded handkerchief.

"It is incredible . . . Yet it is possible. An incident reported directly to sector headquarters. We have done *that* before. Knocking out the post, you know, which might easily happen in a real raid. Henry Bowling would have believed such an incident was authentic," Dr. Wallace thought. "If one of his wardens appeared with such a message—"

"It would not have to be a warden," said Kenmore. "Anyone posing as an incident umpire might have delivered such a message directly. Or a member of the household might have carried such an envelope to him, pretending it had just been handed in at the front door of the house. We are not going to solve the problem by deducing the identity of Henry Bowling's caller. There are scores of persons in La Jolla who *might* have gone there on such an errand."

He shook his head.

"Let's go back to the *modus operandi* . . . to what Henry Bowling did. He put on a mask, after laying aside his pipe and eyeglasses. That is to say, removed the mask from its carrier, inserted his thumbs under the harness straps, and lifted the mask to his face. He put it on, covered the outlet flutter valve with one hand, and expelled a lungful of air around the sides of the facepiece. That is the correct procedure, and as Bowling was a stickler for details he would have followed the rite religiously. In fact, he must have done so. He could not have drawn a breath until the mask got fitted tightly onto his face, and then he drew a deep one.

"And," said Lieutenant Kenmore grimly, "the canister of that mask being loaded with cyanogen *inside* the filters, he instantly inhaled an overwhelming amount of hydrocyanic gas and fell unconscious, if not dead."

Darwina's face showed revulsion. She moistened her lips.

"It's fiendish, it's perfectly fiendish . . . But if Bowling had smelled it in time—?"

She faltered.

"In that case," said Kenmore, "the murderer flung his or her arms around the victim, and as he could not lift his hands to remove the thing—as he had to breathe—he inhaled the poison."

The curious thing was that Dr. Wallace had begun to look a great deal more disturbed than Darwina.

"There is just one thing," said Kenmore. "I examined Henry Bowling's gas mask last night. There was no cyanogen odor about it, either. And besides the inlet valve at the base of the canister was defective. It could not have been used in that way at all."

Darwina blinked confusedly. "Then how can you say—?"

"There were *two* masks, of course. The murderer took away the cyanogen-loaded one, and left the other in its place. And as neither the masks or carriers are numbered or individually identified in any way—"

"*It was mine.*" Wallace barely pushed the words from his throat. "My mask. The one with the defective valve.

"I—that's why I was late at the drill," said he jerkily. "Because I could not find the mask. I had it in my car—intending to exchange it for another in San Diego, you know. And it was stolen from the car yesterday."

"Did you report the theft to the police?" said Kenmore.

Dr. Wallace mopped his perspiring forehead. "No. I did not. I—well, the fact is, I found out at a drill over a month ago the valve was defective. I have said so much about taking care of government property, I was ashamed to admit I had been carrying a quite useless gas mask around in my car all that time."

XV

Always read the postscript of a woman's letter first, because that is where the news is.—THE AUTOBIOGRAPHY OF CATHERINE HOPE.

Although Acting-Lieutenant Arnold had taken personal command of the search, the sub-station officers had not found Lally's brooch or her rings.

"But," said Arnold, "I want to show you something else."

His uniformed figure led Kenmore from the front hallway through a passage where the telephone stood, to the back hallway.

"I got to thinking," said the acting-lieutenant, "about that getaway of Al's. He didn't run out the side door because Crush was out there. He couldn't run through the kitchen without risking being seen by the maid or the cook—Mrs. Yellick was out shopping, but Al didn't know that.

"He must have gone along the passage to the front of the house," Arnold decided. "Sergeant Lyon and Heyes had followed Mrs. Axiter upstairs; Ffleming hadn't come down yet; so the coast was clear for a minute. Still, he might not even have got to the front door without being nailed. The jewels were too hot to hang onto. I got to figuring, maybe he ditched those the very first thing.

"Well, sir. Look here."

He opened the basement door.

"Corinne was down here, you know," said Kenmore.

"Yeah. But he didn't have to go downstairs. He could just have knelt and pushed something through here," Arnold pointed.

It was true. The basement steps consisted simply of treads nailed to their supporting 2 x 12 planks; there were no riser boards.

"I didn't find the brooch and rings," said the acting-lieutenant, "but come down and look."

Corinne Axiter watched them descend into the basement. The dark sister sat on an up-ended packing box. She was smoking a cigarette, with birdlike pecking gestures of tapping away the ash before it had a chance to form.

Perhaps not exactly guarding her, but certainly standing watch, was a blue-garbed sub-station patrolman.

Lieutenant Kenmore peered under the stairs. A shelf ran along the wall. He recognized a familiar blue-and-yellow tin.

"It's cyanogen, all right."

There was no dust on the container; or anywhere along the shelf.

"Wiped off," observed Arnold succinctly.

Corinne's heels rapped sharply on the cement floor. She had sprung to her feet.

"I want to make a statement about that!" the dark sister exclaimed.

Kenmore turned.

"Yes; what?"

"It isn't just that. It is the whole thing." Corinne's eyes were darker, soot-colored shadows in her considerably smudged face. "I can explain the poison, cyanogen, if that is what it is. But that's the least—I think you are behaving in an absolutely contemptible fashion!"

Lieutenant Kenmore's grey stare met this attack warily.

"What have I done that is so contemptible?"

She gestured. "Bringing these men in here to search the house. Pretending it's to look for Lally's brooch and rings. Of course, you found those things in Al's pocket. It is just a cheap trick to enter this house without a search warrant!"

She ignored his headshake.

"And that's not the half of it," continued the dark sister. "Look at the perfectly shameless way you manoeuvered mother into opposing the autopsy."

"*I* manoeuvered—?"

"You did. You knew perfectly well my uncle had been murdered. And if you had said so frankly, of course mother and I would have been glad to cooperate in every way. But, no. You had to pretend it was accidental death, and that an autopsy would be just a lot of beastly red tape."

Lieutenant Kenmore drew a deep breath.

"Good God!" said he. "That's ridiculous, Corinne. Lally brought up the possibility of murder; both you and your mother pooh-poohed it. And I did not say the autopsy was red tape. I said it was reasonable and necessary. I told your mother it was no use trying to oppose a post-mortem."

The brunette head tossed.

"Miss Axiter to you. And don't swear at me . . . I say you are deliberately making people think we killed Uncle Henry, and you are not giving us any chance to clear ourselves.

"I won't stand for it," said Corinne. "I demand the right to be heard. I want to make an *official* statement about all this, and if you don't mind, I shan't trust to your police stenographer's notes. I will have a stenographer of my own present."

She crushed her cigarette underfoot, and then ran up the steps.

Acting-Lieutenant Arnold's perplexed gaze followed . . . "What the hell?"

Kenmore shrugged. He was not any more impressed by Corinne's petulance than by her illogical accusations. Both, he thought, had been assumed for a purpose. Corinne would be sufficiently cool and logical when the need arose.

"It wasn't this cyanogen, anyway," said he some moments later. "The spout-cap is rusted fast on it."

Outside, several officers were methodically and quite futilely combing the Laurustinus hedge. Kenmore, watching, thought the task looked like a labor of Hercules.

The lieutenant walked slowly to the curb and the B.I.S. sedan. He unlocked its trunk, and unrolled the newspaper in which Donald Heyes had wrapped a whiskey soaked towel and a broken bottle. The bottle could not have more than three-fingers of fluid, Kenmore thought. He recalled there had been only a moist spot on the rug upstairs.

He stared intently at the towel. There was certainly a smudge of dust on the fabric.

He was puzzling over that when Sergeant Lyon returned from his Shore Club assignment, having taken a sub-station patrol car for the job.

"Well," said the lieutenant, "what have you got?"

Lyon had got the bus schedule. "It leaves the Shore Club at 7:18. Nobody noticed if Al Dearborn got on. The same driver has the run tonight, and we can check that with him."

"And Lally—?"

"She was there in the bar last night. The bartender ain't sure when or how long. A lot of people came in for a quick one before dinner. She was just one in the crowd."

Lyon fumbled in his pocket.

"I cut something out of this morning's *Union* there.

Where'd I put that clipping?—It's about that table tennis tournament last night. Part of it."

The clipping was not complete; there was no headline, only a summary of results. James Scott def. Walter Jones, Buddy Telight def. Ronald Chapman, Edward Chapman def. Carl Kaysen, Albert Preuss def. Whitey Elliot . . . That had been the first round play, and it was not all of it; for the second round drawings followed . . . Kenmore turned over the clipping.

"No," said Lyon, "the other side is about an Army flier that got shot down in the Philippines, when the War broke out. Killed in action, they thought. But what he really did was lay up in a native village until his busted leg healed, and then because the Japs held the islands he had to sneak down to the coast and steal a native boat. It took him more than a year, hopping from one island to another, until he landed somewheres in Australia."

"It was Captain David Wayne," began Kenmore; and broke off.

He was interrupted, in fact. "We meet again," observed Amy Rhine's genteel voice. "*Whatever* do you think? Corinne has asked me to take some *dictation* . . . It is *odd* she thought of me. We were never friendly, you know."

Lieutenant Kenmore heartily—although silently—agreed it *was* odd. I want to make a statement, the dark sister had said. I don't trust the police, I demand to have a stenographer of my own present . . . And she had been thinking of Amy Rhine when she said it.

"What I'm trying to dope out," Lyon was saying, "is how Lally got to the Shore Club. If she went there alone."

"She may have taken a cab. She wore an evening gown."

"I was going to check that next."

"It can wait," Lieutenant Kenmore told him. "Bring in your note book. Corinne has something to say."

"Are you ready, Mrs. Rhine?" said the dark sister. "I want it down in black-and-white why I am taking this step. It is probably unusual. I don't know. I don't care. Conventions never meant much to me, anyway. You can cross that out, Mrs. Rhine."

Amy Rhine drew a line across her page; Sergeant Lyon's pencil jotted an uninterrupted series of Gregg symbols.

"I am taking this step," Corinne began afresh, "of my own free will and on my own responsibility. There is no one else capable of attending to things since his death. My mother was prostrated by grief by the loss of her brother. Then today she received the further shock of learning his death had not been accidental, as we were at first led to suppose by the police and Dr. Myatt, but was murder. On top of that, there came the attack upon my sister Lally. Lally is in the hospital, my mother is at her side, and neither of them is in any condition to defend themselves against the things that are being said and done.

"It may be generous," said Corinne, giving Kenmore a glance that got into neither stenographer's notes, "it may be kindhearted of the police not to intrude upon our grief. I suppose Lieutenant Kenmore is too chivalrous to annoy three unprotected women who are left without a male relative to look out for them.

"I suppose that is why he has gone to the trouble of trying to learn our intimate affairs by questioning the gardener. And Foster Ffleming and Mr. Pemberton and the air raid warden people. Lieutenant Kenmore is just too much of a gentleman to think of wounding the feelings of three women who do not know their legal rights, and have to make all the arrangements for the funeral, and actually have reason to fear for their lives besides.

"I am sure," said Corinne, "he would be simply aston-ished to find out people are saying *we* are suspected. Be-

cause that is what they are led to think, even though
Lieutenant Kenmore would never dream of such a thing.
Would you, lieutenant?"

Kenmore sat intently watching the young woman.
What was she getting at, anyway? She very well knew (for
she had known of Henry Bowling's insurance policies)
that of the 'three helpless women,' two had gained
$100,000 or more by the murder, and the third had got
an assured income for life. Under these circumstances,
they were certainly going to be suspected, and Corinne
knew it.

And in Kenmore's opinion, Corinne was a great deal
too intelligent to waste her breath trying. It was no use
protesting the police had asked questions behind her
back; so long as she remained a prime suspect, it was obvious the police department wasn't going to take her into
their confidence. It was not Kenmore's job to spare her
feelings; he had the task of apprehending Henry Bowling's murderer; he was not going to be persuaded to ask
her permission whether he might question Fred Crush,
Foster Ffleming, or anyone else.

What was she after, then?

He demanded: "What do you mean, *you have reason
to fear for your lives?* Al Dearborn would have no motive
for slitting your throat, would he? That sounds as if you
thought it was not Al, after all."

Corinne looked startled.

She said: "Did I say that? Will you read it back, Mrs.
Rhine?"

Mrs. Rhine did.

"Oh," said Corinne. "I meant that generally. It was
the different things we all had to think about. I meant
mother did not know her legal rights about the autopsy,
for instance. Lally did not have to bother about the funeral arrangements, but her life was in danger. Of

course, *all* that does not apply to each of us, it simply shows the strain we have been under as a family."

Sergeant Lyon looked up. The change in Corinne's voice was not one he could easily translate into Gregg symbols. (*Confused?*)— He jotted down the interpolation without feeling sure it hit the mark.

Kenmore thought she had sounded almost human for a moment. That was not on the program, he reflected; it had not been in her mind at all. Kenmore felt *he* had missed the mark.

I want it down in black-and-white, Corinne had said, *why I am taking this step*. Lieutenant Kenmore suspected that was exactly true. Her statement had a purpose, it meant to convey something she could not say in any other way, but it needed acute analysis to decide where the significant point lay.

And Corinne had needed a moment to recollect herself.

"Of course Al is guilty," said she. "If you would only pay as much attention to his affairs as you have to ours. If you would question his friends and associates instead of ours, and investigate his movements. Because there is no mystery about our actions at all. I can explain them very briefly."

She had got back into her act, Kenmore thought.

"I think," said Corinne, and her voice had the confidence of having prepared and rehearsed all this, "I think I had better start with last night, the last time I saw Uncle Henry alive. That was Mrs. Yellick's and Ella's night off, so we ate at the Loquat House. Early, because Uncle Henry had to get back for his air raid drill. Lally did not come, she had one of her headaches."

Even the pause seemed prepared and rehearsed.

"Well," said Corinne grimly, "since this is a formal statement for the police records, I had better be explicit. Lally had been drinking. So we left her at home.

"We were early enough to get a table at one of the windows on the sea side. Uncle Henry and mother both ordered curried chicken. I had lobster. You see, we ate hearty meals. There was not very much conversation at dinner, because there was nothing very much to talk about.

"Uncle Henry was in better than usual spirits, really. Darwina Roydan came in, and he pretended to admire her hat, and teased mother by asking why she didn't buy one like it. Of course, he was joking. He didn't approve of Darwina at all. The fact that he laughed about her instead of making an ill-humored comment shows he was in unusual spirits, I think.

"I don't mean that he was usually bad tempered. He was simply not interested, as a rule. He would sit at the table, and I don't think hear a word mother and Lally and I said. He was a man's man, and female affairs weren't of the slightest concern to him.

"He took us into his home, when my father died, because he felt mother could not make her own way in the world, let alone do so and take care of two small children. We saw very little of him, actually. His business affairs took most of his time, he would be away on trips, he would go hunting or fishing with other men.

"I am not going to pretend I ever came to look upon Uncle Henry as a second father," said Corinne. "There wasn't that kind of a relationship, but there were never any quarrels and ill-feelings, either. Mother, Lally, and I lived our own lives, and he didn't interfere."

Amy Rhine had ceased writing. Her expression said, this was really too much.

"*Well!*" said she. "Of course, it is *your* business, Corinne. But to me that sounds a *little* extreme. I don't believe he was quite that perfect."

"I did not say so," replied Corinne. "There were little

things. He would get simply furious with mother when she didn't return his suit at bridge. I have known him to roar at Lally to shut off the radio because he detested jazz music."

"Is that *all?* Because I'm bound to say, there were times when the neighbors would imagine there were *pitched battles* in this house."

Corinne shrugged.

"You can't have a battle without a battleground," said she, "and we had no common ground. Uncle Henry spent his forenoons out of doors, puttering about with his flowers and shrubs. The last two weeks, he had been supervising Crush and the carpenter at rebuilding the guesthouse. He rarely lunched at home. He belonged to Kiwanis, and Optimists, and the Chamber of Commerce—he never failed to attend any of their luncheons. There was usually a political speaker, or a War expert, and he would come home and spend the afternoon writing indignant letters to the President, and Congress, and the newspapers. Then he had his bridge club, and he belonged to a garden club; besides civilian defense.

"He was not really interested enough in our affairs, or we in his, to have any disputes. Oh, there were things. He didn't very much approve my smoking, I'm afraid. But you don't kill people for reasons like that. And, anyway, we had no opportunity to do so."

The dark sister turned to Kenmore.

"Mother and I left the Loquat House at about a quarter before seven. We had dawdled over dessert, watching the sunset. It was a spectacular one. Then, as we walked up the street, I noticed a new *March of Time* was playing at the movie.

"We had both already seen the feature picture in San Diego a month ago. But I thought we had time for the other. And easily reach home before eight, when Foster

Ffleming had said he could come about Al and Lally's insurance.

"There was a line, as there always is at the seven o'clock movie. And we couldn't get loge seats together; there were only singles left. At the time, I was annoyed. But it was a fortunate thing, because the girl will remember. She had to place us on opposite sides of the aisle, and half a dozen rows apart.

"The manager will remember, too," said Corinne. "Because I left as soon as the *March of Time* finished. Mother wasn't in the foyer, and I thought perhaps she had gone on out ahead of me. She had not been very keen about going in the first place, and it was getting past 7:35 then.

"Mr. Clemson chanced to be using the telephone in the ticket box. I waited until he finished his call, and then asked whether he had seen mother leave earlier. While we were talking, she came out. She had sat through the preview of coming attractions."

Lieutenant Kenmore thought, in that case, Corinne had nothing to worry about.

"We walked home," said she, "and fortunately again, we can easily prove that. The air raid drill was in progress, and at Toyon and Balboa we passed Ed Norman and two other of the wardens. It had been an incendiary incident, and the auxiliary unit was just then leaving. Since they are supposed to report in when they arrive and leave an incident, you can probably check the time to the dot. It was approximately ten minutes of eight."

Kenmore considered. If the alibi would stand up under investigation, then it became absurd to imagine for a moment Corinne had ever been worried about the conduct of the police.

She had demanded a chance to clear herself; but she could have done so in a dozen words; and her further statements were quite unnecessary. Above all, he thought, she had not needed Amy Rhine to record a statement of fact which would be supported by two theater employees and three air raid wardens.

It was not the alibi she meant to put in the record, then.

Corinne's cigarette arced into the austere fireplace.

"Well," said she, "we reached home just before Mr. Ffleming arrived. Then I went upstairs to fetch Lally. Mother wanted her to sign a paper which would put a stop to that insurance.

"But Lally wasn't in her room.

"And I found her clothing flung on the floor in the dressing room.

"I was in the dressing room when mother came hurrying upstairs.

" 'Girls!' she called. 'Where are you? Something dreadful has happened to Uncle Henry. They say he is dead.'

" 'Mother,' I said, 'Lally isn't here, and her things are all over the floor.'

"Mother began to cry. I don't remember all she said. But it was how terrible if Lally had gone out in that condition, making a public spectacle of herself, with Uncle Henry lying dead at the very minute.

"I told her not to worry. I would attend to Lally."

Corinne paused.

"It may seem strange for mother to have thought of that at such a time," she said. "But she is like that. It is her family pride.

"All those things she told you last night, Mr. Kenmore . . . The New Ulm Massacre occurred in 1862. Grandfather was only four years old at the time. So it is ridiculous to say he was an Indian fighter, or that he came to America to seek his fortune.

"As for the great romance with Jessie Ross, *she* was years younger; of course they were not childhood sweethearts; she had not even been born when Grandfather Bowling left Linlithgow.

"It is just like mother saying Uncle Henry was a newspaper publisher, when all he published was boilerplate and horse medicine ads.

"Mother isn't a liar. She is simply incapable of facing realities. All those tales she tells are fantastic legends.

"Anyway, I had promised to find my sister. Luckily, I had the presence of mind to look among Lally's things, and her white evening gown was gone.

"So far as I knew, she had not been invited to any party, and there aren't many public places in La Jolla one would appear in that kind of a dress. The Shore Club seemed the likeliest possibility; either there, or one of the hotel bars.

"I came downstairs just as Crush ran in to telephone a doctor. I told him to go to the Shore Club and look for Lally. Then I tried to call Dr. Myatt at his home, and learned he was participating in the medical corps end of the air raid drill, so I told his wife to call and have him sent here as quickly as possible.

"Finally," said Corinne, "I finished by going around to the hotel bars looking for Lally myself, if she was not at the Shore Club.

"But you don't care about that, because neither Crush nor I found her, and she got home by herself. She said she had been at the Shore Club all the time, and perhaps Crush did not look very carefully there.

"It was probably a mistake to send him. I should have realized servants are always resentful and halfhearted when they are asked to do anything beyond their regular duties. He had on his work clothes, and he may have been embarrassed to attract attention by walking in there. As far as my sister was concerned, I did not make an issue of it, because she wasn't sober enough to talk last night. And in the morning, I had to go around with mother about the autopsy.

"I think that is all," Corinne said. "Except I suppose you want to ask your questions."

Lieutenant Kenmore was not going to undertake cross-examination in Mrs. Rhine's presence.

Or, he thought, until he had heard Lally's account.

"I think that is enough for the present," said he.

Corinne frowned.

"Oh. I nearly forgot. I meant to tell you about the poison. That has been sitting on the shelf for years. There was a swarm of bees in Mrs. Rhine's garage—the garage was torn down to make room for the tennis court, afterward.

"Uncle Henry had a deathly fear of bees. I suppose because of his poor eyesight, he could hear them buzzing about and couldn't clearly see them. Anyway, he bought the cyanogen to exterminate them," said the dark sister. "You remember the cyanogen, don't you, Amy?"

Mrs. Rhine did not reply; her pencil had abruptly stopped; above the tensed fingers, sinew and vein showed where the thin wrists disappeared into their ruffled cuffs.

"I am *sure* you do," said Corinne. "Because while the bees in your garage wall dropped like a hail of *bullets*, the others hung around and got overcome by the fumes, and for a couple of days your yard was like a *battleground*. Crawling with sick, dying bees. You must remember it, for you were *furious*. You threatened to *arrest* Uncle Henry for trespassing on your property, and he threatened to sue you for maintaining *a public nuisance*. Actually, the neighborhood simply rang with a regular *pitched battle*."

Corinne's eyes gleamed under their lashes like spear points of obsidian.

Amy Rhine stiffened to the assault.

"No," said she. "I didn't remember it as cyanogen. Whatever he used. I did not know it by that name."

"Indeed?" murmured Corinne. "But you knew what it would *do*."

XVI

If I had been beautiful, this would have been a very different story. Did you ever stop to think, a beautiful woman lives in a different world? Because men are nice to her and women aren't; but with me, it has been the other way around.—THE AUTOBIOGRAPHY OF CATHERINE HOPE.

Donald Heyes' report did not advance matters very far.

"There's a valise in Dearborn's apartment," said he. "Packed. The usual toothbrush and razor and pajamas in it. Of course there are fingerprints around the place. I think they are mostly his, and then those apartments have maid service. So I would have to fingerprint the maid as a preliminary."

"It was just a wild gamble," Lieutenant Kenmore confessed. "I thought perhaps you might stumble onto Lally's prints there."

Heyes stared.

"Why?"

"Because it is not yet clear where she spent Thursday evening. I haven't got that girl figured out, I'm afraid."

"Al is the one I'd be figuring out," Heyes said. *"His* prints were in *her* room . . . How is he going to explain that?"

Kenmore thought, "It's no use trying to close in on Al from one angle. He has got to be surrounded and cut off from retreat.

"Anyway, we've got a lot else to do. Lyon is working

in the guesthouse, typing out Corinne's statement. I want
to study that before asking her any more questions.

"We'll have to check her alibi at the theater and the
wardens in Ed Norman's post. And meet the Greyhound
bus and find out if Al paid him a cash fare. I am going
to ask you to do all that, because I have to go to the hospital, and I want to see Sam Elliot."

Lieutenant Kenmore went on to the hospital, where
Dr. Myatt warned him to make his questioning brief.

"Mrs. Dearborn has not a skull fracture, but it is a
severe concussion. She is not in any condition to be questioned at length, and it would be useless to try."

"I only want to know what happened today."

"Yes," said the physician. "Unfortunately, it often oc-
curs in concussion cases that the patient's memory is
temporarily affected. You may find that she does not recall details. Accident victims are frequently not able to
give a coherent account of the circumstances leading up
to such an injury, and it is useless to press them.

"I thought it best," said Myatt, "to send Mrs. Axiter
home because she is hysterical about all this. There is
nothing to be gained by arguing with Lally now, and because of the shock she has suffered, a great deal could be
lost."

"Yes. I'll cut it short."

Kenmore entered the hospital room. "Mrs. Dearborn—"

"I wish you'd *stop* calling me that," came the intense
whisper from the pillow.

"Lally. Do you know who I am?"

He bent over the pillow.

"Yes," said she faintly. "The cop that looks like a football coach."

"I must ask you how this happened," said Kenmore.

Lally's blonde head moved slightly, negatively.

"I don't know . . . I was sleeping on the bed. The room seemed hot and stuffy. I got up and opened the window . . . And then they were telling me to lie still for the X-rays."

"Yes," said Kenmore. "Do you recall what woke you?"

"I don't think anything did. I was too miserable to notice."

He frowned. "Are you sure you opened the window?"

"Yes . . . I remember that . . . The fresh breeze felt good."

The lieutenant's frown deepened. There had certainly not been any breeze in the room.

"You were sleeping," said he. "Was it just sleep, or had you been drinking?"

"No."

The ghost of a blush colored the girl's cheeks.

"You won't believe it," said Lally, "but I've sworn off drinking. I mean it. I would have given anything for a drink, but I wouldn't have taken one for anything in the world, either." Her lips twisted. "Mother has some sleeping pills and I took two of those, but they didn't help much . . . My God," said Lally shakenly, "it should have been the happiest day of my life, and I wasn't happy. I was just horribly, beastly sick."

Lieutenant Kenmore looked down steadily at the blonde sister.

"Happy?" said he. "Lally, was it because of Captain Wayne?"

"I—can't we leave him out of it? It wasn't Dave's *fault*. It was just the lousy way life is . . . No, it wasn't. If I hadn't been such a damned little fool," Lally said bleakly, "and married Al . . . But there wasn't any time to change that. There wasn't time enough to get a divorce. He just went and that was all there was to it.

"And when I think we could have had those few weeks,

and we didn't—" Her voice rose. "Because, God damn it, we *couldn't!* Dave was *decent.* He was an officer and a gentleman. He wouldn't have an *affair* with another man's wife, thank you. And he was right. We could have tried, and it wouldn't have been any good, and I knew it as well as he did."

She began to laugh. "Isn't it funny? Because everyone will tell you what a perfectly rotten little tramp I am . . . When the one man I ever loved, the one man I ever wanted—isn't it *rich*—never even *touched* me. Because neither of us wanted it that way. I was going to divorce Al and then I would go to Manila and we would be married there."

"All right, Lally," said Kenmore. "But you had better rest now."

She kept on talking. "Well, it wasn't just that he—that I thought he was dead. It—it was the horrible mess I made of everything for him, and now I could never make that up at all. So what was the *use* of anything?"

"Of course," said Lieutenant Kenmore. "You drank to forget—"

"No. I got drunk to remember him. You won't understand that," said Lally, "but it's true. I found out I could get into a haze where anything real wasn't real any more . . . I could get *so* drunk all that slipped away, the War, and death, and time. Do you know what it was like?" said Lally dreamily. "It was going into a tunnel with a candle burning at the far end . . . When you go into a tunnel, the first thing is you leave daylight behind you. That is one stage, the lights and voices and faces fading away. It is the easy part, it needs only a few quick drinks, and you are inside your own private tunnel where Al or Corinne or Uncle Henry or nobody can follow you.

"Then there is a second stage which isn't so nice. Because as you go along, it gets so dreadfully *dark*, groping into a horrible blackness. That is the bad part. When the daylight is left behind and the candle is still so far away like a star at the end of the tunnel. And it seems you will never get there. But you have got to keep struggling toward it, and gradually that gets brighter and you can begin to feel the warmth finally. And you know the wonderful part is just ahead.

"I always thought," said Lally, "I would find Dave there. I knew he was. But I never made it. Because I always fell down in the horrible dark middle of the tunnel, and it was only half a dozen times I got to the warm, bright end. And then I passed out, anyway, just when if I could have taken one more step—"

"Here," said Lieutenant Kenmore. "Stop that."

The tears were brimming from Lally's eyes.

"I know," said she. "It doesn't matter now. He is alive, and I am going to stop . . . I have stopped. It was just that I had such a wretched hangover, and the sleeping pills made me groggy."

"One more thing," said the detective hastily—Dr. Myatt had opened the door to put an end to this interview. "There were some cards of Amy Rhine's in your purse."

"I know, Al stole it."

"Al Dearborn stole—?"

"Well, *kept* it, anyway. It's a long story," began Lally.

"If it's a long story," said Myatt firmly, "it will wait until tomorrow."

Lieutenant Kenmore, as he trudged to the hospital elevator, wore a highly abstracted look . . . He was not very much surprised by these disclosures. When a young woman decides to go to hell in a hurry, there is generally a man involved; and he hadn't supposed Lally cared that much for Al Dearborn. The intriguing query was, had Al seen today's paper? If he had, *if he knew David Wayne was alive,* then he must have expected Lally would begin divorce proceedings.

From a phone booth in the hospital lobby he telephoned Sam Elliot's home, and learned the district warden had already dined and left for the Friday evening session of his bridge club.

"Already?" The lieutenant felt less surprise as he consulted his strapwatch; it had got to be ten minutes of seven.

"They meet early," said Elliot's wife, "because so many of the men have defense jobs in San Diego, and have to get up early."

"Yes; where do they meet?"

"It is at the Shore Club."

Lieutenant Kenmore found the glare of the setting sun irritatingly in his eyes as he drove down Toyon Street; the street dipped sharply toward a molten sea; and lowering the windshield visor did not help.

Under the circumstances, he did not think two logical thoughts until he had parked in the Club lot.

The bridge games had not started when he found out the small room off the lounge; Lieutenant Kenmore's appearance occasioned a sudden and surreptitious silence; he knew they had been talking about the murder, and probably predicting his inability to solve it.

The Catherine Hope Case had left in La Jolla no very high esteem for the San Diego police.

Sam Elliot asked, "You want to go outside and talk?"

"I thought we might drop in at the bar." Lieutenant Kenmore supposed he could get a sandwich there?

"You can have something brought into the lounge," the district warden thought. "I doubt if there's a booth to be had in the bar, and it's so damned noisy we'd have to yell at each other."

He beckoned a waiter; Kenmore ordered beer and a chicken sandwich; and they retired to a corner of the lounge.

Sam Elliot did not know how the ninth incident had got reported two minutes before it occurred.

"Things like that happen," the district warden said. "Even if Ed Norman had the right time, he was working with a flashlight. Bowling is the one who should have spotted the mistake, and held the report up if it came in too soon."

But he did not think it curious Henry Bowling might have overlooked the discrepancy.

"His eyesight was not good, you mean," said Kenmore, thinking of the alarm clock the sector warden had kept on the desk before him besides the watch he wore on his wrist.

"No, it wasn't good. He would overbid at bridge because he'd glance down and read the score all wrong. I remember once I opened with a psychic three heart bid—"

Sam Elliot plunged into a post-mortem of the three heart bid; he had it up to six hearts doubled when the waiter appeared with the beer and sandwich, switched up the lights in the lounge, and drew the black-out drapes on the ocean side of the room.

"—so we went down four tricks," the district warden concluded. "I guess I wasn't so smart. I had no business making a psychic. But then, Bowling didn't have to force me up to a slam, either. He had mis-read the score. It was as much his fault as mine, and anyway it's only a game. There was no need for him to get so damned sore and insulting."

Lieutenant Kenmore recalled Corinne's phrase. "He had a blunt tongue."

"Yes. Of course, this Friday night bridge gang are old warhorses, we're not a bunch of pansies. Blunt things get said sometimes . . . But I tell you, Henry Bowling had a queer side to his nature. It isn't just that he got mad because his partner misbid a hand. I think he enjoyed hurting your feelings.

"I'll tell you how I mean that," said the district warden, "so you'll see it isn't personal with me. When Dave Horton first came out here, he used to belong to the club. That is before his marriage. He married Ginny Ffleming —Foster's ex-wife—Ginny Jedicoe, she was. It was one of those whirlwind courtships.

"Well. Right after the marriage, the postman began leaving all sorts of mail in plain wrappers at the house. Stuff addressed to Dave . . . Literature on sex, those so-called art photographs, advertising leaflets for patent medicines for men only, medicines that claim to develop the female bust—and then lots of Lonely-Heart literature from mail order marriage outfits. Poor Ginny didn't know what to make of it. After all, she'd only known Dave six weeks or so when she married him. Of course, *he* wasn't responsible. It was Bowling's idea of a practical joke. He had answered a flock of *Police Gazette* ads in Dave's name."

Kenmore looked very thoughtful.

"I didn't think it was so funny, either," said the district warden. "It was pretty rough . . . I don't mean he was dirty-minded. After all, nothing downright smutty gets through the United States mails. But when he supplied Dave's home address, of course he knew Dave was at the office all day, and he knew *she* would be startled. To tell the truth, the whole thing struck me as being darned juvenile. And pointless. It's like the nicknames he invented for the club members. Calling Rob Smith, the postmaster, you know, the *G-man*. Fred Billings was *Bullpup Bill,* if you can see what's humorous in that."

"It is a newspaper term, I believe," said Kenmore. "The earliest edition of a Sunday paper is the bullpup."

"Oh. Well, I never got it. Billings is always the first man here, ahead of everyone else, so Bowling had a point. But none of us understood it," Elliot said. "It maybe amused Henry Bowling; no one else."

A sense of humor, Kenmore thought, that was heavy *and* secretive . . . He wondered, how that aspect of Bowling's personality seemed to the killer?

"I'll tell you how it struck me," Elliot was saying. "I had a feeling sometimes he was laughing up his sleeve at us."

Lieutenant Kenmore delved into his pocket and brought forth the ninth incident pink sheet.

"The question is whether it actually was reported early. Whether you made a mistake in writing this."

Elliot frowned.

"I'm not sure that I did write it."

"It isn't your handwriting?"

"Oh. The report's in my writing . . . I'm not sure I noted the *time,* I mean. Because that is at the bottom, the last thing. I remember when Bowling called that in, after he made the report, he wanted to speak to Dr. Wallace and I told him Wallace had not come in yet.

"I don't know what ailed Wallace last night," the district warden said with a trace of annoyance. "He made up this new form, planned a drill especially to use for the Commando raid, and then came late. I was left there trying to do his job and mine, too, trying to take down all those incidents onto a new form I'd never before handled, trying to answer both phones.

"Well, I think now the other phone rang just then,

and I answered it without having filled in this time space, because my attention had been distracted when Bowling asked to speak to Wallace."

"Do you remember what the other incident was? We could fix the time by that."

"It wasn't an incident. It was Dr. Wallace saying he had been delayed and would be right along."

Elliot shook his head.

"It doesn't matter now. But all that irritated me. I'd given up going into San Diego—my kid was playing in a table tennis tournament there—on account of this drill. And then Wallace himself was not interested enough to be on hand."

Lieutenant Kenmore glanced at his watch it was now 7:18 o'clock; time for the Greyhound bus to appear at the door.

"Yes," said he, rising. "Well, I mustn't keep you from your game."

It was at this moment Dr. Wallace entered the Shore Club lounge.

"Sam!" said he.

And then: "Inspector!"

Kenmore afterward thought, Dr. Wallace had come in search of Sam Elliot, had looked around to discover him, and had been startled to discover Kenmore present.

At the moment, the lieutenant only thought Lauren Wallace looked extremely perturbed.

Sam Elliot thought he looked excited, and three girls who had just come in from the bar thought he looked frightened.

The Director Emeritus had entered by the opposite, ocean side of the room; and whether perturbed, excited, or frightened, he neglected to close the door behind.

The breeze ruffled Dr. Wallace's white shock of hair, and fluttered the girls' dresses. In which sense, it was probably true one of them felt a cold chill at sight of him.

He could not have seen the girls at all.

He came a step into the room.

"Do you remember Cath—" Lauren Wallace began. It was as far as he got.

The shot stopped him.

The shot thundered, as the three young women heard it. What Sam Elliot heard was a crack. To Lieutenant Kenmore's ears it sounded thusly:

Pun-n-n-n.

The Director Emeritus could not have heard it at all.

Dr. Lauren Wallace seemed to hesitate. His eyebrows went up toward the white shock of hair. His eyeballs rolled up, and only their whites were visible. And the corners of his mouth lifted. In this moment-long grimace of agony, every facial muscle was irresistibly drawn toward the top of the man's skull.

He fell.

Lieutenant Kenmore knocked over his plate and beer glass, drew a revolver from a holster on his hip, and ran to the open door.

He reached the door before the three girls screamed.

It was very nearly dark now; it *was* dark, to the officer who had been sitting under an electric light. He crossed an eight-foot sidewalk at almost the one stride. With the second stride, he stumbled in ankle-deep beach sand.

He was at very nearly the upper end of the Shore Club's beach; ahead of him, at a distance of perhaps thirty yards, fell the white flank of a wave. To the left, at an indecipherable distance, the beach melted away into murk. Behind him, the Shore Club showed a dimmed-out exterior to the sea. On the right advanced a series of jagged rock forms that strode into the surf.

Something moved there.

Kenmore shouted, and ran toward the rocks.

He did not see the danger until it was fairly upon him; indeed, until it sprang at his throat. Then, a good deal faster than conscious thought, he got his arm in front of his chin.

The impact knocked him down; an excruciatingly painful pressure pierced his forearm; and the revolver fell from his numbed fingers.

Someone yelled, he did not hear what.

Lieutenant Kenmore, rolling, flung a snarling and furry weight from his chest. He raked his free hand in the sand and did not find his revolver.

There came a second yell, now directly overhead.

Kenmore, sitting up, stared at the bared gleam of a bayonet. The dog stood growling beside the sentry's khaki-clad leg.

XVII

It is always the men who do parlor tricks.—THE AUTOBIOGRAPHY OF CATHERINE HOPE.

PFC Charles Tazewell, ——st Company, ——st Battalion, had passed the Shore Club moments before the shot.

He had not seen Lauren Wallace, or anyone else there. The sentry was picking his way through the rock formations when he heard the shot; he turned; but the boulders hid the Shore Club from his sight now.

Reconnoitering rapidly, sentry and dog emerged from the rocks as Lieutenant Kenmore ran onto the beach; the dog perceived an armed man apparently charging upon them; and what happened thereafter was a matter of canine corps training.

"I thought she'd tear your gullet out, sir," said Private Tazewell.

It was not the first time he had challenged strollers in the vicinity of the Shore Club.

"Drunks, generally," said he. "I don't think she'd have gone for you, except she saw the gun, and how could she tell you were a cop? That gun was *bad.*"

Private Tazewell had not observed anyone else making off along the shore. Kenmore, as he stood rubbing his arm, could see no one else; that was to be expected, considering the killer had only to dash around either corner of the building.

"Go back!" he shouted. "Inside! All of you!"

For the doorway had suddenly poured forth Sam Elliot and Wyeland and others . . . It would not do at all. Kenmore thought the murderer might very well have flung down his gun, and run around the building in order to enter it upon the other side. In that case, he had only to return, join in the search, and under cover of the darkness hurl the weapon into the sea.

"Inside! All of you!" said the lieutenant. And to Tazewell: "Will you watch it? Don't let anyone onto the beach at all until the police take over."

He entered the lounge, now a scene of inconceivable disorder. At the sound of the shot and screams, the members of the bridge club had streamed in one doorway, and the patrons of the bar in another. (Many of the latter had brought their drinks with them. A dozen cocktails got spilled upon the lounge floor in the jostling confusion.)

"Stand back. Stand back," appealed Lieutenant Kenmore, forcing his way through the knot about Lauren Wallace's fallen form.

He had been shot with what was probably a heavy caliber revolver bullet that had entered the base of the skull.

Kenmore stood, gesturing with an exceedingly sore right arm.

"You will all have to clear this room . . . Elliot,—" he glanced around "—Wyeland, will you lend a hand? Get these people back. No one is to leave the Club, but you cannot stay in this room."

Wyeland caught at the painful arm.

"She *saw* who it was . . . That girl there."

Lieutenant Kenmore forced his way through a smaller knot assembled around the eye-witness. He wasted some moments upon her, until he discovered she had not seen him leave the lounge; or rather, she *had*. For her description of the murderer plunging from the doorway, pistol in hand, was of Kenmore himself.

"Back. Out of the way, folks. Keep *moving*."

The lounge was cleared at last.

"All right. If you men will each guard a door," said the lieutenant, perspiring. "Where's a phone, Elliot?"

"There's a phone booth in the bar."

It was a doorless booth, and Kenmore found Foster Ffleming wedged inside it.

"No. No message, Ella. I'll call back later," that gentleman was saying.

He turned and bumped into the lieutenant.

"Ffleming," said the detective, "no one will be allowed to leave here unsearched. Do you mind—?"

The insurance man shook his head stiffly.

"All right," said Kenmore a moment later. "Now dash out to the parking lot and tell the attendant no cars are to go—absolutely no one is to leave the Club."

The lieutenant pressed into the booth and dialed Seaview 3-3609. "Henry Bowling's residence," said a voice at the other end of the wire.

"Is that you, Ella? This is the police . . . Mr. Ffleming was just on the wire; what did he want?"

"Miss Corinne," replied the maid, "but she's gone to the hospital to fetch Mrs. Axiter."

Kenmore reflected Mrs. Axiter had left the hospital half or three-quarters of an hour ago . . . He rang up Seaview 3-2119.

"Lyon, I want you to drop that job and get down to the Shore Club *fast*. Notify Arnold; Dr. Wallace has been shot; but leave a patrolman there at the house. Tell him I want to know what time Jessie and Corinne Axiter come in."

Until these officers arrived, it was necessary to post Club employees at the doors; though it did not seem very likely it would be hard to prevent people leaving; quite the contrary.

Kenmore had to fight his way back to the lounge, and he did not at all like the temper of the crowd that barred his way. He was perfectly aware of the danger of mob psychology . . . In twenty-four hours, Henry Bowling had· been murdered, Lally Dearborn severely assaulted, and now it was Dr. Wallace . . .

Lieutenant Kenmore did what it was possible to do under the circumstances.

First off, who could be eliminated as having been in the bridge clubroom when the shot was heard? William Wyeland named off a list: unfortunately, he assured Kenmore *Sam Elliot had been there.*

The lieutenant sighed and massaged his bruised arm. The bearded lawyer had arrived after the district warden left that room, he had subsequently encountered Elliot in the lounge, and he assumed the other had been in the clubroom that was where, on Friday nights, Elliot invariably was.

Sam Elliot, for his part, thought Lauren Wallace's last words were: "Do you remember *has—*"

It was not the district warden's fault his auditory nerve connected with a brain and not with a wax recording disc. *Cath,* as a syllable, meant nothing to Elliot; his mind therefore rejected it; and by a process of reasoning substituted a semi-intelligible *has.*

Foster Ffleming returned and reported Dr. Wallace's car was parked at the street-end curb with its motor running.

"I looked there," said Ffleming, "because it wasn't in the parking lot, and I saw him only about a quarter of an hour ago at the control room. So if his car was not here, it would have meant someone brought him . . ."

Among the hundred-odd persons present, Ffleming alone displayed any capacity for clear and incisive thinking.

Lieutenant Kenmore went outside, looked into Wallace's machine, and saw a gas mask carrier lying on the front seat.

He did not have to remove the mask. It was enough to unsnap the carrier flap. The odor of cyanogen assaulted his nostrils, for the poison was spilled loose in the canvas bag.

A chatter of typewriter keys greeted Lieutenant Kenmore as he entered the Legion Hall; Darwina Roydan looked up from the machine.

"Hello," said she. "Dr. Wallace and I had a perfectly brilliant idea after you left . . . Because if Bowling was killed by a false incident envelope trick, that could best be done by someone who knew how a civilian defense drill is run. I have been going over the list of persons who are enrolled in the defense corps, and comparing it with the incident reports last night.

"Do you see what I mean? For instance, Ed Norman is familiar with the routine, but he is known to have been at Toyon and Balboa Streets. So we can check him off. Will Wyeland knows, but his movements aren't of record until he met me on Cathcart Way at a quarter of eight, so he is on the list of suspects. As a matter of fact," continued Darwina, "I am a suspect, too! Because I left Ed Norman's incident to deliver Wyeland's envelope, and so it would have been possible for me to have killed Henry Bowling between 7:20 and 7:31 o'clock! Then, there is Mrs. Chapman—"

Kenmore interrupted. "Darwina, when did Lauren Wallace leave here?"

"When? Why, just a few minutes ago. He stayed late to talk to Wyeland about taking Henry Bowling's job as sector warden."

"Wyeland!"

"Yes," said Darwina. "What's wrong with that? Wye-land is the logical choice, after Bowling. He has an office here in La Jolla, and can be reached almost any hour of the day." She stared. "What is it? What has happened?"

"Lauren Wallace was shot to death in the Shore Club lounge at 7:18 o'clock tonight."

Darwina's face became rigid.

Several seconds later she managed faintly:

"Who—?"

"Nobody knows. Nobody," said Kenmore, "except of course whoever did the job." He pulled up a chair and sat down. "You had better tell me exactly what happened here tonight."

"Yes," said Darwina Roydan numbly. She needed some moments, however, to pull herself together. "Well, in the first place. Wyeland came in. To talk about that, you know."

"At what time?"

"I'm not sure. Half after six, I suppose."

"Exactly what was said?"

"I don't know. I was getting up this list, here in the office, and so Dr. Wallace walked out into the control room with Wyeland. Of course, he didn't want him to see what I was doing. So I didn't hear what was said, that is, I didn't listen."

"No mention of Henry Bowling's death at all?"

Darwina frowned. "There was something about the pink report forms. Dr. Wallace explained they were an experiment, each sector warden had got only three, and they would not be used again. Because they did not work out as well as the old forms, after all."

"He didn't say anything about a *missing* pink sheet?"

"Dr. Wallace? Heavens, no."

"Go on."

"Foster Ffleming came in."

"You still suspect him, do you?" said Kenmore.

"He is not on the list of suspects, because he is not in civilian defense at all. He merely brought in a bundle of things Corinne had packed together. Apparently she cleaned out the guesthouse files today. But I don't think he would be running errands for Corinne if she was not an heiress.

"And by the way," said Darwina, "*he* mentioned Corinne had not been able to find Henry Bowling's armband and gas mask. You had better shut his mouth about that."

Kenmore shrugged. The gas mask was not any secret now.

"Well," said Darwina, "then Amy Rhine came in."

Discouragement appeared on the lieutenant's angular face. "What was it, open house tonight?"

Darwina replied that the control room was kept open every night until nine. "By volunteers. Friday is Amy's night. Usually there is nothing to do except answer the phone—wardens calling in and leaving numbers where they can be reached in case of an alert. She had some work with her, some notes she intended to type, and was going to use this machine. Naturally, I didn't want her around while I made up a list of murder suspects. So I told her I had to use the typewriter myself. And as I would be here the whole evening, she could take the night off. It would be more convenient for her to work in Wyeland's office, anyway, where she wouldn't be bothered by the phone ringing.

"But then, as she turned to go, Dr. Wallace came in— he said he had something of hers in his desk."

Darwina paused.

"Yes?" said Kenmore. "What?"

"That's just it. He didn't say. Because it wasn't in his desk."

Brows knit, she peered in the direction of the desk as if trying to visualize Lauren Wallace's form there.

"I am trying to remember his exact words. *'That's odd . . . It was here . . . I wonder if Elliot . . .'* He didn't finish the sentence. He was muttering under his breath," said Darwina, "and of course at the time I didn't think much of it, not then. But perhaps he didn't want the rest of us to hear."

"You were all in this room at the time?"

"Yes. Wyeland had come in with him, and Amy and Ffleming had been here all along."

The lieutenant's grey eyes speculated. "But didn't Amy ask him what it was?"

"Yes, she did. He muttered something about her sister, and then Wyeland—come to think of it, *he* acted very strangely . . ."

"In what way?"

"Why, he seemed to lose all interest in everything else when he found Amy here. He got restless and fidgetty— I don't know how to describe it."

"Pulling at his beard?"

"Yes, he did *that* . . . Well, anyway. He said he had to go or he would be late at his bridge club. And he told Amy to come along, he would drop her at the office. The more I think of it," said Darwina gravely, "the more I'm convinced he rushed her out through the door before there could be any discussion of *what* was missing from Dr. Wallace's desk."

"Don't jump at conclusions," said the lieutenant, with equal gravity. "As you say, he was restless *before* that got mentioned."

"But *why* was he, at all?"

Kenmore asked, "Had Mrs. Rhine mentioned the nature of her typing?"

"No-o."

"It was a statement of Corinne's to the police," the detective guessed. "It wasn't very discreet of Amy to bring that to a semi-public place for typing, where almost anyone might wander in and read what she was doing. If Wyeland rushed her outside, it may have been on that account. He may be retained by the family, if they haven't already asked him to act."

He paused.

"Then Dr. Wallace left here without saying what he had had in his desk?" Kenmore resumed. "Did he say where he was going?"

"He did, yes, that he was going to see Sam Elliot. But I thought that was an excuse at the time. Ffleming was trying to talk to him about that missing mask of Bowling's—Ffleming's no fool—and I think Dr. Wallace hurried away, so he would not have to tell him you had taken a mask from the guesthouse."

"And Ffleming went with Wallace?"

"Yes, no, I'm not sure in what order they went. I was busy going over these reports. Dr. Wallace may have *said* that to get rid of Ffleming . . . and then decided to go to the Shore Club for some other reason; I don't know."

"There is just one more thing . . . If you have these volunteers here nights, who locks up the building?"

"*They* do, and leave the key in the mailbox."

"Good God!" said Kenmore.

He stretched a hand toward the phone on Lauren Wallace's desk.

"Oh. Is this an extended service line?"

"No," said Darwina, "you'll have to go into the control room and use one of the phones there for that."

Lieutenant Kenmore had to call Deputy Coroner McGheen.

An hour later, the Shore Club had been emptied of eighty-three persons, none of whom left carrying a gun. A squad of uniformed officers were searching the building and the beach in front of it. Donald Heyes had taken his pictures, and vainly tried to discover incriminating fingerprints on the gas mask and inside Lauren Wallace's automobile.

And Dr. Lauren Wallace lay on that mortician's slab where Henry Bowling had been placed the previous night.

Lieutenant Kenmore, as he proceeded to take charge of The Victim's clothing and personal effects, thought the testimony he had collected at the Shore Club was scarcely worth the labor of sifting.

(Dr. Wallace's wallet, penknife, watch, keyring, fountain pen, pencil, card case, and cuff links accumulated in a pile at the foot of the slab.)

Kenmore had told Lauren Wallace not many hours ago, it was not difficult for an experienced investigator to separate wheat from chaff . . . For what any witness sees in an event is nine-tenths what he expects, or is led to expect, to see.

(Dr. Wallace's shoes got tied together by their laces.)

"All right, Ed," said Kenmore to Deputy Coroner McGheen. "Probe and see if you can find the slug."

The lieutenant stepped onto the mortician's porch, and lighted his pipe. A fog had begun to advance upon La Jolla; the downtown streetlights were already erased.

Kenmore rubbed his aching arm . . . It had been a piece of bad luck, running into the military sentry. But had the murderer relied on his doing so? He thought not. A minute earlier, and Lauren Wallace would have encountered Private Tazewell face-to-face. A minute later, and the sentry would not have heard the shot at all.

There had been luck involved, but it could not have been presupposed in the murderer's plan. The assassin, discharging the bullet into Lauren Wallace's brain, had not counted on the sentry's help; and if the sentry had not appeared, still neither the gun nor its owner could have been found. Lieutenant Kenmore considered that an extraordinary feat of legerdemain had been performed at the Shore Club tonight.

"Every move of that was planned in advance," he thought, "like a magician's trick."

And the accounts of the witnesses (insofar as anyone had witnessed anything) were precisely the accounts of an audience that has seen such a stage trick performed . . . who have seen every move except the vital one.

And the vital one had not happened until after the shot, of course.

"No," Kenmore's thought ran, "I will never get it that way."

His thought turned in the other direction. "Drop the gas mask for the moment," he reflected.

Do you remember Cath—? Dr. Wallace had said to Sam Elliot, who might have taken from Wallace's desk whatever was there. "Something that was not important at first glance, or Wallace would have told me of it before now." It was in fact something that had not seemed of the slightest importance until Lauren Wallace, opening his desk drawer, found that article had disappeared. At that moment, exactly because it was missing, the significance must have dawned upon the incident officer.

McGheen appeared in the doorway. "I got it for you."

Kenmore studied the misshapen, flat-shouldered object. "That's a .357 Magnum slug."

"It shouldn't be a hard gun to trace."

"We'll try. But I suppose the easiest way is to find out who killed Henry Bowling. We have made some progress there—and I don't see why we should drop all that and start a-fresh from nothing."

The fog preceded him up the hill. He parked on Toyon Street; inside the guesthouse, Sergeant Lyon again punched at Henry Bowling's typewriter; the approaching glow of a flashbeam belonged to a sub-station patrolman.

"Lieutenant? Say, I can't find that damned brooch or rings anywhere. If you ask me, we're licked."

"We'll broadcast the description," said Kenmore. "Has the family come in yet?"

"Yeah. Awhile ago. 7:30."

Kenmore opened the guesthouse door.

"Just finishing," said the sergeant.

"Yes. Come along. We are going to take another statement from Corinne."

"Great grief!" said the sergeant.

Corinne, swathed in a dressing robe, answered the front doorbell.

"Well"—she did not suggest they step inside—"what is it now?"

"Miss Axiter, you left the house this evening. I must ask you why, and where, you went."

"It was to the hospital. To bring mother home."

"And only that?"

"Yes."

Lieutenant Kenmore said, "But your mother left the hospital at about a quarter of seven, didn't she? And you didn't return here until half past seven."

"Mother was nervous. I told Crush to drive us around awhile. I thought the drive would do her good."

"Where did you go?"

"Up the canyon road aways and back."

"May I see your mother?"

"You may not. She is in bed. I gave her several sleeping pills," said Corinne. "If you want to know, ask Crush. If you don't believe me."

The door slammed.

Lieutenant Kenmore walked around to the garage; he found the door unlocked; Crush, a whiskbroom in hand, was sweeping out the tonneau of a green Cadillac.

"Just a minute," said the lieutenant, and looked; there was certainly beach sand in the Cadillac.

"Hello. Where'd all this come from?"

The gardener's congested tones were surly. "That goddam Lally . . ." He reddened. "Well, it's a fact. She goes bumming around in the car, and then I catch hell for the shape it's in. A man could pick up after that girl all day long."

"Who gave you hell?"

"You guess . . . Corinne, of course. The car ain't fit to ride in, the tennis court ain't fit to play on—"

"Yes," said Kenmore. "When did she give you hell?"

"When don't she? Tonight. When I got out the car for her. All the way *to* the hospital."

"And after that?"

"They wanted to go joy-riding. I ain't done nothing but work all day, so's it's a pleasure for me. Driving by them goddam dim-out lights," said Fred Crush, "with the old lady bawling her head off and Corinne yapping at me, *Don't drive so fast,* and *Watch out, there's a car coming.* I'll say that was one hell of a joy-ride."

Lieutenant Kenmore, when he returned to the guest-house, picked up the typewritten report.

"Corinne turned the tables on Amy Rhine," he thought, "but was that only a feint?"

If that had been her purpose, the body of the statement was utterly superfluous.

And, he reasoned, that feint was not exclusively in Mrs. Rhine's direction. For if she had known what cyanogen would do, so had Corinne known, and Lally, and Jessie Axiter.

Lally had no alibi. Was that what Corinne meant to say?

Kenmore doubted it; because it was unnecessary for Corinne to say so. Lally's lack of an alibi was a fact the police could be relied on to discover for themselves. Just as they could be relied on to learn Corinne and Jessie had sat through a *March of Time.*

"It is not anything like that," the lieutenant thought. "There is a circumstance or inference she had to put into the record, and could not except by taking the bit in her teeth."

In fact, the whole form of the statement was extraordinary.

"As if she wanted to say something," he mused, "she could not have put into a reply to a question, if I had questioned her."

He picked up a pencil and began underscoring those portions of the statement which did not seem to have any bearing on the issue at all.

"The unimportant and dragged-in bits," he reflected, "are not unimportant or dragged-in. You could throw away everything else but that."

The pencil drew a line: *There is no one else capable of attending to things since his death.* And another line: *I suppose Lieutenant Kenmore is too chivalrous to annoy three unprotected women who are left without a male relative to look out for them.*

"She has said that twice—and here is the same note

again—*wounding the feelings of three women.* Trying to drive that home."

Lieutenant Kenmore leaned back presently and re-read these underscored passages.

He took us into his home, when my father died, because he felt mother could not make her own way in the world, let alone do so and take care of two small children . . . I am not going to pretend I ever came to look upon Uncle Henry as a second father . . . It may seem strange for mother to have thought of that at such a time. But she is like that. It is her family pride . . . Mother isn't a liar. She is simply incapable of facing realities. All those tales she tells are fantastic legends.

Lieutenant Kenmore stretched a hand to the desk drawer.

The hand froze.

He stared for a long while at the sheet of pink paper protruding from under the stack of *Valley Press* stationery.

A very long while he looked at that, before he lifted a piece of the stationery and scribbled off a message.

He dialed operator.

"Franklin 1101, please." And then, to the night man at B.I.S.:

"I want you to send a telegram to the County Prosecutor, Mankato, Minnesota.

"Request information re Frank Axiter, husband Jessie same, brother-in-law Henry Ross Bowling, all formerly your city.

"Reply collect.

"Sign that John Kenmore, Lieutenant, Homicide Detail, San Diego, California."

XVIII

I don't understand business. I leave all that to the brokers and lawyers.—THE AUTOBIOGRAPHY OF CATHERINE HOPE.

Messrs. Kane & Ffleming occupied elegant offices in a downtown San Diego bank building; at nine o'clock Saturday morning, neither of the partners had yet come in.

"You might talk to Mr. Telight," the girl thought, "if it is a business matter."

"It's about a joint insurance policy issued to Alvah LeRoy and Lalitha Dearborn."

Mr. Telight was, by contrast with his surroundings, an almost threadbare man. Mr. Telight was what executives speak of as a "detail man." He was one of those small, shrunken, and impersonally efficient underlings, who are invariably found to have the whole of the company's business at their fingertips and no least bit of it within their grasp.

"I never heard of it," said he. "Dearborn, Dearborn, that is not in our files. What is it, anyway?"

Kenmore explained.

"But that is not our line at all," said Mr. Telight. "A five thousand dollar policy. It would not be worth carrying on our books. We do not *sell* insurance. We buy it. We represent the client, not the underwriters. Do I make myself clear?

"Well, let us suppose you are operating a business, a

large business"— Mr. Telight's manner implied this to be an extremely unlikely supposition—"with warehouses, a fleet of trucks, and so on. You would have to insure your physical properties against fire and earthquake hazard; then you would have to insure your stocks of merchandise; you would be under the legal obligation of complying with the employee compensation laws; you would have to carry personal and property liability insurance on your trucks. It would need weeks of your time merely to see all the salesmen representing the dozens of companies who compete in those fields; and you would need an enormously expert training in order to weigh the merits of the hundreds of complex policies you might possibly buy.

"It'd be cheaper in the long run to turn the whole thing over to an insurance brokerage house. Which, of course, is precisely what Kane & Ffleming's clients do. We are specialists in our field, just as the investment counsellor knows infinitely more about stocks and bonds than the ordinary person can ever hope to.

"And it would not be worth one of our representatives' time to run down a mere five thousand dollar policy. Particularly, a policy that was about to be discontinued. There could not be any profit in *that* at all.

"I am afraid," said Mr. Telight, "you are mistaken in the matter."

He had barely finished saying so, however, when Ffleming came into the office. Espying Kenmore, the junior partner promptly came that way.

"Oh, hello, lieutenant," said he. "Don't tell me Telight has fallen under suspicion of the law?"

Foster Ffleming looked unusually pleased with the world this morning. Saturday being a half-day, he was garbed in a costume suited to an afternoon round on the golf course. An Airedale trotted at heel.

"Have you seen the paper?" he asked. "I don't mean the front page"—the murder of Dr. Wallace occupied most of the front page—"but there has been another reduction in maritime risk rates. It means we are whittling down the U-boat menace . . . Of course, that was a shocking thing last night. But the War is still far more important.

"Still, speaking of that," said Ffleming, "did you hear the Home Fronter on KGOY last night? I wonder where he gets all his information?"

Lieutenant Kenmore thought it was because that political program had a pipeline into Captain Harry Whipple's office, but he did not say so.

"We were speaking of that," said he. "I came in to ask about Al Dearborn's insurance."

"And I told him—" began Telight.

"Oh," said Ffleming. "The firm isn't handling that. Jessie asked me to look into it, and I did so as a personal favor. Telight here will tell you it costs us about twenty dollars in overhead merely to put a client on the books."

"Twenty-three dollars and eighty-five cents to be exact, Mr. Ffleming."

"Reminds me, Telight. I'll want Beed Brothers' account this morning . . . Come along, lieutenant." Ffleming led the way into a private office. "I was handling the thing on the cuff, so to speak. And now what about it?"

Lieutenant Kenmore glanced interestedly about the junior partner's office. Its window framed a view of the harbor. The executive's desk and chair were big, without being too big. A globe stood on a bookcase filled with solemn, encyclopedic business volumes. A parchment on the wall announced that Foster Videll Ffleming, as a member of Ethical Insurors of America, would conduct his professional affairs on the very highest moral plane.

The one picture was of the Statue of Liberty. It seemed to Kenmore the one thing in the room that wasn't entirely impersonal was the Airedale which, as they sat down, stretched himself at his master's feet.

"I wondered how Al got the insurance at all, if he has a heart ailment."

Ffleming blinked. "What makes you think he has?"

"He's a 4-F; he told me, because of a bum ticker."

The other threw back his head in brief laughter. "Al's an automatic 4-F. Because he was dishonorably discharged from the Air Corps back in '34 or '35. He posed as a commissioned officer, passed a flock of bad checks, and drew a court-martial."

Lieutenant Kenmore said that had not been known to the police . . .

"I don't know that he served time for it," replied Ffleming. "I know it is so, because I live in that apartment building, and I couldn't help overhearing some of the quarrels. Lally found out, I imagine from Dave Wayne, and it was one of the things that disillusioned her about Al.

"She should never have married him in the first place," Ffleming thought. "She was three years younger then, she was just a kid, and she was taken in by the glamor of the aviator. Al used to work for a jitney plane outfit, flying wedding parties to Yuma. Lally went along on one of those jaunts as a bridesmaid, and came back a bride."

"I didn't know he was ever a licensed pilot, either."

"Well, maybe he wasn't. Maybe he was just a grease monkey, and they let him take up a ship once in awhile. I don't know the details, but I do know it was a damned shame. It's Al who got her to drinking like a fish. He is just a stinking bad egg all around.

"But," said Ffleming, "I thought he was in the clear. He couldn't have killed Bowling, according to what is in the paper and on the radio. Or Wallace. He was in jail when that happened last night."

Lieutenant Kenmore observed that Al Dearborn had not been put under arrest for either of the homicides. "Did he try to kill Lally? Is it safe to assume all three crimes were perpetrated by one and the same person?"

Foster Ffleming stared. "You don't think they were?"

"It isn't what I think. It's what I can prove. I've got to investigate Al, if only to clear him. If Dearborn tried to kill her independently of everything else, that is one thing. If the attempt on her life was made for the same reason Dr. Wallace was shot, then that is something different."

"It certainly never entered my head—"

Ffleming paused.

"Well, why *was* Wallace killed?" said he. "It was because his mask was borrowed for the Bowling murder, and he had found out who borrowed it. Wasn't it?"

"It was not necessarily that," Kenmore thought. "It was not that at all, if Lally shared the knowledge. In that case, the common knowledge probably related to Dr. Wallace's discovery something belonging to Mrs. Rhine —or *Mrs. Rhine's sister*—had been taken from his desk."

"What?" said Ffleming. "I don't get that at all."

"You didn't hear Wallace tell Mrs. Rhine he had something of hers?"

Ffleming's confused expression relaxed.

"Oh," said he. "Yes. But I didn't understand it that way. *Of* hers? I wasn't paying much attention to what was said, but I thought he told her he had something *for* her. I understood, something or other he wanted typed. Some civilian defense notice. I wasn't really listening, I was trying to get a word in edgewise about the gas mask."

"Go on," said Kenmore.

"There's nothing much to tell. Corinne had what's-his-name, Crush, clear out the guesthouse yesterday; she told him to return that bundle to the control room; he was growling about everything else he had to do. I said I would take care of it."

"Yesterday afternoon?"

"It was in the morning," Ffleming said. "I stopped in . . . I thought I could help them about Bowling's insurance, you know. And, well, I walked in on a council of war. Wyeland was there. They were discussing ways and means of blocking the autopsy. Wyeland said it couldn't be done by legal action, but maybe by political pull it could."

"Yes, but getting back to the bundle—you didn't return it until last night."

"I didn't think there was any hurry. I got tied up in that council of war thing, and I was late as it was. I had the dog here in the car because the vet is giving him some shots. So I didn't stop.

"Well, then. In the afternoon there was that attack on Lally, and I simply didn't get around to the control room until evening.

"The whole thing about that was," said Ffleming, "Corinne knew the armband and gas mask were missing, she was worried about that, and I told her Elliot and Wallace had been there last night. I thought Wallace had probably taken them, and I said I would ask him when I returned the bundle. I did, and I must say he acted very upset about it." Ffleming stuck out a toe, prodded it gently against the Airedale's ribs. "Of course, you've guessed by now . . . That was why I tried to telephone Corinne. To tell her Wallace didn't have the mask . . . that he had rushed off about it, and then turned up shot to death."

"It wasn't," said Lieutenant Kenmore, "to find out

whether she was at home to answer the telephone a couple of minutes after the shooting?"

"You mean," said Ffleming coolly, "do I think she's a murderess? No, I don't. Look here," suddenly. "You've probably dug up some unpleasant facts about Henry Bowling by now. Let me tell you how he impressed *me*. I think he came to La Jolla with the notion of playing the big frog in our little puddle. But he picked the wrong puddle. La Jolla has too many retired moguls, and too many visiting celebrities. It's just like Corinne's tennis. She was probably a star back home, but out here she ran up against these Southern California girls who have the national rankings."

"Said," Kenmore smiled, "like a native son."

"No, I'm from Michigan. But we *do* have the tennis talent here, just as they have the All-American football teams in Minnesota . . . Anyway, that's just an example. My point is, Bowling wanted to create a bigger stir in La Jolla than he ever succeeded in doing."

Lieutenant Kenmore's nod was almost an involuntary one. *I want to introduce you to a murderer,* Henry Bowling had said, instead of simply notifying the sub-station and handing over his evidence to the first cop that appeared. Kenmore thought he *had* wanted to create a stir in La Jolla, he *had* wanted to hold the center of the stage. So he'd phoned Kenmore, he'd tried to phone Wallace . . .

Ffleming shrugged: "I think he resented it, tried to take it out on us in various little ways. With his practical jokes and his nicknames and all that.

"Well. I don't know if you're aware Al Dearborn was mixed up in a patent medicine racket, some scheme based on extracting vitamins from sea weed. He peddled a lot of stock in that, and some people think it was Bowling's stock. In plain words, that Bowling bought into the thing and got a hundred thousand or so shares at a discount, and then Al Dearborn retailed the stuff for him. I know Al came to me with a big sales-spiel about Bowling having invested in the thing, he showed me a list of others who had bought, and some of them had bought far more than they could afford. Poor Amy Rhine, for instance, must have had every nickel of her savings in it. Another of Al's claims was that the product was based on a scientific study made at the Marine Research Institute. So when the pills got on the market, the government seized a shipment of them, Lauren Wallace got called as a witness. He testified, of course, those statements were entirely false and misleading. It was settled out of court, finally. The promoters agreed to keep the stuff off the market, and the government agreed not to send them to the penitentiary.

"Just between you and me and the dog," said Foster Ffleming, "I think you will find when you get it all dug up that these murders occurred because *somebody* had lost a lot of money. Which wouldn't have happened if Henry Bowling had not unloaded those shares as he may have. Or if Dr. Wallace had not testified as he did."

The junior partner looked up.

"Oh. Come in, Telight."

Mr. Telight brought in the Beed Brothers statement.

"It doesn't explain," said Kenmore thoughtfully, "what happened to Lally, does it?"

"I wonder," remarked Ffleming. "Maybe it was intended to punish Bowling by murder, and Al Dearborn by a murder frame-up . . . I don't know, I'm not a detective, thank God, I'm only in the insurance business."

Mr. Telight lingered, curiously smiling.

"That will be all, then," said the junior partner.

"Yes, sir. Buddy won last night, by the way."

"Good for Buddy," said Ffleming.

Mr. Telight's curious smile effaced itself into his formerly colorless and threadbare personality; he retired.

Foster Ffleming chuckled:

"Telight's the proud parent of a pugilist! He has a son who's heavyweight champ at the Naval Base. The old boy himself can name you off the winner in every title bout since Corbett whipped John L . . . Goes to show how hard it is to tell what's really inside people."

Lieutenant Kenmore thought otherwise.

"No," said he, "it goes to show the opposite. What is inside anyone gets found out sooner or later, not always as easily as that came out."

He went on to the Market Street station, and found the B.I.S. anteroom besieged with reporters. Besides the San Diego men, two reporters had flown down from Los Angeles to provide special coverage for their papers; there was an A.P. man, and another from the U.P. . . . Lieutenant Kenmore brushed aside questions, would not pose for a picture, and escaped into his own office— and found Harry Whipple there, seated in Kenmore's chair.

Captain Whipple's almost nobly-Roman features radiated triumphant good humor.

"What the hell do you think, John?" said the special division commander. "Mrs. Dearborn's brooch and rings have turned up."

"Where?"

"In Los Angeles," said Whipple. "Reported by the pawn shop detail there. Al Dearborn hocked those things, of course. But the red-eyed son-of-a-bitch did it *Friday morning.*"

There was a long pause . . . guarded on Kenmore's part.

"It is a tough break, in a way," said the captain, less triumphantly. "Did you tune in KGOY last night? The

Home Fronter said you couldn't make that pinch stick.
Of course he'll remind the public of that tonight, and it's
bound to make the police look bad." Captain Whipple's
expression did not contrive to appear entirely sym-
pathetic. More than a trace of satisfaction lingered upon
his handsome countenance. "For you can't make it stick,"
said he. "Dearborn must have stolen those trinkets before he got on the bus Thursday evening. If he admits
that, it will explain neatly how his fingerprints came
to be in his wife's room. And when he makes that explanation, then, you have got no physical evidence to
put him there in connection with the murder attempt
yesterday."

"No," said Kenmore. "Well, if he wants to admit that,
we will charge him with burglary instead."

Whipple smiled.

"Yes; but who will make even that charge stick? I
understand Nathan Stacey is going before Judge Hendryx
this morning and ask a writ of *habeas corpus*. Which
means he is willing to go into court, and wants to go
there. "Okay, *you* go in against him. But suppose Stacey
has Al testify he went there and Lally Dearborn gave or
loaned him her jewelry? Are you sure she won't say she
did just that? Or if she denies it? And Stacey brings out
she was intoxicated, and probably unable to remember
whether she did or did not? No, John. We've got to
have a better case than that to hold Al Dearborn."

Captain Whipple selected a cigar from his pocket case.

Meditatively he trimmed its end and moistened the
trimmed tip.

"It isn't fair to burden you with this when you've got
your hands more than full already," said he. "It isn't
fair to the police department. Because the Home Fronter
is going to say, what the hell kind of a police department
is it? Where the homicide detail drops two unsolved

murders to track down a mere burglary. When the burglar is the one guy who couldn't have committed either murder!

"The way I look at it," said Harry Whipple contentedly, "you're over a barrel both ways. KGOY will pan hell out of you if Dearborn goes scot-free now; but if you, or any homicide detective of yours, go dig up the evidence to convict him, you will get twice as much hell for doing that."

It did not escape Lieutenant Kenmore that Whipple was uncannily able to predict the future course of that radio program. He thought Whipple wasn't merely providing tips, he was running the show.

It sounded as if the detective division commander wanted to take the burglary investigation away from Kenmore entirely, and assign that to a special squad of his own; that would extend the pipeline from KGOY to La Jolla directly.

"Well," said the lieutenant, "suppose you assign me Marks and Delevan from Jenning's detail."

Captain Whipple expelled a wreath of cigar smoke.

"Marks and Delevan aren't big enough for the job," said he; and Kenmore thought, Good Lord! For the point of his superior officer's Machiavellian tactic became clear, even before the captain had uttered another word.

"Al Dearborn has got Stacey to bat for him. Okay, we'll put in our first team, too," Harry Whipple resumed energetically. "I won't stand by and watch them crucify you, John. I'm going out there to La Jolla myself, and I'll personally get so much on Mr. Al Dearborn no mouthpiece alive can beat the rap for him—"

Lieutenant Kenmore didn't listen to the rest. He'd heard enough; he knew the captain wasn't interested in pressing the burglary charge. Whipple was not the man to send himself on a plain clothes man's errand . . . or on an unselfish errand. Captain Whipple's motive, as always, was political and personal. *He thought he could solve the La Jolla murders.*

"And show me up," Kenmore realized.

The alarming question was whether the captain hoped to do so by virtue of superior ability, or by some significant information known only to himself.

"What's he got up his sleeve, anyway?" crossed Lieutenant Kenmore's mind for the second time in twenty-four hours.

XIX

Show me a woman who cries, lies, and faints to get what she wants, and I will show you a man who is an old-fashioned household tyrant.—THE AUTOBIOGRAPHY OF CATHERINE HOPE.

San Diego had been sunfilled. But La Jolla was fog-bound. Lally Dearborn's window overlooked a shoreline that was barely visible through a veil of wet cotton mist, and only advertised its presence by a rumble of surf and the hollow coughing of a seal.

"I hate hospitals," the blonde sister said. "Couldn't I confess to something and go to jail instead? I would rather be in jail any day."

"You look very comfortable," said Lieutenant Kenmore. And Lally, though unwontedly pale, certainly seemed a great deal better than she had last night.

"A jail," contributed Captain Whipple brightly, "ain't any bed of roses, either. You can ask Al if he thinks so."

This jocular remark had its little point. Captain Whipple had hoped to draw an unguarded response from Lally for the benefit of Sergeant Lyon's notes.

When she did not reply at all, Whipple pounced on her non-committal silence instead . . . "You aren't surprised to hear we locked him up?"

"No. Mother was here this morning; she said you had."

"Yeah. Well, were you surprised when *she* told you?"

"Nothing," said Lally, "that Al could do would surprise me."

"Not even stealing your jewelry, and trying to kill you?"

"Nothing," said the blonde sister wearily.

Whipple bent toward her. "Yeah! Okay! So he did steal the brooch and rings?"

"I suppose so, it wouldn't surprise me in the least."

The captain looked up at Kenmore triumphantly.

Lieutenant Kenmore's expression was not so pleased.

"No, Lally," said Kenmore. "It is not enough for you to answer with *you suppose so*. It is not a question of whether or not you think Al capable of these crimes. The question is, have you any knowledge of the fact? That he robbed you? Or tried to kill you?"

"No," said the blonde sister. "If you put it that way, I don't know for sure."

Captain Whipple's face knit with annoyance. Lieutenant Kenmore's, with thought . . . The facts, he reminded himself, were these: Lally had been attacked by an assailant unknown to her. If it was Al, he had to approach the house by broad daylight, either along Laguna Terrace or Toyon Street, in full view of whoever lived or chanced to be passing upon those streets; or from the alley, passing Crush at work in the rear yard. He had to enter a house in which were Lally, her mother, her sister, a house-maid, and presumably a cook as well. He had to discover his victim alone, he had to risk her outcry if she saw him, and when he had committed the silent and stealthy attack, he then had to escape from that house and neighborhood unseen.

Lieutenant Kenmore considered those were long odds, since Al (if it was he) could at least have waited for darkness.

"You know what she means," Harry Whipple was saying. "He must have stole the jewels, if she didn't give them to him."

But Kenmore was not so sure he knew what Lally meant . . . A forceful conjecture suddenly thrust into his mind.

"Lally!" said he. "It was directly after lunch you went to your room yesterday?"

"Yes. About one o'clock."

"And you had no conversation with anyone until you regained consciousness under the X-ray apparatus? Do you recall who was present then?"

"Dr. Myatt . . . some nurses . . . my mother."

"Yes. What was said to you?"

"Mother kept asking me if it wasn't Al who did it. Dr. Myatt wouldn't let her talk to me very much . . . After you left, he gave me a hypo to make me sleep."

"Then the first conversation you had with your mother was this morning. Did she tell you the result of the autopsy? That your uncle had been killed by means of cyanogen poison?"

"In his gas mask," Whipple added.

Lally Dearborn stared at them, her eyes slowly widening and rounding.

"No," said she blankly.

But then her eyes began to narrow. She moistened her lips.

"Why!" said Lally, "that is why—! Al tried to kill me before I could tell about his quarrel with Uncle Henry."

"What quarrel?" said Kenmore.

"It was the day before. Wednesday. They came out of the guesthouse, shouting at each other. Uncle Henry said he would give Al until the banks closed Friday."

"At what time Wednesday?"

"It was just before dinner. About six."

Several thoughts struggled for mastery in Lieutenant Kenmore's mind, among them the fact that Al Dearborn's fingerprints in the guesthouse were explained by this story.

"Well," said he, "did Al see you then?"

"I don't know. I dodged around the corner of the building."

Lally blushed.

"I had been uptown and bought a bottle of whiskey. I couldn't keep it in my room, or mother would find it and pour it down the drain. I had a new hiding place. It was behind one of the sandbags at the guesthouse.

"I had just come in the Toyon Street gate," she said, "and I didn't want Uncle Henry to see the bottle, so I stepped around the corner."

Captain Harry Whipple's composure broke.

"God Almighty!" cried he. "Excuse me, Mrs. Dearborn, but you never kept whiskey in your room?"

Lally shook her head.

Whipple stared at Kenmore. "But then, hell, whoever slugged her, had to bring that bottle in from outside!"

Kenmore's frown admitted it was a perplexing factor.

"Getting back to this quarrel, Lally. What else was said?"

The blonde sister remembered, "Uncle Henry said Al was worse than a woman."

"Worse . . . what did he mean by that?"

"It was just an expression. If anyone did anything wrong, it was *just like a woman*. If it was frightfully wrong, it was *worse than a woman*." Lally's expression was half a smile, half a frown. "I think Uncle Henry must have been jilted when he was young. He was such a woman hater. So when he said Al was worse than a woman, it only meant he was disgusted and angry with him. I suppose Al had borrowed money and promised to pay it back and didn't."

"You suppose. But do you know so for a fact?"

"No, but that's my guess."

Kenmore inquired, had Henry Bowling been in the habit of advancing Al money?

"No," the blonde sister admitted.

"Then what makes you think he did?"

"It's just that Al has been trying to get money in a hurry. He even wanted to cash in our insurance policy, but I wouldn't let him."

Lieutenant Kenmore stared. "Al wanted to give up the five thousand dollar husband-and-wife policy, and *you* wouldn't let him?"

"No, I would not. I think it was Monday he wanted me to sign a paper with him, and I refused. It was at the Shore Club bar. We sat in a booth and argued for half an hour."

Lally's eyes were pleased. She seemed proud that she had been firm in the matter.

Harry Whipple blurted: *"Huh? Why?"*

"Because," said Lally, "he hated me, and I thought he wouldn't dare kill me while we had that insurance. Everyone would know he did it for the money."

Captain Whipple, who had opened his mouth to say something, found himself made speechless by the girl's naive logic.

"Yes," said Lally, "he's a brute and a bully and he's insanely jealous. But I thought he wasn't insane or jealous enough not to back down from real danger. I thought that insurance policy would make him think twice. I told him I'd pay the premiums myself if he didn't."

Lieutenant Kenmore said that at any rate, Al had needed money. "Did he bring the matter up again?"

Lally laughed. "I think he wanted to. He called Thursday evening and wanted me to come to his apartment and get my purse."

"Your—what was he doing with your purse?"

"He picked it up, I suppose. I must have left it in the booth at the Shore Club on Monday. Because, when I got uptown and wanted to cash a check, I'd lost it. But I didn't know then whether it was at the Shore Club or the postoffice or where."

"In that purse," said Kenmore, "there were some Christmas cards of Amy Rhine's. Where did they come from?"

"Oh," said Lally indifferently, "when I left the house Monday Uncle Henry gave me some things. There were some reports to go to the control room, and letters he wanted mailed, and those cards belonging to Mrs. Rhine. He found them when they tore out the fireplace in the guesthouse. They had slipped down between the mantel and the wall. I thought it was silly to even bother Mrs. Rhine with them. Anyway, I lost the purse and Al must have picked it up. I wasn't fool enough to go to his apartment, but I didn't want him to think I was afraid to, either. So I said I had a date with somebody else. He asked where, and I said at the Shore Club. And he said he would bring it to me there. So I went upstairs and put on that white dress so he would believe I really did have a date."

"Did he meet you there?"

"No. I waited and waited, and I had one drink too many. I was getting into the *dark part of the tunnel,*" Lally said, "and I went out and sat on the rocks. The beach is patrolled, you know, and a sentry came along. He was pretty stern. I think he believed I had gone out there to jump from the rocks."

"Yes," said Kenmore. "But if Al did not meet you, how did that purse get back into your room at home?"

"I don't know. Is it there?"

Captain Whipple shrugged.

"That part's all easy," said he. "Of course, Al didn't show up. It was a trick to get Mrs. Dearborn out of the house Thursday night so he could steal her rings and brooch. Then yesterday he came back to kill her. He brought the purse with him. So if he got caught in the house, he could say he was there just to return the handbag to Lally."

Kenmore did not think that was the explanation. He said: "Well, Lally, how did you get to the Shore Club Thursday night?"

"Uncle Henry drove me. I asked him for the keys to the car, and he said he would take me. He thought he was doing me such a favor, because I had had a headache, and I swear I thought we would never make it alive! I just sat tight and prayed the rest of the traffic on the street would see it was Henry Bowling's green Cadillac coming, and give us a wide berth." Lally giggled. "It was funny about Uncle Henry. He was so bitter about women drivers, and yet he drove *worse than a woman*. He just wouldn't look. He'd sail through stop signs and cross over the white line and back out of parking places and never see another car coming. Mother and Corinne were always watching out, and they'd scream at him to look out for this, that, and the other. And then he'd get furious. He'd say they were just like a couple of women back seat drivers. He thought they were both too nervous to be trusted with a car, and so neither of them even learned to drive. I didn't, myself," said Lally, "until I learned with Al's car. And then Uncle Henry got a little used to the idea. He would let me take the Cadillac, though he wouldn't ride with me at the wheel, either."

Captain Whipple laughed.

"Excuse me, Mrs. Dearborn," said he, "but wasn't your uncle afraid you'd get stewed and smash up the car?"

"He didn't know how much I drank . . . Mother and

Corinne always pretended I had a sick headache," Lally said. "Of course, if he knew, he would not let me take the car. But then if they wanted to go anywhere *he* wasn't going, they would have had to walk or take the bus, or wait until Crush finished his work and could take them. So it was convenient for them—he didn't know."

"Yes," said Kenmore. "Your uncle took you to the Shore Club, *but who brought you home?*"

Her blue eyes opened at him blankly.

"I don't know. I passed out on my feet, I guess. I don't remember coming home at all."

That, thought the lieutenant, was a lie.

XX

I am really a very simple soul.—THE AUTOBIOGRAPHY
OF CATHERINE HOPE.

"Well," said Captain Whipple on the hospital steps,
"so long. I'm going to have it out with Mr. Al Dearborn.
Before Stacey can spring him."

He strode off into a fog that was dissolving under the
impact of splinters of sunlight.

"Clearing up," Sergeant Lyon observed.

"Yes. It is almost clear now," John Kenmore thought.

Lyon seemed to find a double meaning in this remark,
or in the lieutenant's tone.

"You don't mean it?" said he. "What now?"

"I want you to find the carpenter who helped remodel
the guesthouse and bring him there."

Lieutenant Kenmore presently parked the B.I.S. sedan
in front of the Beachview Apartments. A-3 proved to be
on the first floor. He did not approach the door, but
walked around to the side window . . . Directly under
the window flowered a bed of Cosmos. Kenmore parted
the leaves and peered down at an inch-deep, semi-lunar
depression in the soil.

He straightened, looked about, finally circled to the
rear of the building. A row of garbage pails had been set
out for the city collection truck. He returned with one
of these. Inverted, and leaned against the side of the

building, its rim fitted into the half-moon depression exactly.

Lieutenant Kenmore started toward the block-distant Shore Club; the tide was now out; the fog had lifted. A brilliant sun streamed upon the sand scarf of beach where the sub-station police were combing the terrain with garden rakes.

"No luck?" said Kenmore.

Acting-Lieutenant Arnold said no luck. He added that Gilbert and Sullivan had hit it smack on the nose. "A cop's life is a hell of a ways from a happy one. Playing thimble, thimble, where's the thimble. Yesterday, that brooch and rings. Today, that gun . . . I suppose it will finally turn out the Magnum was pawned in Los Angeles hours before Wallace got shot with it."

Lieutenant Kenmore did not really think the gun would be recovered on the beach.

"We have got to eliminate all the wrong possibilities, though," said he, "in order to pin it on the right one."

"You think you're ever going to pin anything on anybody?"

Kenmore thought so. "When Lauren Wallace's murderer is arrested, you are going to be surprised how many people knew it all along.

"Excuse me," he added, turning.

His name had been shouted, from the rocks.

Darwina Roydan's headgear today was a bathing cap. In one hand she carried a diver's face-plate. In the other, a gunnysack.

She balanced on one foot in order to remove a large, black rubber fin from the other. And then, on the other foot to remove the second fin. And carrying these, waded through the tide pools toward Kenmore.

He met her halfway; that is, as far as he could advance dryshod.

"Well!" said Darwina. "I've got it."

Lieutenant Kenmore's grey glance dropped to the gunnysack. It must be admitted, incredulously.

"No," said Darwina. "Not the gun. I've been diving for abalone. But that isn't the real reason . . . It is because I *think* best in the water. There is something about the motion of the waves."

"Yes: What is it you've got, then?"

"A theory," said Darwina, "about those murders. But you will laugh at me when I tell you."

She looked up at Kenmore. Beads of sea water glistened on her face, detracting somewhat from her extremely solemn expression.

Lieutenant Kenmore did not laugh. "What is your theory?" said he.

"It is a long story . . . I'll give you an abalone for lunch. I can tell you while I am fixing that."

The lieutenant glanced at his strap watch. "I can't stay for lunch. Let me carry the sack for you, though . . . Well?"

"I think," said Darwina, "the murders were committed by different persons, and there is no connection between them."

The Institute headland lay beyond the Shore Club. As they walked along the shore, flights of gulls were frightened up from the sand; a formation of cormorants skimmed the crests of the incoming waves; in the troughs of the sea, a seal barked hollowly.

Landward, the beach lapped against a retaining wall of concrete; above were the stark forms of aloe and century plant; the whole topped by the graceful fronds of date palms.

"I've been thinking about the psychology of it," said Darwina. "As a matter of fact, I sat up late last night reading . . ." Darwina's theory recalled the criminal mind's preoccupation with a special *modus operandi*.

The psychological truth was, she argued, murderers rarely ever changed their method. And it was certainly not in a poisoner's psychology to vary from a narrow pharmacopoeia of death. She mentioned Dr. Pritchard's antimony and aconite; and Dr. Cross's arsenic and strychnine.

"Henry Bowling," said she, "was poisoned with cyanogen. But Lally got struck with a bottle. Poor Dr. Wallace was murdered with a gun. And as for Catherine Hope, *she* was strangled."

Lieutenant Kenmore nodded, rather absently. "That is all true . . . It is probably the most striking feature about all these crimes. The murderer is trying to repeat the general pattern rather than the exact *modus operandi*."

"What?" said Darwina. "From all I can see, there isn't the slightest similarity!"

"On the contrary, I am impressed by it . . . How did the killer come to think of using cyanogen in a gas mask, do you suppose?"

"To pass it off as accidental death," Darwina Roydan thought, "of course."

"Do you really believe that? Considering the reluctance with which insurance companies eye a claim running into several hundreds of thousands of dollars when death is by misadventure?

"No," said Kenmore, "the criminal may have *hoped* to evade an autopsy, but not *relied* on doing so . . . No. It was an attempt to repeat a pattern that had been stumbled on in the Catherine Hope Case."

He kicked a kelp "baby" toward the water.

"Look here," said the lieutenant abruptly. "I have a

theory about Catherine Hope! . . . Her flashlight was found in a waterlogged condition, but found high and dry on the rocks out here. The tide had not reached those rocks at all, or of course the lard pail would have floated away. I think the chances are she had dropped the flashlight during the grunion hunt, it was rendered useless by the accident, and so she came home early—and I think, caught an intruder in the house.

"It was not a planned murder at all, as it seems to me. Whoever was there, had no business being there; was into her private correspondence or notes. I daresay this intruder got into a panic at being caught, grabbed her by the throat, and then had to go through with the thing . . . The reason for removing her body from the house was an instinctive impulse to direct police attention away from her home, her private life, her ordinary movements. It is my guess the murderer first thought of dumping the body off the rocks into the sea; but because the moon was rising, and because of the numbers of grunion hunters on the beach, did not dare go through with it. The fish tank occurred as an alternate possibility; the corpse was left there, stripped to create the semblance of a sex crime, and the flashlight, lard pail, and bathing suit dropped on the rocks to make it appear that was where the crime got committed."

"It is odd," said Darwina, "you didn't think of that at the time."

"I did not conduct the investigation," replied the lieutenant. "But let me finish this . . . In one sense, I say, it was hardly a planned murder at all; but in another it was far and away more brilliantly conceived than anything that has happened since. The murderer imagined the *police* had been outwitted because there were not any fingerprints or discoverable motive and because suspicion had been foisted onto an unidentified sex fiend.

"But in reality something far more difficult than outwitting the police had been accomplished. It was this, that the whole town of La Jolla had been outwitted. It was not possible for me, or any other detective, to find out the truth unless someone told it . . . I suppose that murder could have been solved by the disclosure of a single, simple, apparently irrelevant fact."

Darwina stared. "What was that?"

"Of course, no one told it . . . The crime was thought to be a sex-fiend slaying. And it was not possible for *anyone* to recall a simple circumstance correctly when *everyone* is seized by a hysterical mass-suggestion. The factual truth about Catherine Hope was never told because it was never remembered. The people who knew the truth dropped it to run after something else that didn't exist. They were all looking after Peeping Toms, they were all playing detective. And their very wish to help solve the murder led them to interpret and modify their testimony to fit the popular theory."

Lieutenant Kenmore paused to get out his pipe. He built a shelter around its bowl with the one hand, and with the other struck a match. The act of shaking out the match afterward caused him a grimace; that arm had twinges in it this morning.

"Well," said he, "the killer had blundered, had instinctively walked into that set of circumstances . . . So when it came to murdering Henry Bowling, there was a natural—this time, a conscious—effort to recreate that set of circumstances.

"Catherine Hope had been slain against the confusing background of a *grunion hunt* . . . A tremendous strategic advantage to the killer resulted from having played that murder against a background of crowded activity, involving all those scores and hundreds of people. Very well, Henry Bowling was to be killed during a Commando raid *defense drill,* an activity which likewise involved scores of persons.

"Although," said Kenmore soberly, "I am inclined to think that was not the first plan that came to mind. I fancy Lauren Wallace got executed as the result of a murder scheme that had been originally devised for Henry Bowling's benefit. Bowling belonged to that bridge club, he would normally have gone there Friday night, and I think the murderer toyed with the notion of killing him against the *confusing background* of a bridge club meeting involving a dozen or so suspects."

Darwina Roydan looked thunderstruck.

"You mean," said she, "I was supposed to draw up a list of all those suspects!"

"Someone would, certainly . . . My point is, the thought of using the Paratroop invasion drill came first, and then the notion of employing the cyanogen in a gas mask followed as a logical sequence of that. The *backgrounds* are a point of resemblance in all three murders. There is another similarity," Kenmore observed, "arising out of the fact that in the Catherine Hope Case, the police search got distracted because of a lot of meaningless accessories. As for example, the 'diary' that proved only to be Selected Readings from the autobiography."

Darwina gasped.

"Then the envelope—?" she conjectured. "And the pink sheet—?"

"I was thinking," said Kenmore, "of the gas heater in the guesthouse, of the whiskey bottle that did not belong in Lally's room, and of the cyanogen-filled mask in Lauren Wallace's car. The envelope, or rather its contents, are a third and different similarity. It is clear from the result of the Ermel test, Catherine Hope 'had something' on someone. I think it is equally clear Henry Bowling and Lauren Wallace 'had something' on the

same individual that has by this time been destroyed . . .
as the intruder must have destroyed whatever evidence
Miss Hope had among her correspondence or family
papers."

Darwina moistened her lips.

"If we only *knew!*" said she despairingly.

"You don't solve murders by crying over spilled milk.
What's gone, is gone," the lieutenant answered philo-
sophically. "We have got to fight with what weapons and
clues are left. It is really incredibly lucky Bowling closed
that envelope away in the telephone book . . . So lucky,
I suspect he did a bit of quick thinking at the very end.
When the door opened and the murderer walked in.

"And what else is left," said he, "is a fourth resemblance. Which is that in the Catherine Hope Case, the
investigation got misdirected toward an unknown sex
offender. And that there has been a pretty clear effort
to misdirect this investigation in one way and another
. . . What is it?"

"I was thinking," blushed Darwina, "I did that. When
I accused Foster Ffleming."

"I don't mean that. I only wish Dr. Wallace had confided his suspicions to me, instead of trying to make sure
of them first . . . No, that is not my point. Ffleming has
nothing to kick about; if you accused him, *he* had vir-
tually accused Amy Rhine."

Darwina stared.

"How on earth does he—?"

Kenmore told her.

Darwina shook her head. "I don't think he has it right
at all," said she. "I'm sure Dr. Wallace never imagined
Bowling was behind that. My impression is that Henry
Bowling looked the model of a hardheaded, conservative,
sensible businessman, but he had another streak in him.
I suppose he took a gamble on the scheme, and lost like

everyone else. If Al Dearborn told Ffleming that Bowling was backing it, he was merely using a salestalk to make the thing seem like a sound investment.

"And then," said Darwina, "how was Wallace shot? The murderer must have been concealed in the rocks, thirty or forty yards away. If not in a boat or on a paddleboard in the water! It is simply ridiculous to suppose Mrs. Rhine is capable of *that* kind of shooting."

Lieutenant Kenmore said he did not think that was the murder method. "But it's beside the point. It is the deliberate falsehoods I've been told, about the movements of these people. You told me yesterday, you had seen Fred Crush, and that he had a cold in his head. But that followed your discovery of Dorothy Wyeland's shoe, did it not? The question is, was Crush sweeping the tennis court at that time?"

"He was not *sweeping* it, but he was in the back yard. He had been in the guesthouse, I think," said Darwina, "and came out when he heard the gate creak open."

"Why do you think so?"

"Because," said Darwina, "I'm sure I heard a door close . . ."

John Kenmore's expression made his face more angular than usual.

"Yes," said he. "I'm sorry about the abalone lunch, but it will have to wait until another time."

Sergeant Lyon and the carpenter awaited his arrival at 222 Laguna Terrace rear.

"Bring Crush in here," Kenmore told Lyon, and escorted the other man into the guesthouse. The carpenter was a veteran named Clarence Smiley . . . He stated, in response to Lieutenant Kenmore's queries, that he had lived in La Jolla for the past nineteen years. In the summer of 1940, he had fallen from a scaffold and incurred a hip injury; since that time, he had only labored at odd jobs. The period of his employment by Henry Bowling had been eight working days, terminating on the previous Tuesday.

"What day," Kenmore asked, "was it you tore out the old mantel in here?"

Smiley had not helped tear out the mantel. Crush had done that. "I just worked on the new construction, was all."

Lieutenant Kenmore asked another dozen questions, which were only intended to camouflage the important one already posed. He was about to dismiss Smiley when Sergeant Lyon abruptly entered.

"You're too late!" said the sergeant, loudly and bitterly. "Whipple beat us to the punch—the pinch!"

"He's put Crush under arrest?"

"Yeah! Only Crush ain't Crush! He's Frank Axiter!"

XXI

The old family album was fascinating.—THE AUTO-
BIOGRAPHY OF CATHERINE HOPE.

Lieutenant Kenmore entered the sub-station as a flash-
bulb flared and limned Captain Harry Whipple's almost
nobly Roman profile for the benefit of tomorrow's Sunday newspaper readers.

"I never forget a face," the captain was telling the gentleman of the press. "The minute I laid eyes on him, I
remembered the whole case. It was back in '32," Whipple
continued, "and of course I haven't had a chance to re-
fresh my memory on all the minor details. But the general outline runs about like this—"

The general outline ran, that had been an election
year. It had been a year when voters in Minnesota, as
elsewhere, were principally interested in the presidential
contest, and hardly interested at all in another proposi-
tion on the ballot . . . a local highway paving bond issue.
But Henry Bowling had been interested in that, had been
advocating the project in the columns of his newspaper
supplement; indeed, was being paid for doing so. But
naturally, not in the form of a direct payment by means
of a traceable bank check.

"Here," said Captan Whipple, "is where this Frank
Axiter, Bowling's brother-in-law, cames into the picture.
He worked for Bowling, and he was delegated to handle
a little black bag transaction involving $15,000 in slush
funds. He handled it all right. He skipped with the
money, and with Bowling's private secretary. *Her* name
was Crush. He had a crush on Miss Crush, you might say."

Captain Whipple continued . . . Frank Axiter and Miss Crush and the little black bag had presently reached San Diego; the pair had registered at a San Diego hotel under her name, since the name was gold-stamped on her traveling cases. There had been no particular secrecy about it; they had assumed Bowling would not go to the police because the $15,000 had not been honestly come by; he could not prosecute them without exposing himself as a grafter.

"Only," said Whipple, "Jessie Axiter got found in a pool of blood with her throat cut. She afterward said it was an attempt at suicide. But at the time she was too near dead to say anything. The Mankato cops suspected murder, and they started a hunt for the missing husband."

(Which, thought Kenmore, explained the scar on Mrs. Axiter's throat.)

Harry Whipple was not certain whether Miss Crush had got frightened by thinking Axiter really had murdered his wife. Or whether she intended to doublecross him all along. At any rate, she crossed the Border to Tijuana and the $15,000 went with her. Frank Axiter got picked up alone and flat broke. "We locked him up awaiting extradition. That was my contact with the case," said Whipple, "and it ended when the Mankato police dropped the charges. Either because they thought it *was* suicide, or because they couldn't prosecute if she wanted to say it had been."

But, the captain continued, Bowling had had private detectives on the case as well; he had accumulated sufficient evidence to threaten Frank Axiter with a Mann Act prosecution, and Axiter had knuckled down under that threat. "He signed promissory notes for the $15,000, and signed some kind of a confession, too. I don't suppose Bowling ever expected to collect on the notes, yet he could always threaten to collect on any property Axiter ever accumulated. And at the same time he was protect-

ing himself against blackmail of a political nature,"
Whipple thought. "Axiter could not open his mouth
above that slush fund deal, because if he did so his own
confession would put him behind bars. Bowling simply
fixed it so the man didn't dare show his face in Mankato
again."

Lieutenant Kenmore, as he listened, recalled Corinne's
choice of words: Henry Bowling, as she said, *took us into
his home, because he felt mother could not . . . take
care of two small children.* But Corrine had not been such
a small child in 1932; it was ridiculous to suppose she had
not recognized her father in 'Fred Crush,' even though
she had not seen his face in the intervening years.

Kenmore decided Corinne knew very well who 'Crush'
was . . . The question in Corinne's mind must have
been, could she conceal this family skeleton? He began to
understand why she had wished to make her statement to
the police in front of Amy Rhine. Corinne had to know
where she stood. She dared not rely on a lie which could
be exposed.

Amy Rhine was an enemy. She had lived next door and
within earshot of the family. She had made it her business to investigate Henry Bowling's past, and doubtless
she had gossiped a little, so some part of the sailor's story
might have reached Corinne at third or fourth hand. So
Corinne had begun her statement cautiously, testing
whether Mrs. Rhine would deny Frank Axiter's death;
finally she had deliberately attacked and goaded the older
woman; if Amy had known or suspected the truth, she
would surely have flung it into Corinne's face then.

But Kenmore wondered whether the girl had reckoned
on exposure from another direction. There was William
Wyeland. The bearded lawyer had been intrigued by the
will. Had he guessed Bowling's money was devised so
Jessie Axiter's husband could not eventually come into
a cent of it?

Captain Whipple's voice ran on: "Then in 1939, we find Bowling moving to the West Coast . . . By and by, this man Axiter pops up again. He was another kettle of fish now, because after all those years Bowling couldn't reopen Mann Act or theft charges. In a way, Frank Axiter had the upper hand. *He* had nothing to lose by admitting his right name wasn't 'Crush' and it would have been damned embarrassing to the family to admit Jessie's husband, and the girls' father, was an ex-crook turned common gardener."

In fact, Jessie Axiter's propensity for inventing family legends had got her into a position where she could not admit it.

Whipple urged this point. "It was a blackmail set-up," he declared, "except for one thing. Crush had tangled with Henry Bowling before, and got all the worst of it. It looks to me as if he hired Crush and kept him on the place so he could have an eye on him; and Crush feared and hated him. But if anything happened to Bowling, then Crush had only his wife and the girls to deal with, and he wasn't afraid of *them*."

Lieutenant Kenmore knew very well this fell far short of being a satisfactory solution to the affair. And yet it could be twisted into very nearly that. You had only to say the envelope had been left as a red herring to divert suspicion from 'Fred Crush'; you had only to argue that, though 'Crush' had not murdered Catherine Hope, he had studied that case intently enough to model his murders upon it. You could say then, Lally's life had been attempted because she was the one member of the family least likely to be silenced by the fear of scandal; and Lauren Wallace's life had been taken because he had caught 'Crush' in the act of returning the exchanged gas mask.

Other thoughts than his were running in this channel.

"Yes," said the Los Angeles *Times* representative. "But

are you going to charge him with killing Dr. Wallace?'

Harry Whipple held up a flat palm.

"My investigation is not yet complete, of course," said he. "The details have to be worked out. Lieutenant Kenmore has had charge of all that since Thursday. I myself have only taken a hand in the last hour."

The captain's pause seemed designed to let the comparison sink into his hearers' minds.

"Still," he resumed, "I think I may say I have uncovered some highly suggestive facts.

"Frank Axiter, *alias* Fred Crush, was found to have in his garage a fully packed suitcase.

"He had in his pocket when arrested the sum of $500 in $20 and $10 bills.

"It appears he was prepared for instant flight when apprehended."

"Hasn't he got any alibis?" asked the *Times* man.

Harry Whipple shrugged.

"On Thursday evening he claims to have been in his room over the Bowling garage. That stands, of course, on his unsupported word.

"Friday afternoon, he was discovered on the tennis court a few minutes after the attempt on his younger daughter's life.

"Friday night, he states he drove Mrs. Axiter and the other daughter into the country. I have, however," said the captain, "an eyewitness who places him within two blocks of the Shore Club at almost the time Dr. Wallace was shot."

The reporters leaned toward the speaker, pencils lifted and poised over their notepads. They looked not unlike a pack of birddogs which had scented quail.

"Last night," said Captain Whipple in the impressive manner of a man who has got a clinching point in mind, "at approximately seven o'clock Mr. William Wyeland and his secretary, Mrs. Rhine, left the civilian defense control room where they were among the last to see Dr. Wallace alive. William Wyeland is a highly respected local attorney. Mrs. Rhine has been employed by him for a number of years, and is herself a witness of the highest veracity. I may add that I have known them both in another connection.

"Mr. Wyeland had proposed leaving Mrs. Rhine at his downtown office as she had some typing to do. She declined the offer, inasmuch as it would necessitate a long walk home along darkened streets. She said that she would do the work on her portable machine at home. Mr. Wyeland then offered to drive her there. She again declined, saying it was only a few blocks from his destination, the Shore Club.

"They therefore parted company at the Club. It was then some five or six minutes past seven o'clock. The time is established on Mr. Wyeland's part by the fact he entered the Club some minutes before the shooting occurred.

"Mrs. Rhine meanwhile proceeded along the waterfront. At the foot of Penguin Street she came upon Henry Bowling's green Cadillac. The machine appeared to be empty as she approached. Nine passersby out of ten would have thought it *was* empty

"Mrs. Rhine, fortunately, glanced inside as she passed the car. She saw Frank Axiter, known to her only as 'Fred Crush,' in the front seat. He was sprawled across the seat, pretending to be looking for some article in the glove compartment.

"She passed by without speaking to him, walking another block and a half to her residence. She immediately got out her portable and went to work, glancing at her wristwatch as she did so as she was to charge for her typing by the hour. The time was then a quarter past seven, or three minutes previous to the shooting of Dr. Wallace."

XXII

My sister and I are very fond of each other—at a safe distance.—THE AUTOBIOGRAPHY OF CATHERINE HOPE.

Motorcycle Officer J. S. Dugan removed his cap and showed a villainously bald and scar disfigured scalp. "H'yare," said Officer Dugan, from the corner of his mouth.

Officer Dugan looked as if he had been projected bodily from the pages of the kind of comic magazine that clergymen and educators deplore and condemn; there was something Neanderthalish about his brow, and something nether-worldish about his eye. J. S. Dugan, it was apparent on the surface of him, enjoyed an extensive familiarity with death-rays, stolen bombsights, and heroines trussed into electric chairs.

His scars, however, were honorable; his manner of speech owed to a broken jaw; J. S. Dugan had crawled into a flaming, overturned automobile and got two children out of the wreck, and he would have got out a third if the machine had not blown up in his face.

"H'yare," said Dugan, and Lieutenant Kenmore ripped open the telegram Officer Dugan extracted from the lining of his cap. The message was under a Mankato, Minnesota, dateline; it had been put on the wires at 9:43 a.m. Central Time; the hour of its receipt in San Diego was 9:12 a.m. Pacific Win-the-War-Time; the body of its contents he already knew; for it was signed *Lawrence Bowling, County Attorney.*

Lieutenant Kenmore thought: "The hellion never forgets a face, does he?"

For of course the message had been phoned to *John Kenmore, Lieutenant, B.I.S.* before the written copy of it left Western Union; only Kenmore had not been in at 9:12 a.m.; it was Captain Harry Whipple who had lifted the desk phone and graciously received the record on Fred Crush, *née* Frank Axiter.

In spite of all, Kenmore had to laugh.

After that, it was not very surprising to learn that Amy Rhine had also telephoned the B.I.S. very shortly after nine o'clock. Directly, in fact, she reached William Wyeland's office. Mrs. Rhine had not *even heard* Lauren Wallace was dead until then. But when she heard of it, she could not help recalling Fred Crush's very *strange behavior.*

"Especially," said Amy Rhine, "because of the *gun* you know."

What gun?

It appeared Amy Rhine had purchased a firearm not very long after Catherine Hope was murdered. A lone woman did not feel *safe* in her bed at night after that tragedy.

"Was it," interrupted Kenmore, "a .357 Magnum?"

"I don't know what its *name* was. *Smith & Weston,* it seems to me."

"*Smith & Weston.*"

"You could ask Jerry Grew—no, you *can't,* he is dead —but I bought it from him *second-hand.* Anyway, it was a perfectly *huge* gun, and I was *afraid* of it, and this morning it was gone *chamois bag and all.*"

"Where did you keep it?"

"Under my pillow at *first.* But then later, in my desk. I would never have *missed* it," said Amy Rhine, "except to be on the safe side I made a carbon copy of Corinne's statement, and I went to lock that away in the desk, and the gun was *gone*."

Now, said she, was that why Fred Crush had tried to *hide* from her? At any rate, she had thought it best to call police headquarters directly and a very *gentlemanly* officer had promised to look into it *personally*.

Finally, she did not know *what* Dr. Wallace had been *talking* about last night. Mrs. Rhine did not *have* a sister.

Sergeant Lyon had gone around to the three La Jolla banks. "Corinne," he reported, "drew $500 from the Bank of America branch. This morning. In $20 and $10 bills."

"We had better see her about that," Kenmore thought.

La Jolla was a flash of tropical color under a dazzling afternoon sun. The sky beyond Laguna Terrace was a Mexican pottery blue only marred by some flecks of anti-aircraft shells. The bursting shells made a sound like the angry slamming of a basement door.

From some mysterious source had appeared quantities of handbills advertising that the inside story of the La Jolla Murders was to be gotten by tuning in KGOY at 8:15 o'clock every weekday night.

There was such a handbill flung down on the walk at 222 Laguna Terrace.

Corinne, said Jessie Axiter, had gone out . . . Anyway, said Jessie Axiter doggedly, on Friday night the green Cadillac had not been anywhere near Penguin Street; it had been on the canyon road, and she and Corinne had been in it.

"Amy Rhine," said she bitterly, "is a spiteful cat. I hope you are not going to take her word against mine and my daughter's?"

"It is a question of your husband's word, isn't it?" asked Kenmore.

Mrs. Axiter looked at him indignantly. "I suppose that is a typical police trick," she decided. *"He* hasn't changed his story. Why should he?"

"Because he is going to be charged with murder if he sticks to it."

A reverberation of anti-aircraft shook the windows in the baronial living room. Jessie Axiter waited until that was over.

"Because he wasn't there?" said she. "But if he admitted he *was,* you would let him go? You see, you're being ridiculous."

Lieutenant Kenmore shrugged.

"Your husband is not under arrest for having been within two blocks of the shooting, Mrs. Axiter . . . Eighty-three other people were much closer than that! It is suspicious, not that Amy Rhine saw him parked on Penguin Street, but that he denies it."

He could not read any response in Jessie Axiter's eyes. Lieutenant Kenmore had thought at their first meeting, she could cling to beat the very devil . . . She was evidently going to cling to the canyon road alibi.

"Where did 'Fred Crush' get $500?" he asked.

"I'm sure I have no idea."

Kenmore told her where Axiter had got $500.

Jessie did not look very dismayed. Kenmore had not thought she would, really. It is only the relatively truthful witness who can be routed in confusion by being caught in a flat falsehood.

"Oh," said she, "I can explain that," and walked to the dragon-limbed table. "Here."

Lieutenant Kenmore looked over the second telegram of the day; or rather the first, since this was headed Mankato and 8:42 a.m.

TAKING PLANE EARLIEST RESERVATION ARRIVE SAN DIEGO
MONDAY TEN ACK EMMA   LAWRENCE

"Who is Lawrence?"

"Lawrence Bowling. My cousin. It is very simple," said Jessie Axiter breathlessly, "and it explains *everything*. Why we did not want the autopsy. Why we set the funeral for Saturday definitely. Because if I wired and said Saturday, he couldn't take the train and I didn't think he would fly just for the funeral. He must have been very lucky to get a plane reservation as it is . . . Good heavens. Don't you see? It wouldn't do at all. Because he knows *all* about that old trouble, and he would know who 'Crush' *was*. So that is it. They could not both be here."

The lieutenant said, "And 'Crush' had to go? You told him to pack a suitcase and you gave him the money?"

This had the ring of truth, or of part-truth, he thought. The difficulty was, Jessie Axiter was so very skillful in eluding full truths. *All those tales she tells are fantastic legends,* Corinne had said; but Jessie had not made up the Henry Bowling legend or the Lally legend out of whole cloth, either. Mrs. Axiter, thought Kenmore, had not pinned her faith upon any one single whopping Maginot Line falsehood. She possessed a defense-in-depth consisting of a great number of little lies, exaggerations, and omissions; and these pillboxes were all camouflaged to resemble the natural landscape of truth at first glance. And these fortified positions had been taken to defend the last citadel of all; her respectability; which was the thing she would cling to until the bitter end.

"But that is not all," said Kenmore. "The telegram only came this morning. And the canyon road alibi got made up between you and Corinne and 'Crush' last light."

"It isn't an *alibi*," Jessie Axiter retorted indignantly. "Because it's *true*."

She frowned.

"Last night proves it," she argued. "Because we did not know then he would be arrested. So you see we didn't have to make up an alibi to shield him."

Kenmore gave a headshake.

"It is the other way around. You are relying on him to shield someone else, and you'll find he won't do it."

Jessie Axiter's reply to that never got voiced. The front door slammed noisily; Mrs. Axiter turned with relief.

"Corinne," said she.

And then, helplessly: "Oh, *Lally!*"

Lally?

Lieutenant Kenmore sprang past the dragon-limbed table, up the three curved steps into the front hallway.

Corinne Axiter, a feminine thunderstorm incarnate, was glaring lightning bolts at her blonde sister. Lally was wearing a Chinese orange splash of mandarin robe and a vacuous smile and presumably nothing more than that. Lally's feet at any rate were bare, and she stood swaying on them.

"You fool," Corinne was saying. "You damned little fool."

Kenmore's grey glance ranged from the golden-haired to the dark sister. "What's *she* doing out of the hospital?"

Lally giggled at him. "I walked out by myshelf. No fun. No drinksh. I quit. Cold."

"She's sick." Jessie Axiter burst past Lieutenant Kenmore. "She doesn't know what she's saying, she's out of her head . . . Dr. Myatt *said* there might be complications—"

"Mother, for *God's* sake!" This from between Corinne's clenched teeth. "She's *not* sick. She's *drunk*. Now will you *please* go somewhere and cry your eyes out and let *me* handle this?

"Come on, Lally."

Lally didn't come, she'd stopped in front of Kenmore.

"Drunk. I'm drunk again. I'm no good, am I?"

But she sounded, for the moment, stone cold sober.

"Why shouldn't I get drunk?" she asked the lieutenant. "It's my life, isn't it?" Lally grimaced. "Wouldn't I make some hero a swell wife, though? Mrs. David Wayne— *Captain* Wayne's wife. *You* know. The former Mrs. Al Dearborn, Corporal Dearborn that got kicked out of the Air Corps for passing rubber checks.

"I'm *sure* you remember," said Lally thickly. "Henry Bowling's niece. Henry Bowling, the well-known political grafter.

"Lally Axiter, she was, Frank Axiter's kid. The famous thief and murderer."

"I think," said Lally's mother weakly, "I am going to faint."

"She will, too," said Corinne.

And she did, into Sergeant Lyon's arms.

"Christ!" whispered Lally, shuddering inside the mandarin robe. "Isn't it nice for Dave to come home to? Can't you imagine how *proud* he'll be? I'll bet his f-family just can't wait to m-meet my f-folks—"

At this point (and Lieutenant Kenmore was surprised she had reached it at all) Lally went under . . . A sob stumbled from her lips. Her eyelids fluttered and locked shut. The trembling of her slender form became a dizzy, downward plunge.

He caught Lally as she fell.

"You had better carry them both upstairs," said Corinne coolly.

Lieutenant Kenmore, when he had left Lally on the tester bed, walked through the dressing room into the bath and wrung out a cold towel there.

He was pressing that to the girl's forehead when a clap of anti-aircraft shook the house, rattled the sash in the window frame. The door between Lally's room and the dressing chamber began closing.

Kenmore looked around dubiously at the chairs: moved one of those to the doorway; and stood on it.

Ella, it appeared, was not so exacting a housekeeper that she dusted the inch-wide top of the door; along the upper surface lay the grey, powdery accumulation of years wiped clean for a single hand's-breadth at one point.

"That gives you some idea," said Corinne, ten minutes later. "She simply got up and walked out of the hospital. They were frantic, of course, they telephoned to see whether she'd come home, and I knew where to look . . . The nearest bar."

"Yes," said Kenmore, "but where did she hear all that?"

"You should know. The police had been there again."

Kenmore thought, Harry Whipple had been there again.

Corinne's voice ran. "You see what she's like, there's absolutely nothing she won't do when she's in that condition."

"If you mean drunk, she wasn't in that condition when she left the hospital . . . I know what ails her," said Lieutenant Kenmore, "and I know what ails *you*, young lady."

Corinne Axiter said that was very interesting, or started to say so.

"You shut up."

And these three quiet words fell upon Corinne's ear in a way that made the dark sister fall back a step, and gulp, and—shut up.

"Yes," said Lieutenant Kenmore, "I know. You think you are so clever, so brainy, so superior. Lally is not in it with you; your mother is not in it with you, either. It was no trick at all for you to see through your father and your uncle and Amy Rhine . . . Well, there is one person you have not seen through yet."

"You, I suppose," said Corinne, rallying.

"No," said Lieutenant Kenmore. *"You.* Yourself."

And a moment later he added:

"You and your climbing on garbage pails and crawling in windows."

Corinne Axiter was visibly shaken. "Who told you that?"

"You did."

Kenmore's mouth was drawn in a half-smile.

"You're guessing," said the dark sister. "Bluffing."

"No. It's true. You told me that. If you will fetch Amy Rhine's transcript, I'll show you the place."

"I don't believe you . . . It is in my room."

And in Corinne's room:

"Here," said Lieutenant Kenmore. *"There aren't many public places in La Jolla one would appear in that kind of a dress . . . I finished by going around to the hotel bars looking for Lally myself, if she was not at the Shore Club.* But if there are not many places in La Jolla she would wear that dress, the obvious conclusion would be Lally was not in La Jolla. She had gone into San Diego with someone, very likely. And if *that* was likely, there was no sense sending 'Crush' to the Shore Club, there was no use looking for her in the local bars. The sensible thing would have been to sit down to the phone and call those places and then telephone the better class night clubs in town. You could have dialed fifty numbers in the time it took to trot around La Jolla.

"Can't you see what this statement of yours means?" said Kenmore. "You knew very well she was in La Jolla; something had happened to make you think she was with Al Dearborn; of course you went to his apartment."

Corinne hesitated.

"Yes, I did! I'll tell you why . . . Ella had left a note on the memo pad beside the phone for Lally to call Seaview 4-4623. And that is Al's number. So as a matter of fact I *did* go to his apartment. No one answered when I rang the doorbell, but there was a light inside. If I had known then what I know now, I would have realized the light was a trick. Al left it burning so Lally would see it from the Club and expect him along in a minute; she would never dream he had gone to burgle her room. But I didn't know. So I took the garbage pail and stood on it and looked in—I had to open the window because the dim-out shade was drawn—and I saw Lally's purse lying on the arm of the divan."

The dark sister stared grimly at Kenmore.

"What would you think? I thought of course she had been there."

"Go on."

Well, said Corinne, Lally had denied being with Al and on Thursday night it had not seemed especially important since she had got safely home. But then on Friday it developed the gas mask was missing, the autopsy result got known, and there followed the attack on Lally. As if Lally knew something about Al's movements he didn't want told!

In short, she had not been sure whether Lally had an alibi or not. The question was whether Lally had been on the beach with the sentry, as she said; if he would confirm that, well and good. But if not, it would be fatal to inquire into the matter openly. That was why, when Corinne had picked up her mother at the hospital Friday night, she had directed 'Fred Crush' to park the Cadillac at the foot of Penguin Street.

"Penguin Street," said Corinne, "because there are steps there going down to the beach."

Leaving 'Crush' in the car, then, they had gone down onto the beach expecting to encounter Private Tazewell. The notion of the purse occurred to Corinne as an opening gambit; she was going to tell the sentry her sister had lost a purse on the beach the previous evening; and that this purse contained some ration books and ten dollars in cash. The ten dollars she was willing to offer as a reward for the ration books. If the sentry *had* met Lally, thought Corinne, he would probably guide them to the exact spot among the rocks and help look for the lost handbag.

"Instead of that, we heard a shot and screams and the dog—and mother got absolutely hysterical with fright. So I had to bring her home, and I still didn't know where Lally had been Thursday night. That is why I lied and said we had been on the canyon road."

A pause.

"But if the little fool thinks our father killed Uncle Henry and Dr. Wallace, then she can't be mixed up in it herself at all. So her alibi doesn't particularly matter."

Lieutenant Kenmore shrugged. "Lally is a little fool, perhaps. She's not a big enough fool to imagine she is smart enough to outwit the police." He shook his head. "You are trying to outwit a murderer! Lally's alibi— Good God! It is Lally's *life* that matters!"

There was a longer, and somehow a great deal *deeper* pause.

"Thursday night, then," said Kenmore, "you went through the window into Al's apartment and brought home Lally's purse?"

"Why . . . Yes."

"There were some cards in it at that time—?"

"I don't know," said Corinne, "I didn't look to see what was in it."

Frank Axiter protested his innocence in almost the identical words he had used to protest it on a previous occasion. It was true, he had driven the Cadillac to the foot of Penguin Street . . . "God A'mighty! Corinne told me not to admit it! They're trying to protect Lally. They expect me to lie and get in trouble for that . . . What do they care if I rot in jail?"

Lieutenant Kenmore recognized the familiar words, but the voice was not the same. The voice was not now congested. Axiter had been deprived, among other creature comforts, of his nasal jelly.

Kenmore peered across the sub-station cell into the other's brick red face.

"*Skunk-kitty!*" said he.

The gardener recoiled; then his chin dropped onto his chest and his eyes fell. He breathed hard, bereft of speech.

"Yes," said the lieutenant. "Of course. You brought her home from the Shore Club. You couldn't admit it . . . Miss Roydan had switched on a flashlight. You knew we had overheard that. And so you did your damnedest to disguise your voice." The overheard incident, the lip-smacking note of triumph, the secret pleased mockery, became unwholesomely explicable. "Your own daughter," Kenmore said. "I suppose it gratified you to think she had fallen to your own level? No. Don't mistake me. I don't say she had, or could. But it was necessary for you to pretend to yourself it was so."

From the cell cot, a whine.

"Throw it up to me," said Frank Axiter. "Just because I made one mistake in a lifetime."

Kenmore shook his head.

"Don't mistake me about that, either. I don't think it's important you stole $15,000 and deserted your wife and children. The important thing is you were a poor sucker, you couldn't hang onto the $15,000, and you came crawling back."

Axiter had wanted to be near his family. "I admit I lost my temper, I cussed Lally out . . . It isn't so easy for a man to stand by and see his own kids go to hell! A man can't help having his fatherly feelings, can he?"

Lieutenant Kenmore replied he could understand those feelings. "You couldn't bear to tear yourself from the bosom of your family . . . You tried that once. And it involved having to stand on your own feet. You would rather be on your knees than that. I know," said the lieutenant with certain grim pity in his tone, "how it was. Your life did not begin in 1932 when you ran off with $15,000 of Henry Bowling's boodle . . . What was it before then? You worked for Henry Bowling; an exacting, overbearing man with a rough tongue in his head. I wouldn't have cared to work for him. And to be frank, I can't picture Jessie as an ideal wife, either.

"Unfortunately, the woman you ran off with wasn't any improvement. The whole thing of running away, losing the money, being picked up by the police, was not any improvement. And then what?

"It was 1932, with 1933 coming up. You must have sung Salvation Army hymns for your supper, you must have stood in breadlines, you probably raked leaves for the WPA. You'd have liked to go back to your family and your rich brother-in-law then, wouldn't you, Crush?"

But he hadn't dared, not then, and not for a long time thereafter. Not until the brother-in-law had brought the family to La Jolla . . .

"You had jumped out of a frying pan into a fire, and the worst of that was," Kenmore thought, "you'd built your own fire. You couldn't blame that onto anyone else. I suppose that was the beauty of working for Bowling again. You could sit up there in that garage and feel sorry for yourself, you could feel imposed upon and cheated, you could say it was all Bowling's unscrupulousness and the family's selfishness! You could have got plenty of other jobs, you know. But you would have had to *work* at any job, and you couldn't blame it on the slavedriver, Henry Bowling. You'd have been pinched by the meat shortage just the same, and you couldn't have whined that family was eating your share. You—oh, hell!" said Kenmore, and gestured toward the other.

Frank Axiter, cringed as from a fist.

But Lieutenant Kenmore's palm was open, and a gold coin lay on it.

"Remember this?" said the lieutenant.

"No, I don't know nothing about it, I—"

"Don't lie," said Kenmore. "You found this in the guesthouse when you tore down the mantel. Didn't you?"

Axiter's lips worked under their thatch of moustache.

"I—what if I did?"

"I am asking the questions," said the lieutenant. "Get it straight in your head, Crush. *You* are the guy locked in this cell. *You* are the man who masqueraded under an alias and a false alibi. You have a habit of not admitting the truth until it flies up and hits you in the teeth.

"Now," said Kenmore, "I know the truth about this coin. But I am not going to stand here and tell it. *You* are going to tell me."

"Well," said Axiter, "I found it, I didn't steal it."

"What did you do with it?"

"Put in my pocket."

"When you tore down the guesthouse mantel. How long ago was that?"

"Eight, ten days."

"Go on."

"I hid it, you-know-where," said Axiter, possibly hoping Kenmore did not know where.

"In the guesthouse light switch box."

"Yeah," said Axiter, despondently. "On account of Bowling being murdered. I thought I might get asked some questions—well, that gold piece worried me. I didn't know if gold was legal nowadays, if there wasn't some law against it."

"All right . . . Now what else did you find behind that mantel?"

"Just some junk. Nothing much."

"Including a letter," said Lieutenant Kenmore. "Why are you trying to lie about that?"

Downcast, Frank Axiter confessed it was because he had opened the envelope. "Bowling came in just then. I didn't want him to see—I pushed the envelope behind me, inside the gas heater. While he was looking at all the junk."

"Yes, you thought you had broken the law in opening the envelope," said Lieutenant Kenmore evenly. "What was in the letter?"

"I don't know, he took it away before I got a chance to read it."

XXIII

Paris . . . was just like living in a movie.—THE AUTO-
BIOGRAPHY OF CATHERINE HOPE.

Lieutenant Kenmore stared at the blued steel, Circas-
sian stocked .357 Magnum.

"She bought herself plenty of gun, huh?" Sergeant
Lyon thought.

"Amy Rhine? Has she identified it?"

Acting-Lieutenant Ralph Arnold said not. "We just
found it. Wrapped up in that chamois bag and stuck
behind the sandbags outside the guesthouse. It wasn't
there yesterday, we looked when we were hunting for
that brooch and rings."

"Who found it?"

"Well, as a matter of fact," said the acting-lieutenant,
"*I* did. I figured if Axiter hadn't thrown it away at the
Shore Club, he probably had it hid somewhere around
the place. I wonder how he's going to talk himself out of
this one?"

Lieutenant Kenmore kept staring at the gun. "I don't
want anything said to Axiter about this. Or to Amy
Rhine, either."

"You mean," said Lyon, "until you make a ballistics
test?"

"I was thinking of a naphthionate of sodium test."

A fly swam in a slow aerial orbit over the weapon, descended onto the checked tip of the hammer, and then

rose alarmedly under the focused eyes of the three officers.

"That's what they use to trap mail thieves, isn't it?"
Arnold said, almost casually.

"Yes. It is luminescent under ultra-violet light."

"I thought that's what you meant."

Arnold shook his head: "You can't pull anything like
that while you've got the guy locked up."

"No. We'll turn him loose."

Arnold stood, ran his hands down the seams of his
trousers.

"You know, they got a big axe sharpening for you at
KGOY."

Kenmore smiled.

"All right. It's your show. It's your neck," said the sub-
station commander. "If you want to stick it out. But
what's the use? He couldn't be dumb enough to fall for
anything like that."

Kenmore said: "You think so because you are looking
at it through *your* eyes."

"Through anybody's eyes," said Arnold, "it's wrong.
You can't charge a man with murder and then turn him
loose, expect him to go grab the murder gun, when he
knows that's the very thing the cops want him to do."

Lieutenant Kenmore began pacing the sub-station
floor.

"Yes," said he, *"you* know the police department
would not turn Axiter loose and give him a chance to
get his hands on a loaded gun. But does Axiter know
it? Or any of them?" The lieutenant shook his head.
"These people haven't your experience with the police
blotter and the police show-up. Take one of them to a
show-up, and the man *they'd* pick out as the most
dangerous criminal there is J. S. Dugan. Because Dugan
might have walked straight out of a B-movie.

"And that's where they've got their education about police methods—except possibly Wyeland knows better, but he isn't a police court lawyer. I doubt if he's been inside a criminal court in the last twenty years. And then Wyeland loses his head in a crisis, he doesn't stop to think for himself, he just goes along with the crowd. And the rest of them—Good Lord!" said Kenmore. "They'll fall for anything. It can't be too wrong. They'll swallow it, just as they swallow a movie—"

He paused.

He smiled.

"Do you know, I think I've got it?" said Lieutenant Kenmore.

Arnold wore a thoroughly dubious expression. Which was, indeed, mirrored on Sergeant Lyon's countenance.

The acting-lieutenant said: "Okay, what kind of a Hollywood gag is it going to be?"

Kenmore chuckled.

"It won't be one. They've *seen* all the Hollywood gags, it's exactly what they'll be expecting . . . Every move in this affair has been planned ahead of time against us," said the detective. "We are going to change that, throw in a planned move of our own. But it won't be a Hollywood gag, it will be the one thing they can't possibly be prepared for. Our surprise—the one thing they *won't* expect—will be ordinary, everyday, routine police procedure."

"Who," said Arnold, "do you mean? *They?*"

"I'll draw up a list."

Lieutenant Kenmore sat down at the desk.

Arnold took to walking the floor.

"Look," said he. "You're going to wait until after that Home Fronter broadcast, aren't you?"

Lieutenant Kenmore said not.

"Before," he said. "Before the Home Fronter can tell

the world how it happened Lally Dearborn, who was slugged in front of an open window, got found lying beside an open door and beside a whiskey bottle that had been hidden behind a sandbag . . . Here's the cast."

Arnold peered at the list:

AXITER, CORINNE	HEYES, DONALD
AXITER, FRANK (alias FRED CRUSH)	KENMORE, Lt.
	LYON, Sgt.
AXITER, JESSICA	RHINE, AMY
DEARBORN, ALVAH LEROY	ROYDAN, DARWINA
DEARBORN, LALITHA	WYELAND, WILLIAM
ELLIOT, SAMUEL E.	DUGAN, J. S.
FFLEMING, FOSTER V.	

"Some cast . . . Is that in the order of their appearance?"

"Dugan," said Lieutenant Kenmore, "is in the order of *his* appearance."

XXIV

I like to hear a man talk shop.—THE AUTOBIOGRAPHY
OF CATHERINE HOPE.

As a matter of fact, the alphabetical order of Lieutenant Kenmore's list was not at all the order of appearance. Lally, Corinne, and Mrs. Axiter were of course at
home; Amy Rhine was the first to press the doorbell at
222 Laguna Terrace that evening. Mrs. Rhine had
thoughtfully brought along two stenographer's note-
books and a supply of sharpened pencils. The pencils,
projecting from the bun of hair at the nape of her neck,
made that portion of her look a little like a machine
gun turret. Ffleming walked in next; having brought
his Airedale for the latter's exercise (as he said) he arrived afoot and perspiring.

Darwina Roydan was there on the stroke of seven
o'clock, again wearing the Spanish galleon. Al Dearborn
(who was now out on bail) brought the smug look of a
man who had been in jail when Lauren Wallace got
killed; Fred Crush got marched in by Sergeant Lyon.
Donald Heyes followed, bearing under his arm a port-
folio of photographs. William Wyeland was the next
to the last to arrive, and last of all was Sam Elliot who
presumably had nothing to worry about since he had
been at the control room phone when Bowling was
killed, and had been side-by-side with Kenmore at the
moment of the second murder. Sam Elliot looked put
out and put upon, since Mrs. Elliot had made other arrangements for his evening.

It wasn't, he grumbled audibly, as if *he* knew anything about all of this.

Lieutenant Kenmore replied, that was not the idea. The lieutenant stepped to the fireplace and rapped out his pipe noisily, a proceeding which had the effect of a falling gavel in bringing the room to order.

"No," said he, facing about, "I haven't called you people here to hold an inquest. In the movies, of course, there is always that last big scene in which the suspects are all gathered in front of the camera for the detective to pick out the guilty party—who is always the unlikeliest bet in the lot. In real life, it is not a case of one detective in a roomful of suspects. Just the other way around, it is one suspect in a roomful of detectives! And the room is at police headquarters.

"I can promise that none of you will be asked to answer any questions tonight. It is not good police procedure to question one witness in front of others, to let any witness hear what another says, to allow him consciously or unconsciously revise his testimony in the light of another person's testimony. If I thought for one minute any of you had one iota of information, I would have a private talk with that one.

"That clears the ground," said Kenmore, "and we can get on to the real purpose of this meeting . . . I've called you to warn you, your lives are all in danger."

The grey glance traveled around their faces.

"You don't believe me," said Kenmore. "Suppose I told you then, I have considered asking the district attorney to issue warrants placing you all under arrest, protective arrest, as material witnesses?"

Lally stared back at him blankly. Corinne looked skeptical still, and Jessie Axiter had a grim eye fixed on Al Dearborn. Elliot and Foster Ffleming came up from the divan they shared.

"Good God!" cried Elliot.

Lieutenant Kenmore waggled his pipestem. "If I am not going to do that, I have at least got to make you understand the seriousness of the situation. To begin with, there was a telephone call Henry Bowling put through to police headquarters a few minutes before he died—"

He described the phone call, the subsequent discovery of the envelope in the phone directory. "And now, Heyes, if you'll hand around those photographs."

Donald Heyes distributed photographic enlargements of the Ermel-processed envelope. Sam Elliot relapsed into frowning silence. Foster Ffleming's lips moved as he read. William Wyeland pulled at his brown beard. Al Dearborn squinted through a veil of cigarette smoke.

Lieutenant Kenmore said:

"*Katie* is Catherine Hope.

"The letter is part of one she wrote to her sister. It was never mailed because it fell behind the mantel in what was then Mrs. Rhine's home."

"Oh, *no!*" said Amy Rhine. "It didn't. Because I remember *all about* those letters. I put them in my handbag to take to the postoffice, and they were not out of my handbag *at all*. They were not loose on the mantel *ever*."

She sat shaking her head, the pince-nez flashing denial.

"Let me reconstruct that for you," said Kenmore. "We are speaking of the letters Catherine Hope wrote on the last day of her life. She mentions, here, having destroyed a first letter. If she had given you that first letter, she could not have taken it back without your knowledge. It appears to me she did not give you the letter because she was dissatisfied with it; that after you left, she rewrote it and tore up the first version; and then, on her way to the beach, stopped by to leave it with you for mailing. You were not at home; therefore she tucked it into the mantel, supposing it would catch your eye, and instead it fell through between the mantel and the fireplace."

Ffleming objected. "Wasn't the door locked?"

Amy Rhine cleared up that point. "Oh, she knew where I hid my *key*. She used to leave manuscript to be typed." She raised another point. "It would have been *simpler* to drop it in the box on the corner."

"There's a simple answer to that," said Lieutenant Kenmore. "The contents of the letter were peculiarly important. Catherine Hope may have intended it to go by registered mail. If she had lived, I can imagine her telephoning you later that night, or in the morning. 'I put a lettter and twenty-five cents on your mantel last night. Will you have it registered for me?' "

He gestured: "We could spend the night exploring every minute detail of what might have happened. There comes a time when you've got to chop wood, and not stop to reason why every tiny chip falls where it does.

"The important points are definite and undeniable. Catherine Hope *did* write this letter, it *was* lost, and was found six years later by Frank Axiter—to call him by his right name. And that therefore he stands in peril of his life, for the same reason Henry Bowling and Dr. Wallace were in peril of their lives."

All eyes turned to Frank Axiter; who reddened, and cleared his throat, and said nothing.

"Because he found this letter, originally," Kenmore observed, "and no matter how vigorously he denies it, *Catherine Hope's murderer cannot be sure he did not read it*. Mr. Axiter operates under the shadow of an alias. He is a confessed thief. He has tried to hoodwink the police through this investigation. *His* peril is direct, as the first of the series of persons who handled and may

have read Miss Hope's letter, a week ago Henry Bowling
was next, second in the series—"

"Excuse me, sir!" William Wyeland's bearded jaw
snapped out the interruption. "But if this letter contained any such statement as you imply—a clue to a
murderer's identity—I protest that Henry Bowling would
not have waited a week before notifying the authorities.
Whatever his shortcomings, he would not have been
particeps criminis in the situation you describe."

"Good heavens!" said Jessie Axiter. "Of course not! It's
just ridiculous."

"It is *ab hoc at ab hac at ab illa,*" the attorney concluded. "Mrs. Wyeland would say, backfence gossip."

Lieutenant Kenmore, shaking his head, commented
Catherine Hope had not had second sight. "She did not
write, 'So-and-So is going to kill me.' It was, 'So-and-So is
a bastard but I will not tell on him for his wife's sake.'
And Henry Bowling had no notion who *Katie* was. Frank
Axiter kept the envelope from him, pushed it out of
sight into the gas heater, and so the letter (it probably
began, *Dear Sister*) appeared to him to have been, like
the Christmas cards, addressed to Mrs. Rhine."

"Oh," said William Wyeland. The angle of his beard
lowered, and he fell to twiddling his watch-chain.

"It was an essential misconception on Bowling's part,"
Kenmore resumed. "He was not so fond of Amy Rhine
that he saved those cards and the letter as a good-will
gesture. It was quite the opposite. He kept the letter to
return it because he supposed she would be annoyed it
had fallen into his hands.

"It is a question of character . . . in keeping with his
dislike of women, in keeping with his sense of humor to
play such a trick. And to carry the joke farther, by telephoning and apologizing profusely for having read it,
so Mrs. Rhine would know he *had.*"

Lieutenant Kenmore turned his glance upon Amy's thin features.

"Your peril," said he, "is not so direct as Frank Axiter's. And yet it is considerable. Because the murderer cannot be sure how much Bowling said, what hints and allusions he may have let fall to embarrass you."

"No," said the gentlewoman. "Nothing I have not *told* you."

"Unfortunately, the murderer won't take your word for that. Or mine."

Kenmore looked around to the others:

"Getting back on the main line . . . It was not until Thursday night, at some time after seven o'clock, that Bowling lighted the guesthouse heater; then he found the envelope where Axiter had hidden it; he realized he had the whole thing wrong.

"He was not killed on the spur of the moment, though! A murder of that kind, involving the theft of Dr. Wallace's gas mask and the preparation of a false incident message, needed advance planning.

"What was the situation? Henry Bowling knew who had killed Catherine Hope, but until the Paratroop defense drill began, he did not know that he knew. But he had said something, possibly he'd said a lot, about a *letter* and *Amy Rhine's sister* and the *bastard*. He'd talked so much about it that, directly or indirectly, the murderer had got wind of it. That is why we have someone plotting Henry Bowling's death hours in advance— to silence him, and of course get hold of the fatal letter."

He paused.

"So far, we have Henry Bowling killed and both Frank Axiter and Mrs. Rhine in the dangerous position of holding—so far as the murderer knows—a vital clue to his identity. We can add Corinne and Jessie Axiter because there is no telling how much Bowling mentioned in his own home. You all know what happened to Lally. *Her* peril is direct, again, since the letter was handed on to her along with the Christmas cards."

Lally wetted her lips.

"Do you know what? I must have given the letter with the warden reports to Dr. Wallace . . ."

Kenmore nodded.

"Wait," said William Wyeland. "There's the same flaw. I mean, if Dr. Wallace knew—"

"But can we imagine Lauren Wallace reading personal mail that accidentally fell into his hands?" said the lieutenant. "I should say he laid it aside, offered to return it to Bowling on Wednesday afternoon, and then Bowling said it was Mrs. Rhine's letter. So Wallace put it in his desk for her. We can't say now whether he glanced at it, or whether Bowling indulged in allusions to *Amy Rhine's sister* and the *bastard*. But Wallace knew enough to be alarmed by the letter's disappearance. He rushed off in search of Sam Elliot. Because you, Elliot, had been in that desk Thursday and took report forms from it."

Elliot's solid face flushed resentfully. "Hell! I don't go nosing around in other people's mail . . ."

"Nevertheless, you are in peril."

And as Sam Elliot grunted incredulously, "I know," said Kenmore, *"you* don't think so. Lauren Wallace did not see himself as a prospective victim any more than the rest of you do. And yet he was killed, Bowling was killed, Catherine Hope herself was killed because of what's in that letter.

"You have all got to realize," said the lieutenant, looking harshly around at the faces in the baronial living room, "your fate is not in the hands of a court of inquiry that is going to weigh the evidence against you. We are dealing with an executioner. The *bastard* is not going to give anyone here the benefit of a doubt. If you have seen the letter in which he is named—if you have *not* seen it, but there is any reason to suspect you *may* have—then you are potentially as dangerous to him as Catherine Hope, Henry Bowling, Lally Dearborn, or Lauren Wallace."

It was at this moment Al Dearborn laughed.

"That's damned good," said Al, quietly joyous. "I'm beginning to enjoy this. If you could all just see the look on your faces!"

"Yes," said Lieutenant Kenmore. "That is very funny, coming from you."

"Me? Come again. I don't get you."

"I am getting at this," replied Kenmore. "Suppose Lally did not mistakenly hand the letter to Wallace with the warden reports? In that case, it was not lost, it was in her bag at the Shore Club—in short, Al, *was stolen by you*. You are a dishonorably discharged soldier, a forger, a promoter of fake stocks, a gambler without visible means of support, a thief—you are a damned crook. What would you do if such a letter came into your hands. That is not a question," continued Kenmore, "since it answers itself. You'd use it for blackmail."

"Yeah?" The maroon eyes flung a sneer. "Some wise cop! What was it doing in Wallace's desk, if I had it?"

"That question also answers itself. *The original was never in Wallace's desk if you stole it.*"

Lieutenant Kenmore came a step closer to Al Dearborn's chair.

"Now, Al. Let's drop the tough-guy act. You're smart enough to know, if you took such a letter from Lally's handbag, you'd have to make her think she had left it at the control room by mistake. Then the letter in Wallace's desk was a *forgery prepared and planted there by you*."

"That's a God damn lie—!" Al Dearborn jumped up.

So did Sergeant Lyon.

Kenmore shrugged. "I could make out a case along that line. I'll put it this way: On Wednesday, Dr. Wallace handed this letter to Henry Bowling. Bowling saw it wasn't the same letter at all. Did he figure out what had happened? Is it possible, Al, that's what he meant when he gave you until Friday afternoon when the banks closed—since that's when the deposit vaults are locked? Because he intended to take back the original from you and lock it up for safekeeping!"

Al Dearborn's face twitched. He swallowed twice—and decided to cop a plea:

"That's a dirty *frame-up!* It wasn't nothing *like* that! I passed a bum check—it was drawn on that patent medicine outfit—I put Bowling's name on the back of it, endorsed it from him to me. You can ask Harry Whipple—hell, he's known about it for a week!"

That was it, then? Harry Whipple, when he had first heard of Bowling's death, had thought it was Al Dearborn's doing? And had been going to solve it on that basis?

"Sit down and shut up," said Kenmore sharply. "I told you before, you are not going to be judged by a court of inquiry. It doesn't matter whether or not you actually did steal the original letter and plant a forged substitute in its place. The point is, you *may* have done so, and therefore the murderer *may* not yet have gotten hold of the complete, unabridged, and damning original. If he thinks so," said Lieutenant Kenmore, "he is not going to run and ask you or Captain Whipple or anyone else. That is *your* peril, Al."

And Al Dearborn, collapsing spently into his chair, looked as if he appreciated it.

Lieutenant Kenmore turned on his heel.

"Darwina Roydan and Ffleming," said he, "get off more

lightly. It was merely their misfortune to be present when Lauren Wallace found the letter had been taken from his desk. They are not in any danger at all, unless there was more to Wallace's muttered remarks than anyone has testified. With you, Wyeland, the case is different."

Kenmore by this time had traveled nearly the length of the room. He reached to the dragon-limbed table and picked up one of Heyes' photographic reproductions."

He began, "When Catherine Hope began . . . *and says*—or rather, ended that sentence—it is not very difficult to surmise she had written *Wyeland says*—"

There was a crash, a yell, and darkness.

Sergeant Lyon roared: "I got him if he comes this way!"

There was a second crash.

"I got him!" panted the sergeant.

XXV

*Grandfather had a sonorous voice and an excellent
memory. I can still hear him declaiming Gray's lines:
"Each in his narrow cell forever laid—" and Shake-
speare's,*

> *"The sepulchre,*
> *Where-in we saw thee quietly inurned*
> *has o'pd his ponderous and marble jaws."*
> —THE AUTOBIOGRAPHY OF CATHERINE HOPE.

The lights came up.

It was Lally who reached the doorway and found the
switch ahead of Kenmore's hand; Corinne had dashed in
the other direction and was discovered brandishing a
poker snatched from the fireplace set; Mrs. Axiter had
fainted. Mr. William Wyeland, struggling up from his
chair, had his clenched fists raised in a John L. Sullivan
pose. Foster Ffleming, bending, held onto the collar of
a stiff-limbed and growling Airedale.

Amy Rhine had, for an unclear reason, mounted a
chair and stood there clutching onto her skirts. Al Dearborn had dived under a divan. Pawing along the inner
wall was Frank Axiter, blindly seeking the side door; if
he had found it, he would have run into the arms of
Darwina Roydan and Donald Heyes, who had both
thought to block that exit.

Lieutenant Kenmore's grey glance absorbed these details; everyone else was staring at Sergeant Lyon.

"I got him!" the sergeant had cried, and in fact, he

had got J. S. Dugan. "Holy smokes! It's *Undertaker Joe* Dugan!"

"What?" gulped Darwina.

"He's a burglar specializing in funerals, wakes, and burials," said Kenmore, advancing toward the cringing and guilt-faced Dugan. "Undertaker Joe knows when anyone dies, the personal effects of the deceased get dredged up out of trunks and bureau drawers and bank vault boxes, everything is sorted over, the valuables laid to one side. All very handy for a lightfingered visitor!"

One of Arnold's uniformed officers breathed loudly from the top of the curved steps. "He was hiding in the shrubbery out back! I ain't twins—I can't watch all four sides of a house at once—"

Kenmore interrupted. "As a matter of fact, the idea of a prowler crossed my mind when I found Lally knocked out, her brooch and rings gone."

"Nah-h!" cried Officer Dugan, shrinking in his shabby plainclothes attire. "Ya ain't gonna hang that bum rap on *me!* The dame was already—"

But here Dugan stopped short, dropped his villainous eyes, and clamped shut his warped and sinister lips.

"Already what?" said Lyon.

From Dugan, silence.

Lyon said to Lieutenant Kenmore: "By God, he *was* in here yesterday. He got scared off without any loot, that's why he's back now."

A whining sound issued from the corner of J. S. Dugan's mouth. He was offering to turn state's witness . . .

"Yeah?" said Lyon. "What you got to testify about?"

"Something *you* don't know, copper," replied J. S. Dugan. "I tell you, the dame was already kayoed. That ain't all. It wasn't me put the bottle onna door, it was—"

"No! Shut up!"

Kenmore's shout drowned Dugan's whine.

"Get him out of here!" said the lieutenant to Sergeant Lyon. "Around back. Take him to the guesthouse." He turned to the others. If he had hoped to read anything on anyone's face, the hope was vain. Al Dearborn's maroon eyes and Amy Rhine's mousey ones bulged equally; Foster Ffleming looked as stunned as Jessie Axiter; Darwina's color was as high as William Wyeland's.

"Excuse me. I'm sorry," said the detective rapidly. "You understand—nothing personal about it—mustn't let him talk in front of all you witnesses—*matter of police procedure.*"

He darted after Sergeant Lyon and J. S. Dugan. "Wait a minute!" Lieutenant Kenmore was heard to call down the connecting hall. "Wait'll I get the handcuffs on him! We don't want him to make a break—"

For the second time, the lights went out in the baronial living room.

"Hey!" said Arnold's uniformed officer helplessly. "Who done that? Stand still, everybody. Don't anyone—ah-h . . ."

"Good luck, Dugan!" whispered Lieutenant Kenmore prayerfully. "Keep your eyes open, both of you!"

The glimmer of metal at the end of J. S. Dugan's sleeve was not a handcuff, it was a gun. He and the sergeant moved ahead into the darkness. Lieutenant Kenmore, crouching with another gun in his own hand, heard the scuff of substantial shoe leather upon the tennis court. It was only one among a variety of sounds that reached his ears. Something very like Bedlam had let loose inside the house.

Lieutenant Kenmore's lips fitted like drawn rubber bands across his teeth. A rattle of hardware propelled him from the side door toward the back, service porch step . . . A blaze of flashlight exploded against his staring pupils.

"Damn it, Darwina!" he exhaled. "Turn that thing off!"

"But, John! The lights—some one ran by me—"

"Shut up!"

Lieutenant Kenmore flung around at the *pun-n!* of the shot.

"Oh, hell!" and ran toward the guesthouse. *"Dugan!"*

Flashlights had come alive at the corners of the big house, from the roof of the guesthouse, down from the garage windows.

"Dugan!"

"I'm okay," said that officer. "Just skinned my nose on the cement." He scrambled up from the tennis court doubles alley. "Where's the sarge?"

"Here," said Lyon, emerging from under the silk oak boughs. "I got the son-of-a-bitch for sure this time!"

He had got Foster Ffleming this time.

"You fool!" said Ffleming. "It wasn't *me*. It was Wyeland . . ."

"Nuts!" cried the sergeant, smoothing his hands down Ffleming's slender person. "What'd you do with the gat?"

"I never had one." Ffleming turned an intently screwed-on expression into the glare of Darwina Roydan's flashlight. "You monkeys, you've let him get away with it again! It was Will Wyeland, I tell you. He ducked behind one of the window drapes and jumped from the window onto the lawn. I was after him when this blithering idiot tackled—tackled—"

He stopped, swallowing.

Acting-Lieutenant Ralph Arnold came toiling along the walk from the Toyon Street gate; stooped and awkwardly; he was hauling a reluctant Airedale by its collar.

Man's four-footed friend gripped in his jaws a chamois-holstered revolver.

"Yes," said Lieutenant Kenmore. "Your dog is trained to carry home packages, Ffleming . . . Before you say anything more, let me remark you are under arrest for murder. I will be fair with you. The gun was treated with naphthionate of sodium . . ."

"I think," said Mrs. Axiter faintly, "a little brandy, Corinne—"

"I think," said Corinne, "we could all use a drink after that!"

Amy Rhine murmured: "Well, perhaps a wee drop."

"I believe it is customary," said Darwina Roydan, "to explain *everything* at this point."

"It is not customary at all," Lieutenant Kenmore said, returning from the hall telephone. "The district attorney wouldn't thank me for giving away his whole case. I've talked too much as it is. I'm probably going to be accused of putting testimony into your mouths—yes?"

Acting-Lieutenant Ralph Arnold came heavily down the three curved steps into the living room.

"He had some capsules of that cyanogen, calcium cyanide, in the cuffs of his pants," said the sub-station commander.

Kenmore stared.

Arnold nodded; said, "He asked for a cigarette. That must be when he popped a couple in his mouth . . . We were going to book him at the station; we drove to the hospital instead; he was dead when we got there."

"Well, in that case—" Lieutenant Kenmore reconsidered "—I think I need a drink myself, Corinne."

The lieutenant presently set aside his half-emptied glass, and began tamping his pipe bowl.

"I had better begin," he observed, "with the motive. It was before us in the fragment of Catherine Hope's letter that could be reconstructed from its envelope . . . She had not applied the term, *bastard,* as an epithet reflecting on his character. She meant that literally, in the legal sense of the word."

"Filius nullius," murmured William Wyeland.

"Exactly. It posed the question, who was the bastard? Did she mean Foster Ffleming? In an off-guard moment he let slip he was from Michigan; naturally, he did not say New Gilead, Michigan. In her *Autobiography* Miss Hope mentioned the difficulty she had in obtaining a passport. New Gilead was founded as an off-shoot theological community where, in the early days at any rate, the marital customs were polygamous; but then any such practice, being illegal, was necessarily practiced secretly and not as a matter of open record. Catherine Hope had to explore all that thoroughly to obtain a birth certificate; such a certificate being, in peace-times, practically the only conceivable obstacle in the way of anyone's getting a passport granted. To write her *Autobiography,* and this is another point, she had accumulated a lot of early family papers and letters. Her grandfather, as a preacher and founder of the sect, would have left correspondence and records throwing considerable light on the community life. There is a reference to the discovery of copper on the Videll farm; Ffleming's full name was Foster Videll Ffleming.

"You could add that up," said Kenmore, "and say, if, in 1937, Ffleming had needed to establish *his* birth certificate for any reason, it would have been natural enough for him to have turned to her—the self-appointed community historian—for aid. And if he had been born out of legal wedlock, equally natural that she should have discovered the fact."

Wyeland tugged at his beard. "Of course that was it!

I recall now, she had asked me some questions along that line, questions relating to a collateral kinship. That is, deriving from a common ancestor. A bastard having no legal ancestor cannot claim collateral kindred. But I did not suspect she had *anyone* in mind."

"No. You supposed you were being encouraged to 'talk shop.'" The detective smiled. "There is a point of suggestive evidence to indicate she *had* been consulted along those lines. Miss Hope wrote as the spirit moved her. What moved her to work at Chapter I—*I Am Born*—just before she died? The answer might be, her thoughts had been directed into that channel by going back into the family letters and papers to ascertain the facts respecting Ffleming's parentage."

Darwina Roydan said the trouble with that theory was, Foster Ffleming had not inherited any property at the time of Catherine Hope's death. "It was several years later."

"That is not the main obstacle. Large estates are not settled overnight, and the Videll property might have been in probate several years.

"No," said Kenmore, "the argument in his favor was, he had inherited a fortune, and to do so must have satisfied a probate court of his legitimate parentage. He was, apparently, the one person involved who had proved himself *not* of illegitimate birth. On the face of it, the one the letter could *not* mean."

"Still, if you had thought of that," Corinne observed, "it seems to me you should have found out about him. Instead of trying to trace that letter to one of *us*."

But Corinne, the detective said dryly, had wanted him to confine his investigation to Al Dearborn yesterday . . .

His pipe had gone out. He relighted before resuming.

"I would have needed a good many weeks to run down the fact of his bastardy, if it could be run down at all. And in the meantime, *he* was trying to trace the letter to one of you, and I did not know how many deaths might result from it.

"It shaped up about like this:

"Catherine Hope had not, as she said, *let on* all that she knew. But the documentary proof was among her papers, and if they had looked those over together, he was aware of the fact. I suppose on the night of 15th April, 1937, he went to her home to destroy that proof. I think it is probable he found a torn-up letter, the one she did not mail to her sister, and was able to reconstruct from it exactly how much she knew.

"The police had made an extremely thorough search of Miss Hope's home six years ago. We did not find then any destroyed letter, or any documentary proof pointing to anyone at all. Evidence of that sort could only be dug up in New Gilead, and only there, as I say, by long and patient work. And it might not be found after all. Therefore, as a practical matter, I had to work with the material actually at hand."

He aimed the pipestem at Darwina.

"You told me you didn't like Ffleming—he had divorced his wife, he had dropped his old friends, when he inherited his money. But was that it? The money mightn't have changed him so much as the realization he had *gotten away with murder.*

"Catherine Hope's killer, I believe, blundered into committing a practically perfect crime. And it must have cost him nights of lying awake thinking of the possible ways in which he *might* be found out . . . It'd take awhile before the other realization dawned. That he *had* gotten away with it, he *was* smarter than the police, he was altogether too *clever* for his ordinary wife and friends.

"He had really become a murderer, then," said Kenmore.

And after a pause

"But there was ·· · my need to employ his remarkable talents until Henry Bowling turned up with that letter in hand. For of course he knew Bowling had it, it was quite in keeping for Bowling to have joshed a victim. 'What's all this about you and Amy Rhine's sister?'— something like that.

"It must have come as a terrific shock to Ffleming— knowing who Katie really was—and knowing pretty well what was in the letter, from having found the torn-up first draft six years ago. But," said Kenmore, dryly, "he was upheld by an inner conviction—he could get away with murder—it only needed a little planning, a repetition of what he'd managed before. Not in the crude sense he would drop Henry Bowling into a fish tank . . . It was the general pattern of confusion and misdirection he wanted to repeat.

"That is why we find him plotting Henry Bowling's death before Bowling himself had any suspicion what the letter meant. And it would have been the same had Henry Bowling not found the envelope at all."

Lieutenant Kenmore paused a moment on this point. It had seemed to him from the first a most significant angle in the enigma. "I know, I've created the impression Ffleming acted from fear it'd come out he'd killed Miss Hope . . . Bowling saw the letter in that light. But Henry Bowling was only an amateur detective; he had no notion of what, really, it takes to prosecute a case in court. We might all feel convinced Ffleming had murdered Catherine Hope, but on the evidence of motive alone a jury could not say it was proved beyond a reasonable doubt. After six years, it is not actually very probable the slayer could ever be sentenced for that crime.

"The danger—the real and pressing danger," said Kenmore "—in the letter pointed at Ffleming's comfortable income. He had got his inheritance by fraud, and I dare say forged records of his birth. He might lose it if anyone reopened the question of his parentage.

"If Miss Hope had not been murdered, if she had dropped dead from a heart attack on the beach that night, Ffleming's attitude toward the letter would have been essentially the same. He'd still need to destroy it— and he'd still have to shut up Henry Bowling from making any wisecracks about bastardy.

"We come to Thursday night, then." And here the lieutenant turned an unsympathetic glance upon Al Dearborn. "When you helped confuse the trail."

For the murderer's moves (Kenmore continued) had been basically simple. Thursday was the servants' night off. Thursday the family dined out. The hedge screened the premises from the streets. It promised at the least an uninterrupted hour in which to exchange Wallace's cyanogen-loaded gas mask for Bowling's, and to make a preliminary search for the letter.

"Necessarily, the murderer had the household under surveillance. He could hardly risk going to the guest-house by daylight if any member of the family remained at home to glance through a window and see him. In fact, Lally had not gone out to dinner. But then Al Dearborn came to the rescue. He put through a phone call so that Henry Bowling drove Lally to the Shore Club—between six-thirty and seven o'clock. That was when Ffleming got into the guesthouse (needing only a skeleton key to do that).

"And, later, you helped him again. You robbed Lally's jewel case, and of course he saw you. What time did you leave the house?"

Al Dearborn began incautiously, "Ten after—" and stopped, grew fiery red, blurted, "You go to hell."

Kenmore shrugged. He had not been fishing for a confession. Al's moves were clear. He'd delayed the burglary to the last possible moment before the bus's departure, so Lally should not discover the theft before he was safely on the bus. If she discovered it later in the evening, he had taken the precaution of not buying a ticket at the bus station. Supposing she had called the police, and the sub-station men suspected Al, there was no witness to tell them where he had gone. Reaching Los Angeles with the brooch and rings in his pocket, he would not find officers waiting for him . . . Kenmore's point was, at ten after seven, the murderer was in the vicinity of 222 Laguna Terrace with his fake incident envelope, and so saw Al.

Ffleming was an insurance man by profession. He knew very well the underwriters might demand an autopsy if the police did not. He had killed Bowling before seven-thirty. Jessie and Corinne did not return until nearly eight. During that time Ffleming had Henry Bowling's keys and had access to both guesthouse and the home. But he had not found the letter. At a quarter before nine o'clock, Lauren Wallace and Sam Elliot lingered to talk to Kenmore. Ffleming then had the chance to go to the Legion Hall, take the key from the mailbox, and insert 7:15 o'clock into the record of Bowling's second incident.

7:15 was very nearly the time Al Dearborn left 222 Laguna Terrace—the change advanced the earliest possible moment of the murder so that Al's alibi hung by a thread. And the change put to question the veracity of Ed Norman and Darwina; it was both misdirection and confusion.

"We come to Friday," said Kenmore. "It had occurred to him, by then, the letter might have been returned to Amy Rhine. I presume he used his skeleton key to get into her home that morning, after she had gone to Wyeland's office. It explains why, when he needed a gun, he knew where to get the Magnum.

"And it's clear why he made himself so helpful to the

bereaved family! He did so to play the role of Undertaker Joe in dead earnest. Because, by hanging about, he
might find a chance to make a still more thorough search
for the missing letter . . . We know he was upstairs at
one time without your knowledge."

"When he tried to kill me," said Lally.

"Except that he didn't try to kill you."

The blonde sister's eyes widened.

"For the reason," said Kenmore, "that at that time he
had no suspicion you had ever handled the letter. As far
as you are concerned, Lally, the theory of a murder attempt becomes untenable when we realize your assailant
wasn't frightened off at all. Ffleming was not in your
room, he was downstairs, and this is how it happened.

"He got into the house unseen, he knocked you out
(but with no thought of doing worse than that) and
carried you from the window to the open dressing room
door. On top of that door he parked the towel-wrapped
bottle. The theory was that in five or ten minutes you
would begin stirring, you would strike the door with
your arm, and bring down the bottle. In the meanwhile,
he would have slipped outside, walked up to the front
door, and rung the bell; he would be downstairs talking
to your mother when the crash was heard. And while you
did not stir, the rattle of anti-aircraft brought down the
bottle instead."

Corinne shook her head.

What, said she, if *she* had come upstairs and walked
from her room into the dressing room?

"The thing was," said Kenmore, "you would have had
to open a door to enter either your room or Lally's; he
had closed the window; and the current of air caused by
opening another door would have moved the dressing
room door enough to have brought down the bottle. And
if it had not, if you had walked in and found the set-up,

nothing in it involved Foster Ffleming. *His* fingerprints were not on the scene; Al Dearborn's were; it would be thought the device had been engineered by Al in an effort to provide himself with an alibi. Ffleming was on the face of it the one man who could *not* be involved, since he presumably did not know where the whiskey was hidden."

Lally colored. "If he was here Thursday before seven, I suppose he saw me take a drink then." Her blonde brows puzzled. "The question is how he got in and out of the house Friday in broad daylight."

"That's easy. When Frank Axiter heard the autopsy finding, he went and concealed a gold coin in the guesthouse. And as concealment was his purpose, he naturally closed the door. He was not working in the back yard all that time.

"The long and short of it is," said Kenmore, "Ffleming had nothing to lose by faking an attempted murder, and if he could establish a direct alibi by it, had a great deal to gain."

And that, he added, disposed of a murder and an attempted murder.

"Bringing us," Wyeland commented, "to Dr. Wallace's death."

"Yes, bringing us to Friday evening when Ffleming returned that bundle of warden supplies. You, Wyeland, and Dr. Wallace were in the control room. Darwina overheard something said about the pink sheets; he, of course, overheard that, too; he learned for the first time it had been an error to carry that pink sheet away from the guesthouse. The natural solution suggested itself: He had only to take another report form and tuck that away in the stack of stationery in the guesthouse. As in fact he subsequently did, seizing advantage of Sergeant Lyon's being called to the Shore Club.

"His first step was to quietly ease open Wallace's desk drawers in search of a pink sheet to take, and that was when he found the letter. At long last.

"But now Amy Rhine walked in. Wallace went to that drawer for the letter. And it was gone.

"It is not very difficult to follow the argument from there on," Lieutneant Kenmore thought. "Lauren Wallace had not attached any importance to the letter until that moment. He had merely glanced at it, discovered the signature, and then held some brief conversation with Henry Bowling. It was a letter of Amy Rhine's from her sister, Bowling had said.

"But Amy, of course, looked incredulous at that.

"And Wyeland behaved, as Darwina thought, queerly.

"It must have been then," said Kenmore, "the suspicion of *Katie's* identity entered Dr. Wallace's mind. It might have done so by sheer association, since Amy Rhine in bringing her typing to the control room office, recalled the circumstance that she had formerly done Catherine Hope's typing.

"Dr. Wallace was not, unfortunately, a man given to making loose accusations, or loose statements of any kind. It occurred to him that Sam Elliot, in getting out the report forms Thursday night, might have simply chucked that letter into the wastebasket. He proceeded to find out, driving first to Elliot's home. Ffleming hurriedly got Amy Rhine's gun . . .

"There was the same pattern to it, you see. The confused background involving a large number of persons, the misdirection resulting from search for a weapon his dog had carried off, the same effort to involve someone else—in this case, by telephoning Corinne Axiter when he knew very well she was not at home; he had passed the green Cadillac at the foot of Penguin Street when he left Mrs. Rhine's home."

And as if to wind up his conversational effort, Lieutenant Kenmore laid aside the pipe and sipped leisurely at his highball.

"It seems to me," said Darwina, *"you* knew perfectly well who would spring your trap."

The detective gave a wry half-smile.

"There were other little clues . . . Buddy Telight . . . I won't go into that. All of it together was not one-tenth enough to justify an arrest. I might have guessed. I could not have convicted . . . The thing is, I knew he could be trapped!"

The wry smile became a grim one.

"Here was a man," said Kenmore, "who had committed a perfect murder by accident, almost without planning it at all. And who was trying to repeat it by deliberate design! That was the whole thing in a nutshell, the strategy behind every move he made. And I had to meet the strategy, had to beat him at that game . . . It was true enough you were all in peril of your lives, but the purpose of my talk, of course, was primarily to point out the innumerable perils of exposure *he* faced. And then to introduce J. S. Dugan, who—if he had been in the house at that time—might very well have seen Lally's assailant leave her room.

"But it was principally," concluded Kenmore, "to hand the perfect murderer a ready-made scene having the *confused background* of persons, the possibility of *mis-direction,* and the opportunity to *involve someone else*—the stage-setting he would have designed, if he had set the stage himself."

Darwina frowned.

"Only . . . if he had not risked bringing a gun?"

"I hoped to God he had not," said Lieutenant Kenmore gravely, "or that would have been a real bullet fired at poor Dugan . . . When Axiter was arrested,

Ffleming planted the gun here for the police to find. And we had found it, reloaded it with blank cartridges, and put it back in its same hiding place. With a coating of naphthionate of sodium to identify the marksman's hands."

"So it was science, after all," said Darwina, and raised her glass. "Here's to science."

"No," said the lieutenant, "here's to J. S. Dugan."

It occurred to him as a whimsical oddity that the case was closing on the same note it had opened; that he had been toasting another officer's health when Henry Bowling telephoned . . . How much had happened in the forty-nine hours since! For one thing, Lieutenant Kenmore was enough of a detective to observe that Lally had been sitting all this while facing an untouched glass. It did not escape his grey glance that the blonde sister raised her highball with the others, and steeled her lips, and put the drink down before her untasted.